MOON TANNING

Dear Herbert,

May you have great enjoyment
on all your rides through the
seasons.

All the best!

MOON TANNING

Motorcycles, Mechanics, Mayhem

Gwynn Davies

Library of Congress Control Number:		2012910847
ISBN:	Hardcover	978-1-4771-2957-9
	Softcover	978-1-4771-2956-2
	Ebook	978-1-4771-2958-6

This book was printed in the United States of America.

To order additional copies of this book, contact:
Xlibris Corporation
1-888-795-4274
www.Xlibris.com
Orders@Xlibris.com
116021

Table of Contents

Prologue..vii
Chapter 1 – In the Beginning... 1
Chapter 2 – The Crew... 7
Chapter 3 – Night Ride 13
Chapter 4 – Birthday for Hobbers.. 21
Chapter 5 – Pyrotechnics and Mayhem 31
Chapter 6 – A Life Less Dismal... 41
Chapter 7 – Oil Spills 53
Chapter 8 – Dreams and Reality... 61
Chapter 9 – Roadside.. 75
Chapter 10 – Bikes and Tea 89
Chapter 11 – The Days of Our Lives... 97
Chapter 12 – Smells Like Teen Spirit 105
Chapter 13 – I Love the Smell of Burnt Rubber 107
Chapter 14 – Run When You Hear Sirens..113
Chapter 15 – Yahbuts and Such...117
Chapter 16 – A Winter Marshmallow Roast 123
Chapter 17 – Let There Be Light 131
Chapter 18 – Finding the Light.. 139
Epilogue..141

Prologue

The branches of the nearby palms listed slowly in the cool breeze. Their soft drawn-out creaking sounds were the only things keeping me awake. The lawn chair, with its legs protruding deep into the warm white sand, was where I rested on this gorgeous afternoon.

With warm temperatures to lie in and the immensely beautiful scenery to gaze upon, it's hard to wonder how it is that so many people have lived their entire lives without experiencing it. How they have never enjoyed the tropics or lush rain forests with such an incredible abundance of life waiting at the doorstep. Even to experience the amazing beaches where every breath taken as though it had been drawn from that of a dry sauna after pouring water atop the hot coals. Where scantily clad women frolic around to your pleasure on the sand below, playing volleyball, or tanning, underneath the glowing ball above us—ahh, the life.

Think of all the great careers people would be in at this very moment. By placing down all of their tiles day by day on the scrabble board of life, most were unaware of the value of their play: desk jobs with no windows to sit next to devouring up life; perhaps the local garbage-removal employee with dirt and sweat on his palms and forehead mixed in with the sweet stench of week-old filth left to ripen in the global-warming community. The last one that jumps into my mind is the mechanic: oil and grease dyeing the forearms on their blue-collared coveralls while grime contributes to the gritty sandwiches taken from the calloused hands at lunch. The motorcycle mechanic is perhaps an interesting story, for it is where this all began . . .

CHAPTER **1** — In the Beginning

"**G**et over here! What do ya think you're doin' to the forklift anyways? There's no bikes to uncrate," exclaimed Albert, the head mechanic at the local motorcycle dealership. He had woken me up from the grizzling reality that I had fallen asleep at work. Not only was it one of the busiest weekends of the season but one of the hottest as well. The months before had constantly been teasing us with the return of good weather. The sun would poke out from between the clouds for a day or so, luring you back into your summer attire. It would then unceremoniously pelt you with frigid rain or random hail the next, setting you back into a disgruntling manner as you went about your days.

I stared back at him, dumbfounded for a good five seconds, until coming to my senses, if that is what they're called. Hopping off of my 'perch,' I started to go back inside the shop before he could think of a dumb retort to add to his previous comment. He followed on my heels as though I was one of his lost sheep from an insane-asylum herd. Inside the Service Department once again, getting back on track was an easy thing.

In the shop, we have three mechanics full-time: Albert, or Alberto if you want to be a nuisance, who is the old, wise, and weathered character; then there is myself, the well-respected, honest, handsome, and most of all, modest mechanic (the last of those being the best character trait) in his twenties; after myself is Harry, or Hobbers, or Hair-bears, the thirty year old, jet-black haired fool from the other side of Canada. Of course there are many other names for the other two, but those will all be revealed in time. Harry has been at our shop for five years; I have been employed here for eight years (oh god), and Albert has been around since the dawn of creation and has worked here for twenty or something years. I don't even think that I'll be alive for that many more years, never mind be working for that many.

The last thing you could possibly want to do was strike up a conversation with Dillen. Not only is conversation all he is good for, but if you get into an argument with Dillen, it takes forever just to get him off of your back. It is also very hard to describe his job description: he talks to customers in the sales half of the shop for 50 percent of the day, blabs uncontrollably to the up-front staff for 40 percent of the day, and then mentally harasses the mechanics for the other 10 percent . . . He may have once been referred to as our service manager.

When the bikes come in to be worked on in the mornings, I usually pick a decent-sized service that will take up a good portion of the day. The newer the machine and the less accessories being installed, the better. There is nothing more exciting than a customer using the Internet to buy aftermarket parts from companies that apply the term 'universal fit.' If that is their slogan, then nothing in this universe is what it is going to fit. Another highlight is that since the customers buy the parts for a low price, they believe that the installation of them should be inexpensive as well—no modification is ever required, since it is a universal fit and bolts on in minutes . . .

Before I continue, I will give you a lowdown on the kind of bikes we work on at the shop. It is a little German company featuring many innovations on the market, especially in the last two decades. They also go by Bavarian Motor Works. Currently, we have opposed twins, single cylinders, inline 4s, as well as a large inline 6-cylinder—high output for performance while utilizing many different body styles to cover most riders' needs on the road or off. We also carry vertical twins in a medium displacement engine that runs in a dual-sport package for the rider that enjoys a bit of on- or off-road enjoyment. The opposed twin is available in any format and is the staple platform of the BMW Motorrad division.

This morning, I picked up one of the opposed twins for a large service. As I came in a bit earlier than the other employees to prepare the shop for service work, the bikes chosen by myself usually end up on the bench closest to my toolbox—go figure. This particular service takes up a very large piece of the day. Since the shop opens at nine, if all goes well, it is done by 2:00 p.m. This leaves no room for meandering about, and gives just enough time to engulf your lunch between a few blinks of the eye. It is only done at one thousand kilometres, and as you can tell by the time allotted, an intensive service is entailed. To start out, a retorqueing of the cylinder heads is done (no, this is not a later edition dual-overhead-cam model released in 2010 that doesn't require the head torque). To those of the public not mechanically inclined, this means squishing down gaskets because the break-in period of the engine has been completed and things that have loosened up now need retightening. Second, the valve and rocker endplay are adjusted back to the manufacturer's recommended tolerances. Without doing this, your engine will sound like a bag of hammers, and leaving those trade tools with the carpenters is a much better idea. Engine, transmission, and rear-end oil are also dropped out of the machine to be replaced with fresh clean oil, which makes the bike oh so dreamy. Examining the colour and texture of the oil drained gives a very good indication of how the motorcycle is being ridden and maintained: too hard or soft, or like the little bear's porridge—'just right.' While the bike is on the hoist, a favourite pastime is to check out the 'chicken strips.' These are the common names for the sides of the tyres that don't get used in cornering. Since motorcycle tyres are round on top as opposed to the flat surfaces on cars', it is much easier to tell how good at wrestling the bike through the windy sections the customer is. The larger the 'chicken strip' (unused tyre), the less hard core and more obedient of the law he is—you can choose whichever you like. Why do companies give us so many horsepower when there are hundreds of signs limiting how fast you can go? It's a devious trick that officers of the law enjoy ticketing for.

Adjusting tyre pressures and checking spoke tension (only on the bikes without alloys obviously) are very important things to check at service intervals. For any outing on your bike for that matter, it is a good aspect to cover. A quick look over of all the brake components is of vital importance in the long run. Albert looked over at me during the service. "Oh look, that's your third set of valves this week. Good fer me, I'll jest take my time and work 'n' these old clunkers." How do you say this nicely? Albert, over the years, has, well, slowed down quite a lot. Harry and I pick up the slack though, as we didn't have a choice otherwise.

When Harry is not texting one of his hos or doing jaw cardio with the rest of the staff, he can actually get things done. I've found the best way to get work out of him is to turn on the news; he cannot stand it. It must be the informative part that turns him away. He then throws on his headphones and whatever music is being played through them—works like a charm. All services for the day seem insignificant, and the bikes roll off the benches one after another in quick succession. Then of course Albert gets the perturbed look on his weather-beaten face, "Nothin' but comebacks is what'll happen if he keeps that up!" I am quite sure that Albert cannot handle how fast everything happens, and it overwhelms him. "Neh, gonna have some nice cold beers tonight when I get back to the shed (the shed, referring to his tiny decrepit shack on his vast property surrounded by trees).

The day came to a close at about 6:30 p.m. I had polished off another chain and sprocket change by the time we finally put our tools away. Since I had been there at eight, unloading and servicing bikes, I felt like a bag of crap and wanted to head home. I asked Albert what he was planning on doing for the evening, and the usual came up. "Gonna go down to the corner store 'n' pick up some lottos 'n' then, and then get ma beer. Probably listen to the radio until I fall asleep." Albert's voice was medium pitched almost with a southern drawl, even though he had never been over the border. When he laughed or became excited, it would get shrill, and he would cackle through his yellowed and missing teeth. . Hopefully, he fits dinner in between his drinking and sleeping, since beer and radio don't usually supply all the daily vitamins and mineral requirements for your body to function. "Lost the power again too! Gettin' out the gens' ta have some lights tonight. Only difficulty is gettin' the jerrys in my truck to fill the gens with juice. Gotta keep 'em running somehow through the night!"

Together we snuck into the back of our lot to where our reserve stash of petrol was for the bikes. Three jerrycans full of petrol: one full of two-stroke mix, one full of premium, and a last one full of contaminated old crap. We checked to make sure the boss had left before we got busy. As he went to drive the old truck into the parking lot, I toted the twenty-litre jug of premium down the side alley of the shop into the parking lot facing the road. The engine was still running by the time I got within distance, and thin wisps of blue escaped from the tailpipe. The low rumbling reverberation of the exhaust kept the scuttling sounds of my boots quiet, so we weren't given away. After tying the container firmly to the back of the cab, I exclaimed to Albert it was time for his getaway. While rolling his eyes at me and putting an exaggerated look of exasperation on his face, he placed the shifter into drive and rumbled out of the lot on his way to freedom.

It may have been the shop's service petrol, but just think of how easy it would be to move around the empty jerrycan now. Albert would pay us back in other ways later on, hopefully with more of his witty jokes that he says at the wrong place/time. Take, for example, one of our monthly meetings: the service department was complaining that day of how poor the quality of the trade-in bikes were that had been brought to sell. The sales department had been taking in these bikes without getting them properly looked at for mechanical issues/lack of maintenance for resale. Albert had been quiet all morning taking in the information that was being passed back and forth over the table. After a heated debate, we took a brief lapse, and everyone caught their breaths. He suddenly chimed in, "I've got an idea that might help." We all moved our gaze over to the chair where he had been slouching for the better part of the conversations. Harry's glazed-over stare twinkled from the fluorescent tubes above us. "You gonna fill us in, man?" he slurred out. Albert started up, "What do you get when you cross an elephant with a rhino?" Harry's eyes lowered, and his upper lip curled up slightly, "Doesn't have anything to do with this, man! What are you talking about?" Everyone else around the table sat, perplexed, and nibbled uneasily on their donut holes that were keeping their figures slim. Albert stared over at Harry impatiently, saying, "Just answer the question, what happens when you cross the two?" "I donno!" Harry quirked defiantly. "What happens?" "Well, 'ell-if-I-know!" Albert let out between hysterical cackling. Groans went around the table, excluding the ones with the puzzled looks on their faces. They got told after the meeting the joke again, which seemed to help it settle in. This is but one occasion where nothing of value comes from Albert's chair at the meetings.

After he was safely on his way home with his much-needed generator juice, I headed into the back lot to lock up the shop. Harry had already rolled many of the service bikes inside for the night, so the job of finishing up was minor. In the good ole days, most of the service crew would have hung around to enjoy a bevy or two after work, chatting with one another through the billows of cigar and cigarette smoke. For hours into the night, stories would go on, one after another, about old jobs, old vehicles with problems long fixed, the useless sales department, or even relationships and their troubles. That all came to an abrupt halt one night: at the time, Harry had recently purchased a used R1 Yamaha. It was a bit older, brought up from the States, and had a few miles on her, but it was still an R1. We would go riding together, since I had a 2002 R6 at the same time, but a completely different story happened with that bike. Albert and Harry had kept on drinking one night after work until who knows when; I did not. In the morning, I came into work and was absolutely astonished. There were so many beer cans and bottles on the counters that they had resorted to overflowing onto the floor. Mounds of ash and crushed cigarette butts lay scattered in between the bottles, making a larger obstacle course in the shop. I received the call at around 8:30 a.m. A garbled dozy Harry was on the other line. "Don't think I'll be able to make it in till a bit later, man, down at the hospital right now, 'n' I just woke up." My response was a bit slow, as I had no idea what had happened or what was going on. My eyes trailed over the massacre on the benches, and I started to realize more of the situation. "I crashed my bike last night dude, 'n' it's totally smashed up. Hit a deer." I listened intently as he described himself leaving the dealership at nine thirty and then doing a low-speed run. The deer jumped out in front of him over top of a meridian. Since he was wearing a tinted visor and didn't seem to notice in time, the deer ran along his merry way. For Harry, it was already too late. He had swerved to avoid, but since the

R1 had such touchy controls, he went sideways and fell off of the powerful bike as it tumbled end over end. He skidded from his knees to his hip and then further down the road onto his back while the bike hit the same meridian the deer had jumped over. The R1 disintegrated on impact with a merging lane sign. The local authorities got called out from a passerby vehicle, and they found his semiunconscious body propped up on the side of the concrete meridian in an awkward fashion. Harry had managed to crawl out of harm's way with his scraped-up body before passing out. The ambulance men laid him on the stretcher with the helmet still on, since motorcyclists often crush vertebrae or have a damaged skull from an accident, where the only thing keeping the head together is the helmet.

While checking vital signs and assessing bodily functions, he started coming 'round again. Back in the Emergency ward of the hospital, they X-rayed or CT-scanned all of the possible damaged area; Harry couldn't tell me which. Afterwards, they carefully removed the helmet and set it aside to be assessed by the insurance adjusters who would be contacted when Harry 'had the time.' They plugged an IV into his arm for the night to keep his comfort levels high and pumped him full of something-or-other.

At this point in the story, which was for the most part up to date, I heard a knocking on the door up front, and I told Harry to hold on a moment. Albert was at the door but with a full-sized oxygen tank in a rustic orange colour between his right foot and left hand. I yelled out to him, "I'll be two seconds, hold on!" I ended the conversation with Harry, while I attempted to squeeze between the mass of bikes in the showroom. After barely fitting through, I made my way to the front door. The lock turned with a clunk, and Albert reefed the door open. "I don't know how you're going to fit that welding tank through here, since I can't even get through." His expert manoeuvrability skills of rolling acetylene and oxygen tanks around for most of his life helped him position the bottle near the display cabinet against the northwards facing wall. "Can't fit 'er through here right now, but when Trevor clears them bikes outta here, I'll wind 'er through into the back." The other employees trickled in throughout the next half hour, and I waited for them all to be present before sharing the news. In the meantime, I cleaned up the previous evening's horrendous mess. To my fellow employees, the news was a bit horrifying. Most of us knew that one day, something bad would come of the alcohol, but not on this scale. Now to the boss, I PG-rated the explanation of the events. I left out that alcohol and speed were the two greatest factors.

This is when the emergency meeting took place, unbeknownst to Harry. Gerald (boss man) set about instituting a no-alcohol policy. He obviously saw through my white veil. He is a short and bald man, so the intimidating factor is somewhat to be desired, kind of like a small terrier yapping hysterically from behind the glass of an overheated SUV interior. The point was well taken though: no drinks after work at the shop or after work on the weekends at the shop. His reasons were for insurance purposes. The authorities probably wouldn't like to hear that a drunken motorist left the shop and crashed right after having the drinks at the motorcycle shop—also that it happened every night (not usually the crashing part). Instead, the drinking moved to local pubs and bars around the city where those kinds of activities continued. That was that though; no more party life at the motorcycle shop.

I locked up the oil shed for the evening and then went inside to finish locking up the shop. Harry covered the bike closest to the door with a protective cover as I locked and chained the back doors. With the air compressor and nitrogen machine turned off, and the lights as well (all ten different switches), it was time to go! We held still for a moment as I punched in the digits on the dimly lit pad of the alarm box, and then we bolted for the door. Finally, the last key was turned, and the stainless steel gate was locked. We were out for the night; freedom at last.

CHAPTER 2 — The Crew

It's a small establishment with an overall roster of eight individuals working in all of the departments. There are two sections: the up-front staff and the shop staff. The upfront we also refer to as the sales department even though not much of that takes place. Second off is the service department. Endless, painful, drawn-out hours turn into years in the back of the shop. Labour-exploited slaves dwell in the dimly lit caves they inhabit, fixing rusty and unmaintained globules of metal formed into machines. Great will be the day when they can overcome their tyrant masters. Speaking of which, those titles belongs to Gerald and Margaret Stone.

Two years previous Gerald had been in retirement and, getting bored with all of his expensive boats he needed a new hobby—a little side project you could say. Taking over the dealership was not only the worst project you could ever think of but also one of the worst financial mistakes that I have ever seen take place. Margaret is aware at all times of what is going on throughout the building. She moved off of their island home just to be closer to the shop—an older lady, a smoker for most of her life, and a complete disinterest in motorcycles whatsoever. The problem is that their millions lie in the business; therefore, it is held in her withered iron grasp, and nothing ever gets in her way.

Her life consists of paperwork, computer details, and leaving the hindrance of indoors to smoke two or three packs of unfiltered cigarettes per day. Some evenings, her red Audi S4 car winds up at the nearest Blockbuster video to find some alluring title to keep a lonely business entrepreneur occupied for a few hours in the still evening. Gerald as well a busy man: every morning getting the kids from whosoever mother it was that week out to the oversized truck. Out to the open road they go, to the school, and finally to the curb in our shop's parking lot where the tiny man drives overtop of it every day. His large truck sends vast shadows out onto the road as it is so overwhelmingly huge. Strollers make their owners find new routes to move along the sidewalks. Yet in his own little world, Gerald is incapable of seeing the reality going on around him. Walking tall at five feet five inches, his chubby—wait, obese body, moves behind the sales counter, similar to that of a small mouse scurrying around in a maze, hopelessly oblivious to the destination in which the cheese lies. He has a small overcrowded desk in a corner area of where the parts department lies covered with wrinkled sales sheets, used half-empty Styrofoam coffee cups, and generally a large stack of accounts payable. Here he sits in sweat and frustration, hunched over in the plastic fatigued roller chair that holds his weight for most of the day. One thing to be thankful of—not being that chair! Bad trade-in values and bike sales are constantly taking place when Gerald is sitting in that chair, and I often wonder if they are playing a game of 'how much money can you lose in a day' or 'how many free parts can you give away to customers to keep them happy.' It is hard not to let it stress you out when your job depends on sales. For the most part, if the sales department goes bankrupt, so does the whole business. Other times, Gerald can be found in the showroom turning away customers, having an extremely overabundant amount of enthusiasm towards the product, and using unintelligent words to describe their features. 'This bike here is really cool and just has piles of power' or 'this machine is totally awesome and much better than all of those cruisers'; those being a couple of eye-rollers to witness when walking up front and mingling with the customers. It's great when you're excited about what you're selling, but it is also great when you have the technical knowledge in your sales pitch.

Then there is the big figurehead in the showroom—the great lumbering mass of flesh and bone called Duane. He had been a computer programmer for most of his middle-aged life, so I am not quite sure how he actually came into the motorcycle business. At the same time as me, he started working at the shop. I was young then, not really caring about the upfront staff. His parents were from New Zealand, and I had only met one of his relatives, some old uncle passing through on a photo-taking tour with a large group of similarly horizontally challenged individuals. Duane's smile is almost gruesome when it takes place. It appears as though someone pulled steel wires through his cheeks and yanked them straight upwards. Not only can you see his wisdom teeth as clear as day, but his eyes get pulled along as well, turning him into a very fat Asian-looking individual.

About a year back, the boss and his wife were trying to organize the place a bit better by tightening up the funds. One of the things implemented was that Duane becomes the general manager of the shop. I know what you're thinking, 'What a great job opportunity for him. A little promotion should be great motivation for the guy.' Let me tell you . . . far from the truth is your idea! For not only does this GM title give his head a wee bit of an oversize, but also the burden is so heavy to carry he feels as though he needs to hold down the counters even more now! Probably my most favourite part about Duane would be his 'partner.' Yes, homosexual is the first thing that comes to mind for me as well; but no . . . it is a woman partner/common-law. When you picture a lady with a whip in a tight black leather suit, I picture his common-law partner. Now, only the controlling part with the whip, not the visualization of her grotesque body covered in fake animal hide; no thank you. It was just the fact that Duane had been in the whipped position since they had been together. In the morning, his partner unlocks his cage door, and then he quickly comes bounding into work, panting and drooling— quickly, meaning ten o'clock for Duane. Anyways, another interesting feature about Duane is his nerves. Back in the day before the takeover by Gerald, Duane was quite underpaid, did a lot more work, and was verbally abused on a regular basis. Now that the old boss is gone, we in the back decided to continue that last tradition. I believe it frazzles him immensely; his patience has begun to dwindle at a rapid rate, and small outbreaks occur on a more frequent basis, each time escalating slightly. His face goes beet red, and sweat fills his large pores while nipping at the frontal hairs on his forehead, leaving them pointy and wet. His size is on a grander scale but is composed of body fat, so the menacing looming monster is more humorous to look at. I am not sure how long he will keep being mentally stable. The harder we try, perhaps the sooner we can change that around.

Duane had been riding for the better part of his life. Over that life, he has acquired numerous bikes. Many of these in recent years have been dual-sport style motorcycles. Six years ago, he was riding his first Kawasaki KLR. He loved this new bike, with its large front forks and a fancy decal job on the tank. When sat on, the bike disappeared! I suppose you could say Duane was a magician, for whenever the bike was dismounted, it reappeared again—fancy that. Not only did he very much enjoy it, but he also bought two more of them later on.

One amusing story of Duane is from several years back, in the mid-1980s. The Suzuki Gamma was a hot 4-cylinder, two-crank two-stroke that had just been introduced into the market after the famous 1984 Gamma that had won many constructor titles. Duane, being in his early twenties, was eager as ever to have the latest craze and purchased one. His buddies and he had a blast riding together through the old back roads, down through the twisties, and around the lakes. As experience was not present, and not much age was behind the handlebars, one dark night it happened: disaster struck! While taking in some heavy corners and winding little roads, Duane found out the hard way how good it is to have a meticulously maintained motorcycle. The night crept up slowly around each bend in the asphalt. As the bike was held at a deep angle and frighteningly close to the ground, the chain broke! At such a high rpm, the links looped around the sprockets at an unthinkable speed and dug into the left-hand engine case. In a split-second, the tranny locked up and destroyed numerous components at once. Duane's eyes, for a brief moment in time, widened in size. The left-hand fairing hit the pavement and started to rip the bike apart piece by piece. For the fragment of time that Duane was in control of the situation, he realized he didn't know what to do. The bike then turned perpendicular to the side of the road as it scraped along the asphalt. Metal debris and plastic became carnage and flew off in all directions. He found himself being pulled at high speed underneath the motorcycle. His leg that was being squished between the burning tailpipe and the tarmac quickly got eaten away as only thin jean material was being used as protection. The bike continued on its course, right off the road. Both of the Michelin A48 tyres hit the gravel at the same moment. Careening end over end, somersaulting in midair went the machine. Clumps of gravel and dirt, metal and machine went exploding in all direction. The forks hit the first small alder tree that had appeared out of nowhere. They blew apart into useless scraps of aluminum and chrome plating from the stanchion tubes. Where they joined to the frame was a heavy break. Aluminum from the frame looked like last night's pasta dish: distorted and mangled, barely discernible as to what was once a bike. The wheels buckled, and the tyres released their air pressures as more trees and rocks came into play. The lights and signal lenses with their plastic mouldings shattered under all the stress, while the tank was beaten and smashed into a small punctured tub. Petrol and hot oil from one of the cracked blocks sprayed uncontrollably as the bike continued moving deeper into the wooded area. It soaked the surrounding foliage and bushes as it came down on the descent. The entanglement of pipes, hoses, and battered frame pieces came to a rest one hundred metres from the launch point of the road. No lights were to be seen; nothing but a cold eerie moon lit the night sky, and no sound of human or animal could be heard. In the distance, the only noise was that of a cool evening breeze rustling the leaves between the trees, yet chilling those with no coat handy.

Thirteen days later, Duane woke up from the coma. He recollects going off the road, but never the impact after the bike and he stopped sliding—probably for the best, as five ribs were broken, massive breakages on his left leg with permanent muscle damage occurred, and third-degree burns due to the exhaust pipe mashed against his inner thigh! Also slight brain haemorrhaging in the areas that controlled the organization and coordination skills . . . Or perhaps he was born that way. The slightly amusing part about that hospital experience was that all of the money in his wallet had mysteriously disappeared. He had cashed his paycheck days before riding and had placed it in his leather riding jacket's pocket, leaving petrol money in his wallet for quick accessibility. I suppose once the interns saw the first glimmer of bills, they neglected to finish their search for the mother lode. Duane later recovered to some extent and went on in life to continue crashing motorcycles and abusing his body.

After Duane in the sales department comes Trevor. He has only been with us for little over a year but surpasses his young blonde counterpart in the riding experience sector by sixfold. Trevor looks after the parts area of the shop. Not an incredible skyscraper individual at five feet eight inches and 150 pounds, but a great guy all the same. Thirty years old takes him out of the 'danger to society' category and into the responsible and mature section. We joke at him at his young age for already he is losing his hair. Not surprisingly enough, a couple months later, his wife shaved all the hair off his noggin so as to keep the embarrassment down. Previous to landing this 'career,' he was working at one of the high-end bicycle dealerships in town. He worked there in the sales department and as a parts dude, much as he did at our shop, just switching over to motorcycles. Trevor is, in my mind, the foremost authority on mountain biking. Not only as a superior cross-country rider, but his knowledge for parts and accessories, and history of such, is amazing. He is a quiet fellow and usually listens to what other people have to say first. He then adds his own thoughts on the matter if being asked—a rare quality if you ask me. Most people around the shop are blundering idiots, interrupting with rude comments and gross humour just to get a quick rise out of the neighbouring employees. As one of the only people who can manage to stay on task in the front of the shop, it is no wonder that he is the only one that is capable of finishing all of the jobs that he starts, mainly without a word. In his spare time, Trevor can be found riding his mountain bike through the nearby trails or relaxing in his lawn chair next to his beloved wife, both of them stretched out underneath the magnificent sun, grasping a cold beer in one hand while holding each other's hand with the second. Of course, as he has so many Oakley sunglasses in his collection they are always wearing those as well. After coming to work at the shop, he realized the twenty-minute drive in his truck was a large waste of petrol. Therefore, he started eyeing up the smaller single-cylinder 650 that we had to offer, competent little machines manufactured in the Axis country of Italy. It keeps costs down but is horribly engineered. Aprilia produced them under the BMW logo, and in the first few months of receiving the bikes, we had shit-loads recalls. Trevor had one of them sent to our shop from another dealership. It had many aftermarket accessories installed, so he wanted to scoop it up. They sound like 300-pound lawn mowers with one fat piston going 'bwam, bwam, bwam.' Attach a blade underneath, and you are off to go make a bunch of money going from lawn to lawn. At least those bikes aren't being made in China, like some of the rumours of late . . . How degrading would that be? 'Oh do you like my 'German-engineered' bike made in China?' Just like every child's toy. No, I don't think that I'll be partaking in that little arrangement. Since Trevor can zip in and out of traffic so quickly with his new machine, he started to get into work faster than everybody else. It's wonderful: go to work all groggy in the a.m. and all the doors have already been unlocked, the lights are all on, and most of the bikes have already been pushed outside, leaving the service area empty. If only he had started working there years and years before, life would have been so much more pleasant. A downside is that a lot less overtime in the course of those years would be had. To add to that, I even used to spend my time going to get donuts every morning after waiting around in the drive-through. I would order coffees and iced caps for the boss, the mechanics, and our shop girl—each morning, a dozen Boston cream donuts just for her. Nowadays, if I went and bought coffee and donuts and attempted to get the shop to spot the bill, I would have my ass pushed up against a cold brick wall with a firing squad staring me in the face, ready to blast me to hell.

CHAPTER 3 — Night Ride

The day's work had chilled my soul. If struck with a blunt object, it would shatter into a thousand tiny pieces. My inner being would be vanquished, and I would crumble away into nothingness . . . Well, it was a good thing that nobody had any blunt objects around.

The night had come in slowly and quietly, but it lay upon us like a large blanket over a king-size bed. The time was six thirty, give or take a few minutes. I was going on a ride and taking Harry along with me, since the two of us riding together was a rare occurrence. Surprisingly on this occasion, we had similar bikes. My legs straddled the silver 2003 edition R1150R that I now owned. A smooth-lined, classically featured brute, and the best and last of the twin spark R259 model series Beemers with the Motronic 2.4 fuel injection. In 2004, BMW started the new K2X series R1200 motors. With this comes their fantastic (completely exaggerated) new wiring system referred to as CanBus. With this system, every computer on the bike talks to one another via two cables. Don't get me wrong, as it's an ingenious idea, which had been used on their cars since the early '90s, starting on the old 850 series. One of the big problems was there were always problems—sensors, computers, switches, plugs, you name it, they would break down! It was very unfortunate for such a brilliant idea. That is what made me go for a bit older bike as opposed to the flashy new models on the floor. In addition, my model had no ABS; the best decision of my life. Not one of my other bikes had ever had it, nor would any of my future bikes. The ABS for my bike would have been the Integral ABS. One of you out there has a friend with it and hears the constant complaints about the whining motors whenever coming to a stop; sissy little servo motors making you insane.

Harry's two wheels of fury is an R1150R Rockster edition. He purchased it from Albert a couple of months ago because he *had to* ride down to California for BMW training instead of taking the free flight. It was doing nobody any good out in that place anyways. He had left it out in the rain and the snow over the last winter, and it was becoming corroded.

This bike is flat black with an interesting pattern of gloss orange decals strewn about over the tank. The main differences between the bikes besides the colours are the forks; my forks consist of cast aluminum crap, whereas his are anodized milled-down aluminum. Then he gets a carbon front fender and a completely different headlight assembly. The original R1150R comes with one large round unit. The Rockster edition has two smaller glass lenses next to each other with a very small shroud instead of a windshield placed over top. The rest of the bike is very similar.

I closed my visor and began putting on my gloves. Since it was still early in the year, she fogged up right away. "Damn it," I said aloud to myself. After pulling the visor back up, I looked over at Harry to see what he was up to: texting like usual. "Come on man, get your shit together, we gonna do this or what?" I questioned him. "Yeah, yeah, gimme a sec. It's this new chick I met the other day, 'n' she wants to meet up for coffee or somin'."

With my right hand outstretched to the bars, I pressed the grey starter button to give life to the machine. She jumped into existence in an instant with opposed pistons banging away in their appropriate cylinders. The sounds of the explosions rumbled out of the muffler. I had cleaned this puppy the previous eve, and she was looking great in the warm glow of the streetlamps. "I've really got to pick up some antifog spray," I mentally kicked myself. For the past month, I had been debating whether or not to buy an antifog screen. The only con to the situation was that the whole screen was not covered. It left gaps on either side so that your peripheral vision was diminished. I tried on Trevor's, and it felt a little like tunnel vision. I had not bought it based on this. The other option was from Scott Racing. They had produced a spray for the inside of your visor. The product sucked up moisture instead of letting it condensate on the screen. It was only six dollars per bottle, but I had been lazy and had put off the purchase. Because of that, I had to live with the foggy screen.

Harry finished his texting and began zipping and buttoning up all of his gear. He preferred leather for his jacket, whereas I preferred the synthetic textile fabrics. As I was thin boned, I found my gear kept in the little heat my body created better than the leather. Harry wiggled the helmet onto his head and adjusted the chin strap to eliminate any strangulation. From where I was sitting on my bike, his engine could be heard roaring to life. "Vroom, vroom," she said as Harry grabbed a handful of throttle and revved her up. He loved to rev bikes, and I cannot emphasize enough how much he loves to rev bikes: two-strokes, customer's bikes, anything with a throttle. But that is him, not me. I yelled over to him, "You ready for this?" He hollered back, "Yeah, but I'm just gonna follow you fer a bit, 'cause I dunno which way you're thinkin' a headin'." "Yeah, right," I said to myself, since he was always trying to be 'king shit' on our rides.

I chugged up to the end of the parking lot and, after looking both ways like a law-abiding citizen, angled the bike left and rolled on the throttle. A couple of cars were between myself and Hobbers, so I waited at the roundabout for the retarded blonde in the minivan to understand the concept of four lanes all coming to the same circle in the middle. 'What? You take turns? Like, oh my goood, that totally works!' Yes, indeed, it does work! What's even better is when you come to the roundabout, and you don't have to think about it for five minutes before moving your ass. All right, finally past the circle, past a big ole pile of red lights, cross over the highway and fuck: three more damn lights just to get another quarter mile down the road. But no more, it's all go, baby! Screw you traffic lights, and you sissy cruiser riders and your dorky little tassels; I'll pass your ass! Harry was beside me at the last light, and he was bobbing his head up and down whilst grinning towards me. He rotated his throttle to bring up the revs, and I did the same (for once). With my left shoe, I flicked the shifter down into first and matched his revs.

The light turned green and we burst forwards into the intersection. A giant roar erupted from both our machines. The wind pushed my head back, and I slammed the visor closed between shifting. The current of air was stopping my visor from fogging. A car was dawdling along in front of us, so I braked and let Harry overtake on the left. He screamed past the automobile with a vengeance. It sounded like he had redlined in every gear so far. A corner was up ahead, and I didn't get the chance to follow. I'm not real big on passing in the corners, so I waited until the road straightened out, and then I leapt at the chance. My rear tyre spun momentarily on the yellow line, and as I passed by the middle-aged Asian couple in their new Toyota Camry, their dropped jaws, amplified the fact that I was passing them with my tail end going sideways. I burped the throttle and the tyre stuck, regaining traction. Then I pounded through the gears to catch up. Harry would have slowed down a bit to wait for me 'cause he knew I'd be stuck for a moment. I raced over the terrain blindingly fast. After whizzing past three more cars going Mach-whatever, I caught a glimpse of his taillights. He was trundling along—well not anymore sucker, here I come! He caught sight of me flying towards him and grabbed a big mitten full of throttle. I was doing around 6500 rpm (lots for an older boxer) in fourth gear, and I knew Hobbers could only be in third when I caught up. I yelled out towards him, condensating my visor once more, "Ahh, here I come Dogger, like it or not," not that he could hear me. Through turn after turn, we sped with the tyres being taken to their outer limits, popping ourselves from a crouched-over position out on the left-hand side of the bike quickly to the same on the right as soon as the corner transitioned.

By the time we reached the last curve to the turnoff, my lean was already an excruciating angle for how I usually ride, but I had to give it just that tiny itsy-bitsy bit more. If someone was sitting on my front wheel, they could have easily reached out and touched Harry's rear wheel. The corner began to straighten out, and from where I was in my crouched position, I craned my neck to check for traffic—none. The bike got pulled over the slippery line onto the oncoming traffic lane. Harry was pulling his bike upright as well but did not think that I could pass him on the straight; sucks to be ignorant! I crept up in the passing lane to overtake him. I saw him look in his left-hand mirror and snarl out something towards me. He was at max acceleration, but so was I with just a little bit more speed from drafting and concentrating on overtaking. After a moment of tucking completely under my windscreen with my helmet banging on the vibrating petrol tank below, we were head to head. Up ahead, something else was taking place; it was called a lack of space. Both of us were doing awesome-possum speeds for these old R-bikes, yet the road was having none of that and was coming to an end—well, the straight was at least. Another ten seconds tops was how long it could last.

Glancing over my right shoulder and discovering the lead was mine, a smile crept upon my face. He knew what was up the road and did not think it was cool to pass me by. I broke over into the proper lane, and the slick silver lines of my technologically unadvanced Beemer were further along than the more sporty-looking unit behind. Just in time for braking!

I dove into the corner at full speed, wrong-O. I went wide, did a superlean, managed to lose a lot of speed in the process; and when the corner straightened out, Harry was riding up my ass like a porn star. He was probably kicking himself to avoid laughing at me so much. He had taken an extra second to slow down before the short ninety-degree left-hander and chisel a smooth cut in the tarmac. Hey, I did manage to pass the fellow though, as silly as it turned out to be. Not to mention, I was still in front, and there were far too many twisties in the next section for him to repass.

I pointed over the top of my helmet to the right, towards the next part of our journey. Turning onto this road always licked balls. Gravel everywhere! Those damned old people that hate sport bikers and their rice-rocket exhaust systems. At night, a couple house owners would always place gravel out on the tarmac to get the bikers to slow down. It does work for that three metre stretch of road, I will admit. But . . . the pissed-off bikers then go even faster on the other stretches of road as they're cursing under their breath.

After dropping down a whack-load of gears and popping on my indicator light, my speed slowed enough. At an almost vertical level, I turned up the road. Jumping over gravel and other small rocks, I made my way to the top of the hilly road that we had turned onto—oh wait, I meant that I had turned onto. Tucked in an elbow and looking in the mirror, "Ahh, shit. Harry, you dork." He had turned too fast and was taking the bike for a wild ride, while nearly high-siding her as he went from sideways gravel sliding, to upright pavement and traction. I just caught the tail end of the scenario but got the gist of it. Guffaw, guffaw! I let out a quick chuckle as he raised his fist and shook it in my direction. He got his act together and rolled on, ready for some more high-speed action. Both of us buzzed around a couple turns as we became accustomed to the windier road. Never mind the tree branches and gravel on the sides of the road we were on, there was a little red squirrel up ahead. He was a funny little guy, darting to and fro, and half the size of his despised cousin, the gray squirrel. These gray squirrels usually push the red ones out of their own territory, and now there are not many left. With his tail bobbing all around and his zigzagging over the single white center line, squirrely made his way over into the bush on the left side of the pavement. Our bikes flew past while he cleared off the road. Running over any animal in a car is cruel and upsetting, but on a motorcycle, it feels close and personal. You might say I get sympathetic with the poor little buggers when it happens. Besides, they do not know any better! This time he got away.

The night was a little cooler, and I knew that the Metzeler Z8 tyres I had been using on my bike recently would not stick as well as they would on a hot day; therefore, for the rest of the ride, I told myself that I would only push myself to 90 percent of my capable craziness factor for the street.

Up a narrow winding incline we went. The pavement on this stretch was just recently laid, and it felt smooth underneath the motorcycle. Less potholes going up the hill, but on both sides of us were cement barriers and a beautiful twist at the top. As soon as the hill was crested, the road narrowed even more, and a sharp cut to the right had to be made. With Harry at my heels, I dropped a gear in anticipation of the corner and lowered my body over the side of the bike. The seat wasn't damp at all, so my pants slid swiftly to take my center of gravity lower and give the bike more cornering room by distributing the weight better. Both our boxer motors vibrated like crazy, and we shot around the tight little corner. A quick-angled jab downhill to the left shortly followed, and we found it was coated in wet leaves, obviously! For a moment, as I passed over the foliage and slowed, a second was stolen; but as the road straightened out and began to wind downhill faster, I sped up dramatically. Two turns from now, I remembered it was a flattish road for 500 metres or so and passed by the entrance to a lama farm and acreage. Harry's impatience from being behind me was most likely catching up; rolling around on his gerbil wheel, probably thinking that it was his chance for revenge-passing. To the best of my ability, I wasn't going to let that happen. Two corners to go. The first continued downhill and put a bit of pressure on my wrists. No need for heating tonight on these grips of mine, I was hot enough . . . I leaned myself over the left side of the tank this time and pulled back *hard* on the throttle. It was a classic off-camber scenario. It had a steep inclined S-curve bringing up the last corner before the stretch. The second corner tosses you quickly back and forth, also an off-camber, and almost doing a full horseshoe turn until the bottom. I scraped my foot peg on the asphalt as I dove into the curve. Being right on the edge of my tread and at the angle the bike was at, I was surprised that the back wheel wasn't trying to slide out on me. The throttle got pulled even further open. The mirrors were all fuzzy from vibration, but it offered a full view of Harry's headlight and behind it a rider. He was hot on my tail, and I had no time for mistakes. His angle was clean and consistent, and he was riding my ass, this time like a hooker down at the harbour. Harry's bike was not any faster; he just had nicer cosmetic parts, which was good for me, since he couldn't pull out with extra power and overtake me.

The corner tightened, continuing further down the spiral. G-forces began to take a hold on my body (not really). The tension on the grips was hard, and the gritting of the teeth was excruciatingly painful on the jaw. If this wasn't a boxer motorcycle, I would be needing pants with all sorts of knee scrapers bolted on 'cause this corner was hell.

Down at the end of the bend, the road became straight and the descent ceased, but the speed was incredible. Trees and signs seemed simple and insignificant when they were passed. As I was mashed hard against my tank for added aerodynamics, the bugs could be seen from behind the windscreen, exploding into different colours, with pieces and liquidlike textures becoming squished flat onto the polycarbonate structure. The howl of wind in the Aria helmet was comparable to that of a fighter jet screaming past at speed. And here I was still crouched over, tucked in the best I could be, just riding my motorcycle. And to my rear was Harry doing the same thing. No such overtaking would be taking place. He knew it, and I knew it. I raised my left fist in defiance at him. Leaves kicked up from my tyres covered his bike in a multicoloured array that could have looked the same from using a leaf blower.

A few sparrows were up the road about 200 metres eating on the edge of the pavement. I was honestly surprised how fast I passed them. I'm sure they felt the same. We both took a few sweeping turns together in tandem. A few more collections of gravel could be seen in the middle of the lane, this time of no concern to us. Both Harry and I were taking the left-hand side of ours this time. My headlight beam bounced up and down off upcoming hills, and we sped towards them eagerly. I screamed randomly from my helmet, "I will consume you with *fire!*" The Beemer was taken over a nice left-banking corner, and then I dropped her down a gear for the next two. These next two were wild. First, you get tossed like a salad over a poorly maintained section of the road, whilst going through an area of road with two others merging into it in the shape of a *K* (best way to describe it). Afterwards, a hard and long right-hand turn going in between a mildly residential area filled with beautiful abundances of pebbles, gravel, and wonderful sand. Once past the residences, the roadway veers left again with the oncoming side against an embankment, your side on the edge of a ravine, lovin' life. Take the corner like a boss! We both slammed the heavy bikes into the left-hander with vigour. Our left feet both rose and fell with the contours of the asphalt, through the foot pegs. Guess I'd probably be buying some new foot peg feelers once I got back to the shop the next day; if I get back to the shop the next day! Har-har. Around the bend, the bikes got pulled back up straight, and we both sped up the next hill that waited for us up the road.

After that hill was an area I referred to as power-line alley. It was between two districts and about three kilometres in length that no one really cared for, and I don't think that anyone owned. As you can tell, I don't know the details. All I knew about the area is that overhead are a large group of power lines, and that was why it was an unpopulated region. This is the worst three kilometres on a motorcycle: ultrawinding, twisty, up and down. And these all sound good, but the tarmac is like Haiti's roads: big gouges out of the asphalt, extremely poor pouring, and overall bumpy as hell. "Chatter, chatter, chatter" went the teeth inside my skull. "Curse you, stupid road, I smite thee!" Yes, I randomly yell at things. If I went to a doctor, they would probably tell me I have a problem inside of my head; but that's okay, since I am the one that has to live with myself and get up with myself every morning.

The sky was black now. Harry's beams broke through the night into my mirrors and periodically blinded me. We both bounced and jostled over the road until it was finally smooth again. A few deer munching mindlessly got caught in my headlight, and they raised their heads in alarm to see the trouble Harry and I were getting up to. We were both going too fast for stopping and having a chitchat, and now that we were through the power-line alley, we could pick up *speed*. My dried-out eyes from the cool wind squinted as they picked out the upcoming corners. Trees hanging over the roads covered them with leaves and debris, and I ripped expertly over them at insanely dumb speeds. As good roads never go forever, I knew there was about five minutes left before the land of boring returned. Effortlessly, I let my senses take flight and guide the motorcycle through the turns. Even with the wet foliage under the tyres, I couldn't let Harry take the lead, at least not yet. He had been behind me through all of those twisties, but our skill levels were pretty much the same. Maybe if I were up against an R1200S, but not an older R1150R, which was an old dinosaur bike. Those things still use pushrods (well, so do the R12s) that is 1800s technology. Shit, another truck! I came swooping around the left curve into the rear fender of a three-quarter-tonne truck full of furniture—well, almost into the fender. He saw me in his side mirror, and he swerved onto the dirt shoulder. I screamed, "All for Allah!" crazily and dove over the line. His rusted steel mirror mount glared at me as I careened out of its wake. "Fuckin' fuck!" I beat the handlebar with my fist. The truck driver was probably also yelling the same thing, as I scared the shit out of him. I shook my head and kept on going. Don't dwell and move onto the next adventure. Harry gave me the finger, and I shook my head back at him. "Better luck next time," I laughed at him. When the next turn became straight, I saw the drop. While pulling open the throttle, the grin on my face grew. The road went from flat to a forty-five-degree incline and then flat again. The drop went down approximately five metres; and a good five metres it was. The front wheel went airborne, followed by the rear. My butt came off the seat, and I straightened my legs as the bike flew through the air. "Yahoo," the bike smacked back down to the earth, and my knee hit the throttle potentiometer that always stuck out on the boxer motors. It felt as though it had gone under the kneecap; yeesh, it was painful. The throttle dropped to 75 percent, and I had also bit the shit out of my lower lip. I was definitely going to be limping for a few days. We cruised together for a few minutes until the next stop sign appeared. I pushed my right blinker button and pulled over into the gravel of the road side. With the side stand down, I hopped off and hobbled away from the bike as Harry followed suit with his parking.

"Dude, I've never seen that fuckin' jump! That's super crazy, man! We should try it the other way. Man, my jacket's bin buzzin' the whole time from texts. What you doin' hobblin' and stuff? What's this?" I pointed to my knee, "I just smashed up the knee with my potentiometer a second ago on that fabulous drop!" "Oh, bitchin'," he tilted his head back and cackled into his helmet for a minute before calming down. "That's gotta *suck*! Ha-ha, can you ride properly?" "Yah, just give me a moment to let the pain sink in, 'n' then we can cruise back onto the highway. But I'm not doing any 'balls-deep' riding with this darned knee." "K, I'll just make a few calls while you rest."

In a retarded manner, I limped around in circles while massaging my kneecap. At the same moment, the truck driver also decided to make an appearance. I had taken my sweaty helmet off and placed it near the front wheel of my Beemer. From the vantage point in his cab, the truck driver did not seem pleased. "Keep going, keep going," I mumbled from under my breath. Since it was dark, I thought he might not notice a couple bikes on the side of the road, except my turn signal was still on, damn it. Harry had been blabbing on his cell when the low rumbling sound of the truck exhaust made him cock his head over the shoulder. "Ahh, hey, babe, gotta go, call you back in a bit," He hung up the phone. "Hey shit, man, we might gotta bust outta here quick, hey?" He didn't have to tell me twice, "Yah, let's see if he's decent. I've got some Mace if he's too much for the two of us to handle." I laughed uneasily towards him. "Yeah, fuck that. He's probably got a fuckin' sawed-off shotgun behind his seat." Nice and optimistic Harry, nicely done. The truck driver's black truck's (hard to tell because of the light) brakes squealed as he slowed and then stopped, taking up the whole lane. We watched him dismount from the truck, grumbling as he got himself planted firmly on the ground. The truck lights made an eclipse of his body, and I wished that I could have pissed myself. It would have made for a better story. "Choo think yer doin 'n my neck the woods drivin' like some hooligan punks?" 'Oh wow', I kept thinking to myself, talk about Mr. Redneck himself. He most likely couldn't tell if a book had writings in it that were English, French, or German. At least, besides his bear-sized hands, he didn't carry any obvious weapons with him. The man was a brute, a lumberjack, and his scruffy beard and up-turned collar didn't hinder the appearance. Harry and I didn't have enough time to talk about what we would say to him. "Shit," I mumbled under my breath. I guess I would take this one for the team. Harry would probably make the guy go crazier than he already looked. "Hey, bud, I saw you back there on the road a few minutes back. I must say, we did pass you pretty quickly, that's for sure!" I smiled and laughed at the same time to keep the conversation lighthearted. It was dark and hard to tell that both of those were forced. "But it feels really good, now that I found that spot in the bush to pee!" I lied out loud. "I was looking for a safe spot, and this seemed to be the best one, hey?" The lumbering beast trudged towards us on tree trunk–like legs. "All right, white boy, if that's the way yer gonna try to pull the wool over mah eyes, I gun deal with it pretty good. But let a me remind yous, both yous. I jest get meself a new babe gurl last spring, I'll be goddamned if a piece o' racin' trash gonna be messin' with that if she ever be in on that road. Ya hear, boy? Ya *hear*, boy?" At that point, Harry had veered his body into the darkness of the bush, and I had walked all the way back and was leaning firmly against the tail rack of my bike, so he couldn't get the plate number. He loomed over me like a Goliath. I got the point. In a stuttering faggoty-voice, I mumbled something about loving wildlife, all the children of the world, and my mother. After giving us both a last evil eye, he stomped slowly and meaningfully over to the cab of his truck. "Let that be a lesson to you!" he grunted loudly before slamming the door closed and starting 'er up. Harry and I both watched the taillights slowly disappear around the bend. Harry moved over to me from out of the bushes, "What the fuck!" He said exasperatedly. "I thought we were gonna teach him how to fuck right off!" I was just relieved—relieved as hell. Harry's babbling was just idle chatter and jabbering in the background. "Yeah," I said quietly, "we should probably get outta here." It was nice that it did not turn into anything more of an event anyways. We rode home at a medium pace without any theatrics. The crazy trucker had dampened our excited moods, and it was time for a brewsky. Harry and I got back to the shop, so we could get our backpacks and part ways. Not until later that night did I remember that my knee was in immense pain. The next morning, it had morphed into a beautiful blue/black colour.

CHAPTER 4 — Birthday for Hobbers

The world, I was not it, for I had one of my own.

My parched mouth was slightly gapping, and I had dry lips from breathing between my teeth. The time was nine in the morning, and it was a Saturday. The night before, a few good friends and I had made plans to go out and possibly take in a few drinks, and maybe mingle with a few hos. Finally, at four, I seem to remember opening the front door and, a few minutes after that, the part I have no recollection of, falling unconscious onto my bed. Most likely drooling and snoring, with all of my beer-soaked clothes still on, just for that little bit of extra pleasure when you wake up the next morning and look at your lousy self in the mirror. Or before, when you pull the smelly sock covered feet of yours from under the covers and plant them uneasily on the carpet-clad floor. And then, a little bit after when you oversleep your alarm, don't notice, but when you do, hop in your car, zip to work as fast as you can before the windows have any sort of chance to defrost, and your co-workers watch you stagger into the shop, and they reel at the big wave of alcohol smell that hits them like a semitruck without brakes!

That was me at this point in the morning: no shower, no toothbrush, no breakfast, and a bit of clean clothing. It was a good wholesome fresh start. Oh, and I'm pretty sure someone spilt a drink in my hair (I don't know how), so it was all sticky and tangled, just to put a cherry on top. At least I wasn't the only one late. Duane always pretended that his alarm never went off. He got into the shop a good forty-five minutes to an hour after everyone else this time. Good excuse though 'cause new alarm clocks are a whole twenty dollars at the local Wal-Mart. Anyways, I had to clean up. Prince Albert was taking his morning dump in the shop washroom that had no fan. This was great, since above the door was a large hole. Even if you closed the door after he was done, it still smelt like shit for thirty minutes. Just for the record, that is one of the grossest things a groggy sleepy-eyed person could come to work and experience—first thing!

Later in the day, when Albert went in there for his second or third vile adventure, Harry and I got rags doused in brake clean, lit them after balling them up, and threw them over the door to the unsuspecting victim on the other side . . . who was always Albert.

And here I was, as groggy as a drunk, which I still kinda was, ready for the day's work: still hadn't cleaned up and hungry as a third-world orphan . . . maybe not that hungry. Dillen opened the door joining the showroom and service area and poked his head through. "Um, hey, guys, that R1200 for the annual service is in. Want to grab the gate?" Even from the washroom where Albert was crouching, you could still hear his wheezed-out bellowing, "Listen, yah gobbler! Git that damned gate open *yerself*!" "Oh fuck," I muttered. This was going to be a headache coming on in *no time*! Especially with these dorks running around making fools of themselves.

Just then Gerald pulled Dillen out of the way and proceeded into the shop. "My, you all look as though you are a bunch of *belligerents*! Wake up! I do not pay you for this unreasonable behaviour." Harry had previously been outside, stacking crates of motorcycle pallets, and walked in just as Gerald was going into his tizzy. "Ahh, what's he going off about?"

One might say that this was the only day that Harry Edwards had not had substance abuse on the previous eve. For once, he was awake, willing to perform tasks and duties, and he was my exact opposite for the morning. Gerald had a wide stare on his round face and turned his head slowly and deliberately towards Harry before continuing his bantering. He raised his voice just a wee bit higher as well to accommodate for his short stature. "What's *going on* here is I'm paying you three lots of money so that the lot of you may lollygag about and play hopscotch all day! See my point? Go! Open the gate, roll the motorcycle around, and fix it! This conversation is over!" He put his fists to the sides and stormed off in a grouch. Harry looked across the shop from me in despair, "What the shit's going on? I'm doin' piles a' work 'n' stuff!" I started explaining to him about Albert telling off Dillen but got interrupted as he came out of the 'shitter.' "Not what happened!" He squealed, "He's full of shit!" Adding for effect, a huge wave of his hands how full of shit I supposedly was. "Ohh right, sorry about that, Alberto. I guess I'll know better next time. Go put your clothes on, Santa!" Albert, underneath his worn blue jeans and brown oiled canvas jacket wore thermal underwear. They were red, and they were also a one-piece jumper, with a flap at the back with buttons in case of washroom breaks. In addition, he just looked unduly amusing; and whenever we saw it, we referred to him as some sort of Christmas elf, Santa's little helper, or Santa, or started singing Christmas carols. Also, whenever he comes out of the washroom, he has his pants undone and has to waddle over to his chair and take his time to become civilized again—if that's possible for an uncivilized person.

Harry grabbed one of his 'health' granola bars and, with pants swishing away because he kept them ridiculously low, managed to get back outside before a verbally aggravated argument broke out. By this time, I had finally managed to acquire my service clothing and was also getting dressed. The boots were finally laced, and I stood up proud and tall, letting out a long sigh. "I'm ready for work, Alberto!" I yelled over into his direction, "Just after I get a tea!" Whatever day it is, no matter how bad or how good, should start with a green tea. At one time, next to my toolbox, I will have about six or seven different kinds of loose leaf green and oolong teas, just begging to be steeped. Sometimes when I am feeling risqué, I might embellish with a white tea. The taste of these teas is so soft that you have to let it sit and mingle on your upper palate for a good fifteen seconds with your eyes closed to appreciate the delicate and beautiful flavour. After grabbing my tea strainer and stainless steel BMW mug, I took the opportunity to stroll up front and get some hot water from the coffee machine.

All our local dorks were there: Dillen, Duane, a whole bunch of customers that stop by for free coffee every morning and then every afternoon because they are all probably on the brink of divorce, are divorced, or just lonely men that think they can come to the shop to relieve their loneliness. There was also Trevor and Gerald up front who were working steadily unlike the others. Rushing over to the coffee machine at the far end of bikes on the right-hand side of the showroom, I pressed the hot water button twice in quick succession. "Gotta get outta here, gotta get out of here," I muttered under my breath. I grabbed my mug a second after the machine let out an audible beep and raced back into the shop before any customers tried to make eye contact or start up a conversation. I praised myself as I slammed the door shut and had my tea. Things were looking brighter this morning!

When I had been up front, some jerk had put that R1200RT on my bench! That means I had to do work. Urgg, "All right, sucka!" Harry had once again returned from working out back and was leaning against the table of a nearby workstation. In his left hand, he grasped a grocery bag of mixed nuts and trail mix. With his right hand, he was shovelling a mountainful down his throat. "Nom nom nom," he said with loose chunks flying freely towards me from his gaping crevasse of a mouth. "So good," he added, opening his eyes wide and tilting his head back to ram another ungodly portion into his throat. Harry grinned wickedly and met my glare. He was trying to egg me on which was not about to happen. At the speed I was going this morning, I probably couldn't even deliver a proper towel-whipping; what a shit-show this place was. Shakily, I began servicing the bike. 'Oh boy,' I thought. The bike needed an annual service. In addition, the old 2006 beater had Integral ABS. Blast it to hell! On Integral ABS is a wheel circuit with fluid running from the control module to the calipers. Then it was a control circuit with fluid running from the master cylinder to the control module with three bleeding nipples. This had to be done for the front and rear systems; the biggest hassle of them all. With my T25 and T30 T-handle torque-style wrenches, I proceeded to remove the left- and right-side bodywork and my 6-mil Allen I used for the petrol tank. With the ABS, 90 percent of the models besides the K12GT/K13GTs have the ABS pump underneath the petrol tank. "Albert, pass me the brake fluid sucker." He murmured something, and from his stool, he hunched over and pulled the 'sucker' from its home under the number-three bench of Albert.

The furthest wall in the shop from the doorway had a large bench on the left; in the middle was Albert's cabinet and toolbox, which then carried on as a bench until the end of the wall. These were Albert's benches number one and number two. On the perpendicular wall to the number-two bench was the opening to the tyre shed, the tyre machine/tool balancer, and the opening to the metal and machine room. Albert's bench number three, and then the opening to the battery room. His castle only had two walls! I wouldn't put a moat around that as your feet would end up a little wet.

With my seven-millimetre box and open-ended wrenches, I plugged away at the bleeding of the pump. BMW even had specialty tools built for the pumps due to the fact that some of the bleeder nipples were impossible to loosen or tighten with conventional wrenches. Luckily for me, our shop had them. One great feature about the R1200 series bikes over the R1150 series is that they use mineral oil in the clutch master cylinder reservoir. This oil is set for life, as moisture does not affect it the same way that is affects

Dot 3 or 4 brake fluid. This means that you never have to change it unless a master or slave cylinder is being replaced. This was a bit of a time-saver, as the brakes slowed the servicing time down enough. Brake fluid running through braided stainless lines should be changed at least once every two years, and more frequently if riding like a man instead of an infant. Some of the fuckers we have that come by have old rubber lines and twenty-year-old fluid sitting in there with the consistency of glue and the colour of tar. That's good ole cheap for you though: if it still runs, keep on going and don't worry about the maintenance.

After finishing up that job, I started on the alternator belt. At 40K on the older bikes, we replace the fuel filter and the alternator belt. The fuel filters were in the newer bikes for life, so only the belt needed replacing—perfect. The crusty alternator belt cover had small steel bolts that corroded easily from the road salts in our mild winters that people ride in all year long. With my small metal pick, I eased out globs of dirt from the bolt heads. The cover was removed fairly easily, and the belt was changed quickly thereafter. These belts are made of elastomer material, and are much more advanced than the predecessors, so no loosening or tightening of bolts or brackets; and no need of special torque wrenches with special spring-loaded tensioner bolts. The belt is stretched directly over the pulleys and is one more time saver in the days of busy lives and individuals always on the go. Most people hate spending money on service work and maintenance and, this saves them a little. While the belt job was taking place, I dropped all three oils and let them drain while I was performing other tasks. The engine oil was children-burning hot and came out of the drain hole at an obscenely quick rate. Scalding hot, it splashed joyously over my black nitrile gloves. I dropped the drain plug and the 8-mil Allen socket onto the metal bench and tore the gloves from my hands. They were throbbing from the heat but were partially saved from the cancer-causing oil that never touched them. Harry noticed the occurrence and ran over to me with hands raised over his head, waving them around like the maniac he was. In a concerned voice, he asked if they were okay. Then he ran over and grabbed some talcum powder, while I started cleaning up the gloves and the oil that was dripping on the floor. He came back and chugged the talcum onto the droplets and all over my hands. "What the fuck are you doing?" I yelled in exasperation. "Oh, didn't you know? This powder shit is the shit! Heals anything!" With my white old ladylike-smelling hands I grabbed the bottle and threw it across the shop. With a dull thrump, the bottle hit the tyre rack near the shop's rear doors and let a white cloud out into the air. Harry let out an enraged battle cry and proceeded to cower over towards Albert. With his hands outstretched, he grabbed Albert's weak and brittle sides and began tickling him. He doubled over onto the floor, clutching at Harry's meticulous fingers. Yelping like a wounded dog, he lay there; and overtop of him, Harry snickered and let out a howl like a wolf.

Albert managed to pipe up that Gerald would hear him, being his last not really valiant effort to save himself, as I clearly was not going to partake in the little game that they were playing. Harry scrunched his eyebrows into a frown and stood up. "All right, ya jerk, just tryin' to have a bit of fun for once, probs the only one tryin' to do that." Albert staggered to his feet and grabbed the side of his bench to keep steady. From being tickled, he started to pant and sweat. "You go 'ave fun by yourself. Don't wanna be included 'n that *crap!*" After getting his breath back, he went up front and had a coffee and did not come back into the shop for another twenty minutes. I went over to my bench and carried the tranny and rear-end oil pans outside, and finished up the engine oil and filter change.

This whole time, I still had the damned talcum powder all over my hands. Harry's joking attitude today was a little strange, and he seemed overly happy—weird, not really something we knew him for. Most of the time, it was a one-sided conversation on his end, whining and complaining about money, or lack thereof. "So, Hobbers, what makes you be in such a cheery mood today? Have a good S and M session last night or something?" Harry leaned over from behind the Suzuki on his bench and belched in my face. "Wow, I hope you share that with your parents next time they come see you, ya sick fuck!" "Yah, like my divorced folks with their shit-show fuckin' lives are interested in coming ta see me! I'm the only one that got outta that crack-pot city. Know what that means? That means if anyone wants to see anyone, I'll have to go do the seein', 'n' the only person I give a rat's ass about is my sister. An' she already said she'd cruise by this summer sometime." "Ahh . . . Harry? I was merely asking about your night, 'cause you seem more casual and, if possible, friendly today." There might be a deeper-rooted problem here that I most likely don't want to get involved with. "Hey?" "Oh," he shrugged and turned away, tinkering with something between his hands while talking. "You know, just got back to my pad last night 'n' cleaned up the place. My roomy wasn't around, so just hung out by myself and watched a movie." "Didn't have any of your bitches over?" I chimed in. "Naw, them hos are gettin' old. Wanted to really check out that psychology shit I ordered. Got the DVDs 'n' stuff 'n' they seemed legit. Wanna get deeper into people, yah know? See what there really thinkin' 'n' stuff. I mean, I know I know them pretty good already, but I dunno. There's like more or somin'. There's like a deeper connection I could get going on, right?" Harry kind of left me hanging for a second. What in the world was I supposed to say to this whack job? "Well sure, it sounds as though when you know that person better, you could have more meaningful and intimate connections with them." "Yah man, I like that. More intimate. So better sex, right?" I looked at him for a second quizzically. Hmm, maybe he is just messing with my head because he knows that I'm probably sounding illogical and looked docile and dozy, I thought to myself. "Well, I didn't mean sex. I meant that when your chitty-chattying, and you understand that given person's emotional backgrounds and are quicker to find out their interests, humour, or intelligence levels, you could technically have a better chance of enjoying and having a more fulfilling relationship with that person. But, ahh, yes, I guess the sex could be more rewarding as well. Good point." He started talking again while I took a breath. I did not know that I could talk that much this morning. Maybe I should be in a state of euphoria for my awesomeness. "Knew you would understand what I mean, man! 'Cause who wants a deeper conversation when you can have deeper sex right? And I totally understand the importance of . . ." Yah . . . he went off for a bit about nothing important. Well, you know, of course sex is important; I was implying his useless babbling and ramblings were not of much importance.

Checked the tyre pressures, adjusted the tyre pressures, set the clock, read the fault codes in the computer, performed a bleed test for the Integral ABS system . . .

Bla de bla bla, and I'm done. Nice, put her all back together, and it's test-ride time. I bolted all the body panels onto the frame and bolted down the hatches 'cause I was going crazy! Actually, I just went for a test ride. After that, it sounded like lunchtime, which was perfect. A little midday snack always lights the fire. Might even grab a quick eat-fresh today; live large or die trying. Albert, Harry, and I, after some servicing work, left our humble station of employment and ventured off into the realm of town. Harry and I cruised down to the eat-fresh land, and Prince Albert marched on over to the grocery store, the local grocery store owned by a few Asian fellows. Good ole refreshing Asia!

"Got me a sub, got me a drank, got me some chips, let's get the hellll outta this joint!" Luckily for me, Harry only said that after we left the establishment. Keep the owners from putting signs up on their doors with pictures that say 'Do not allow entry.' "Fuck, Berty always takes a frickin' long time to choose his stuff." We were standing outside the grocery store, munching on our snacks and leaning against shopping carts. The store was only a few minutes' stroll from the motorcycle shop, and both the eat-fresh and the grocery store were along the same merry lane. "Albert is most likely getting frisky with that big-ass mamma behind the deli counter, hey-hey? He would love to just slide sensually up and down with that old broad." We chided him for a bit even though he was not present. We then saw him through the window at the till. He had been watching us and started making faces and baring teeth at us. We both pretended not to notice so that he looked ridiculous to the other customers in the store; and of course, he had to have his lotto ticket checked. His joy of the week was getting some paper tickets slid under that blue scanner sayin "YOU ARE NOT A WINNER." Wahoo, never saw it coming! For about five years straight, he had won maybe twenty dollars maximum for what—ten or twenty dollars a week? "Finally!" Harry yelled at him as he smiled his way through the automatic doors. "Yes," Albert raised his fist into the air and pumped it all the way down to his side. "A dollar. Guess who won a dollar!" This was a rhetorical question. "Ahh, let me see, the old lady with the walker by the ice cream aisle? Or no—wait—was it Jared Leto, from the band *30 Seconds to Mars*? Did he win a dollar? Was he in there? 'Cause, man, do I love their first two compact discs—great band." The smile on Albert's face went to a grouchy expression. "Thanks a lot for ruining my fun!" "Oh Berty, I'm so sorry, you know I'm sorry! You won the dollar? You won the dollar! May I see it? Is it shiny?" Harry joined in, "Man, I love it when I get a good shiny loony. Those were my favourite growin' up, before the toonies came out." We had been stalling and were almost back to the shop now. "Yah, 1996, good year that was." "What's that?" Harry inquired. "That's when the toonie came out. Couldn't decide whether to call it the dubloonie, like the old gold coins, or the toonie, since it was close to the loonie, but two of them—go figure." "Oh yah, well, why the heck do you remember things like that, man? Useless stuff that don't help you at all—it's totally irrelevant!" I thought for a jiffy and still didn't know how to respond to Harry's preposterous statement. "Well, Harry, that's the beauty of memory: sometimes you are going to remember things that happened in your life that you completely want to forget and wish they never happened. The best thing is that we can remember all the good memories that we want to keep. Sounds dumb, but you might want to cherish some of those memories. You don't want to forget about all the crazy things you did in high school, right? Or the funky shit we get up to at the shop, right? Or all those rowdy bitches you've spent time with, yah? So don' give me shit about remembering 1996. Besides, that was the year of the wild snowstorms that plagued Canada, you probs got tonnes back east!"

We were back at the shop, but Harry told us both to 'hold on'. "Ahh, um, the reason I was kinda dorky earlier was 'cause I'm waiting for a call from my dad. He always calls on my birthday, so there." Berty let out a snicker, and I let out a breath that had been held in since he started telling us this 'serious piece of news.' So it was his birthday? Well, that explained it all: tiny little Harry had birthdays too.

Lunch went by quickly and not much conversation took place. We all got back to work without interruption, and I managed to sneak away up front. I cruised down to Trevor's desk where he was occupied, looking at new helmets on Parts Canada's Web site. "So, ahh, Trevor, guess what I have to tell you?" He lifted his head off his hand, as it had been propped up on the desk. With a questioning look, he asked what it was that I had to tell him. "Well Trevor, this is the part of me asking you to guess, where you guess." "I'm not going to ask or guess, so just tell me." Holy crap, what a grouch he was today, I thought to myself. "It's Harry's birthday today, so why oh why don't you upfronters grab him a cake. It would look suspicious if I went and bought him one." He pulled off an aggravated sigh right into my face and agreed to do it. Yeesh, something was up Trevor's pie-hole today. It's all good though 'cause the party cake was now on the way.

In the shop again, services were rolling out left, right and center; couldn't have been any other way, as there were only three benches. Harry's Suzuki was having some charging issues, which meant waiting for parts. Albert's chain and sprockets and steering head bearing job on the single-cylinder F650GS was going grand: just the usual smashing, hammering, and bitching. And I had taken on a coolant change on a K1200LT after my RT full-service. This big lug took an hour to get the bodywork off before you could even change the coolant; not my idea of an amazing time—all the while, I was eagerly awaiting Trevor's return. He poked his head through into the service department a small while later. Looking over in my direction, he motioned for me to go up front to him. "Dude, there's kind of a tiny problem with the cake." "Why didn't you just grab a generic one? Like a Black Forest or an equally delicious choice?" Trevor put a befuddled look on his face, "They didn't have any, in all seriousness. No vanilla, no Black Forest, or chocolate even." "So . . . did you get anything, like a blob of icing maybe?" "Okay, here is the deal, and don't get mad." He pulled his choice from the plastic bag it had been carried back in. "You're fucking joking with me, right? It's pink! That's not cool! Harry's not a twelve-year-old girl, only his intellect is!" Trevor beat around the bush and bit his lower lip. "But, well, I managed to get the flowers off the top, and I also got his name on the top, in more manly pink colours." "Oh," I retorted. "Isn't that splendid? It says Happy Birthday Hairy, in blue, and the rest in pink. Tell me what kind it is, that might help." "Hmm, I am fairly certain that Helga mentioned it was a chocolate top, with a vanilla bottom half, with a raspberry goo for filling stuffed between the two halves." "Trevor, you just moved up a wee bit from where you were a few moments ago—spot on. You get these dorks up here ready to partay, and I will alert the media in the shop, a.k.a. Alberto VO5." "Gotcha." A quick high-five from

Trevs, and the ball was rolling. Sidling up to Albert, I gave him a nonchalant whisper and then got back to work. We agreed for four o'clock on the dot. We would light up the candles and surprise little Harry.

Wait, wait, wait some more. Bla, bla, bla, boring as shit. Come on, four o'clock! The hands on the home-made clock from Albert moved very slowly for the next couple of hours. Regular maintenance work was a drag on most days; now that it had become more special of a day, the work seemed somewhat pathetic and useless.

To pass the time, even though Harry was oblivious and clueless of what, we sang a few renditions and changed the words slightly around to better suit the environment of a motorcycle shop. 'Let's get physical, physical, Alberto, let's get physical, oh let's get into physical!' For some reason, Albert was always the most amusing name to put into a song, so why not? 'Take time with a tiny Bert 'cause he likes to heal, he likes to steal. 'Cause he's half the man he used to be.' Slow rock ballad guitar solo, take it! 'Half the man he used to be!' Look at that: all that love, and it was four o'clock already. Good news, since the ingested lunch was beginning to wear off, and I would be damned if I couldn't tell you I was hungry again.

Trevor and the other upfronters clambered into the shop through the one small door. Already lit in Gerald's outstretched arms was the masterpiece of a pink cake. I ran over and grabbed Albert. All of us gathered around Harry's bench and herded him between us. "Ahh, shit," was all he managed to get out before a chorus broke loose. "Happy birthday to you, happy birthday to you, happy birthday to ____ (everybody added their own comment here), happy birthday to you!" Harry raised his head up and opened his mouth to take in a deep breath. He lowered in overtop and blew out all of the lit candles. A big tooth-filled grin spread across his face, and it was obvious that he was trying to withhold all those friendly cheery emotions that we've all let loose once in a while. "All right, thanks, let's get a fuckin' knife happenin' so we can eat some of this stuff, hey?" Trevor was already prepared. What a good little wife he was. His woman must be so proud.

The cake, no matter how repulsive it appeared to be, actually turned out to be quite decent in the tasting department. Duane obviously mowed down half of the entire cake because most individuals that have diabetes want to take in three pounds of sugar in one sitting. It all makes sense to me. Gerald grabbed a sliver and ran upfront to keep a watchful eye on the showroom. Heaven forbid, someone might want to buy a keychain and have to wait for a moment to finalize the deal. Noooooo, five seconds, that was too long! Then again . . . in that time, with no one watching, the dude could pocket the trinket and bust out of the store, and who would be wiser? Albert grabbed a large piece and used his classy spoon to tear apart the main course followed by him devouring the contents. Dillen also took a large piece, making sure to lick the morsels from the fork he was using for every friggin' bite. That sure as hell doesn't bother anyone, "Smack, smack, slurp, smack." "All right, you dimwit," I spoke to the retard, "if you're going to be a turd about eating your cake, get back to your counter!" Dillen bared his teeth, showing off a row of brown, possibly chocolate-covered bridgework, and meandered towards the door. Either that or it was from his boyfriend last night. Harry and I took normal-sized pieces, and I was still only able to finish two-thirds of the portion. To be honest, it's not that I don't like sugar, it is just that it makes me feel like crap if I eat a whole pile of it. Maybe I had the diabetes. Oh well, too lazy to go check it out at the doctors. That is what smart healthy people are supposed to do, right?

Trevor waited until all the other greedy bastards, including myself, had all but finished our first helpings before acquiring a piece for himself. With a mouth stuffed full, he managed to nod his head in satisfaction before trundling up to the showroom, his domain.

All the community, and the sharing and caring, seemed to cheer everyone up a little; not that they were in bad moods, but a lighter atmosphere lingered. Much softer than before Harry even received the call from his dad that he had been waiting patiently for. And with the end of the day coming shortly, it was a relief to see some smiles protruding off of everybody's faces. The only thing we could do now was find out whose birthday came next in the calendar year; this being the next probable chance those smiles would be revealed again. You know what they say: all's well that ends well.

CHAPTER 5 — Pyrotechnics and Mayhem

"It's outta control! It's outta control! Watch out!" The blood-red CBR1000 had flames spewing from the tail section and flammable liquids cascading from every side of the bike. It carried on its way, picking up speed as she went. The rider was impervious to the flames surrounding him, doing catwalks and travelling at speeds greater than any enflamed Honda had been before.

The rubber from the tyres was also getting to extreme temperatures and was beginning to melt. Just then, a huge wall of flame smashed into the front fairing, blackening the windshield and momentarily ceasing the vision of the rider. In the distance, Hobbers was vaguely heard screaming at the top of his lungs. "Great footage, man! Keep on goin'!" Up ahead, in front of the rider was a long metal ramp. Thirty feet past that ramp on the ground lay a pool of fluid. It seemed to be moving and shifting the way the air above it looked. It was gasoline! Not just a tiny pool, it appeared to be a lake of gas! No! If that rider jumped over the pool, not only would the flames coming off the bike ignite the gasoline, but the rider would be smothered by smoke and flames.

He was getting closer to the ramp. The chain and sprockets were making a high-pitched whirring sound, while the exhaust pushed sound waves deep into your ears. The suited rider was in a tuck, helmet smacking into the tank, and the gear of his body engulfed in flame. The faster he went, the shorter he had to live. Albert could also be heard in the distance bellowing threats of fire hazards and police officers, but it was to no avail. The Michelin tyres hit the ramp, and the suspension of the bike compressed. The rider was doing obscene speeds, and only now that he was on the ramp could he see the ensuing danger. He has seconds before the inevitable with nowhere to go, but over the *lake of doom*!

As the wheels flew over the edge of the ramp, the tyres exploded into flame. The wheels were turning still, as the rider had his hand firmly on the throttle. Great gobs of melting rubber flung themselves into the air as the tyres disintegrated. He may have started the jump, but there was no way he would finish it, as catastrophe was bound to happen. The nameless rider entered over the *lake of doom*! In a fraction of space and time, the top layer of gasoline lit. A lake of *fire* had been born, and for the CBR, a bed of death. Urgent screams from Harry pulled the rider into awareness of his surroundings. He had to change his landing. If it was possible to land on the back wheel and keep the bike upright while landing, he could jump off the bike and roll safely to a stop; most of the flames burning up his gear and skin would be put out. Then the bike would keep rolling and explode off in the distance, not harming anybody but the ozone. It was the only thing that could be done. The bike was in midair. He could barely see through the smoke and fire, and the temperature inside the helmet was excruciatingly high. All of the bodywork had been melted and blackened. The end of the lake was getting near. The exit ramp was but a small metal plank in the distance. The rear wheel came down onto it. The cords from the tyre flew in every direction, but the rider held his course, and he held on strong.

The front wheel came down next. As it descended onto the transition ramp, rubber as well spun off into the sidelines. When the full weight of the bike had come down, the bike was riding on the rear magnesium alloy rim, drifting the bike and trying to change its course. Just then, the front wheel collapsed from the stresses put upon it. It broke away, the three-spokes from the rim, yet still turned. The forks became caught in the spinning wreckage. The stanchions cracked, and the front end of the bike plummeted towards the ground. Disaster had struck, and the rider of the destroyed machine dove overtop of the bike's handlebars. The CBR went end over end, and pieces went everywhere: red bodywork to the left, chunks of cast wheels to the right. Turn signals and glass from the headlight followed. As the Honda came to a final halt after digging deep channels into the asphalt with the broken frame, the flames caught up to the petrol tank vent and roared up the hose. She exploded into a triumphant ball of fire with a gigantic sound ripping through the shop. Minutes later, all that remained was a small black puddle of melted and burnt plastic on the ground. Harry stopped filming the show with his cell phone, and I grabbed the plastic model Honda CBR bike with a pair of needle-nose pliers and took it outside. With the garden hose, I gave it a good douse of water to make sure the fire was out. It steamed momentarily and then was strewn into the garbage along with the other things we had burnt that morning. I ran back inside to watch the footage.

As I opened the door to reenter the service department from outside, voices from unknown individuals could be heard talking inside. I walked through. At Albert's bench were a couple, both yabbering with him about their motorbikes. Their top of the line R1200GSA 'adventure touring' bike was in for its one-thousand-kilometre service. At that moment, they were planning on going for a long trip, not that unusual for our customers. With the three large aluminum cases on the bike, one of them served as a backrest for the lady. They also wanted the foam pads for added comfort and a COMM install for their helmets so that they could jibber-jabber back and forth with one another. "I don't do COMM installs or helmet stuff like that. That guy over there does 'em." Albert pointed towards me while talking. They walked over to me and 'warmly' introduced themselves. The husband got quickly to the point. "Now, young man, we are thinking this weekend of travelling down to the States, just a few for a small jaunt. We've already bought these systems here," showing off two of the expensive latest and greatest kits on the market. "But we don't do our own installation jobs." He leaned over in his wife's direction, and a sneer appeared on his face. The kind of sneer that says, 'Oh my dear, we're so rich and amazing. It is these lowlifes here in the blue collars that get to do the simple tasks, such as putting speakers and microphones into our $1,200 Schubert helmets.' She looked up into his eyes and smiled back at him, 'Yes, dearest, let us get you some Cialis on the way home, so this time you might be able to pleasure me!' Oh wait, that is what I thought she said, but she didn't—how silly of me. "I actually do most of the installs. Have you guys booked in any shop time for the required work? They need around an hour for each system to be installed. It's not a very complicated process, it's just the time needed to complete the job." His face contorted a little, and his nose perked up into a scrunch, "Why, that's $200, which seems a bit high, hmm?" What a dork. "Well, the good news is that I don't set the price and just do the work." As I was Chatty-Cathying with them, my right arm took the liberty of directing them towards the showroom. They're the type of people that are *über*friendly and good to you until something doesn't go their way exactly as they had planned. As soon as those 'monkeys' had been put back in the barrel, a.k.a. upfront, I closed the door and wiped my hands of the whole COMM system issue, for now. "Yo, Harry-mamma, those crazy-monkeys almost caught fire they came in here so fast." "What was that?" "Two seconds after I left to throw out the toy bike, they just pounced on Albert!" "Hey, you, kids—I mean, children," Albert stammered from over in one of his corners. "What's that, old man? I can't hear you, I'm too awesome!" Albert grouched up instantly. "You two know what I mean: that burning shit! It's gotta stop, 'n' it reeks in here now. All that brake clean 'n' burnin' plastic an' shit. I don't care if ya kill yerself, but I dun wanna be done-in by yer stupid blowin' shit up an' video-tapin' bullshit!" "Albert? We're not just blowing 'shit' up." I brought my fingers up to my head and 'quotationed' as I said it. "We're burning Hondas, okay? A Honda CBR to be precise. We have the S1000RR anyways, a far superior product to all those Japanese models. You should be congratulating us for our fine efforts to abolish them from this service department." He screwed up his face and started to go off on a tangent, moving his grease- and oil-stained arms around in the process, "I'll abolish *you* from here, ya dirt-wad. I'll break your damned phone too! Yer not allowed them at work anyways!" "Goodness gracious, Prince Albert," I said in a loud motherly tone, "I don't take kindly with you talking in that raised voice of yours. This is a workplace and a place of business! Show a little respect for once. I do not condone this rambling of yours. If you continue to keep it up, I promise you I will file for an aggravated verbal assault. Now then! Let us continue our day's work. Let us all take a deep breath and pretend as though we are starting over. Ahhhh, see how good it feels, son? Really good. Try it with me, Berty, ahhhhh." "I won't fucking try that with you. I'm going outside to 'ave a fag! Yer messed up anyways." Albert stumbled outside with a smoke, and I began to laugh at myself and the situation. I was not the one 'messed up,' but the situation and everybody else sure as hell was. "Hey, dude," Harry swaggered over, "check this crazy getup out," referring to the video we had taken on his phone. "I already watched it while you were hittin' up those old farts for helmet stuff—it's like totally awesome." We started the video over again and had ourselves a few good laughs. To sum it up, it was very dorky yet humorous; and since there was lots of gasoline and everything in the video was on fire, there was nothing that could have possible made it any better. After Albert came back into the shop and finished his smoke, the atmosphere soured a whole bunch. He stayed over by his bench, mumbling and grumbling away; and Harry and I didn't talk much either, since it would have been about our pyro fun we had just had. Since poopy-pants didn't want any part in our fun, we were going to let the situation cool down for a bit.

A distant honking could be heard from outdoors somewhere close by. Duane whipped open our adjoining door and screeched back at us, "Dillen's at the gate with a service bike. Can one of you guys grab it?" He then proceeded to slam the door without waiting for a reply. Berty cried out from his hole in the ground he called a workplace, "I ain't gettin' that! Faggot can get the gate himself!" I rolled my eyes over in Harry's direction, like I had done so many times before. He looked back at me, "Fine, I'll get the gate!" He stomped his feet through our shop doors, and I gave him a playful pat on the back. "Awe, thanks, Harry, I knew we could count on you!" He kept on walking and lifted his middle finger at me as he did. "Harry, you're a horrible person! You've got a demon inside that head of yours!" He turned while walking and with a deranged look in his eyes stuck out his tongue wildly at me. "I'm the god of destruction!" he bellowed. In an instant, he had grabbed a bottle of talcum powder. Where it had come from, I had no idea. He then ran back after me with it. "No, dude, I fucking hate talcum powder! You know that!" Harry bent to his knees for a low spray of talcum. I dove to the side just in time as a big waft of powder landed where I had been just seconds before. "Harry, you're going to die for this." "Hah, you can't stop me; I'm the god of mayhem!" I kept myself on constant alert while we fought, "You just said the god of destruction." Again, I managed to escape a ball of powder that was headed straight for my face. "Well, yah," Harry panted, "I can be like whatever I want—I'm a god!" Albert stomped loudly past us and shot through the service bay doors, grumbling about him getting the gate open for the little gay boy. "I hope your powers can suppress my fury of *shizzam*!" I snuck my way to the rag bin and grabbed a good 'sizer.' Harry knew that once I had a rag in hand for whipping, it was serious time. Two quick whips to the knuckles of his right hand, and he cursed me from the pain, "You fucker! I'm def' gonna show you how to play ball!" "Do it, mamma, I'm right here ready for yah!" "Hiya," Harry karate-chopped the air and then threw the talcum powder at me as a distraction. Always the damned talcum powder! He ran backwards and got an oil-covered rag from our discard bin. "So long, sucka, prepare to be Harry-anated!" I threw back my head and howled, "Game time." He charged, and one of his blows caught me at my elbow. I didn't have a long-sleeved shirt on, and the snap sounded like the cracking of an actual whip. The next one I was ready for. He crouched down to get at my thigh, but I skilfully blocked his attack by stretching my rag between both hands and arresting his advance. He continued on the offensive, and I continued to block his shots: an elbow, knee, hip, hand, all were deflected by my whip-stopping technique. In conjunction with my light footwork, he was beginning to fatigue. My plan exactly: defend, defend, and then pounce. *Bawam*, I made my move. Harry went for another forearm shot, and I jumped to the side. I lunged forward and threw three lightning fast hits: bam, one to his left knee, one to his right knee, bam, the last to his right hip bone. Harry fell back a step and tried comprehending how I managed such a quick and powerful attack. He didn't want to let his guard down, but a large red mark had made its way onto his arm, and he wanted to soothe it with a good rub. "Hah, you're just lucky, you piece of shit," he yelled at me in surprise. "Like, no way you'll do that again—I'll be teachin' you." For some reason, his smugness disappeared when I attacked his red arm again, leaving it purple and throbbing. "Ahh, motherfucker" was all he managed to get out. He was seething, red, and had a bit of adrenaline pumping through his veins. In his left hand, twirled the rag 'round and 'round, and then with the right hand, Harry pulled it taut. Meanwhile, I balanced the weight on my toes with knees bent and ready for war, or to spring away from direct hits. I attempted a quick blow to his leg, but he smacked my rag away, "So long, sucka" (I think he enjoyed this expression). Harry chortled and made his move. He feigned to the left, and I skipped quickly to my left, but he knew that's where I would run to. His hit collided with my right thigh. A huge jut of pain erupted where it landed. Before I had time to defend or counterattack, he struck again on my right wrist. It felt like a backhand from an angry woman. I managed to croak out a 'yikes' and a small insignificant laugh, but had to stay focused. Harry was still quite crazed and needed another lesson. His senses were now heightened, and it was going to be more difficult to strike. I was thinking he might try his last move again, see if I had learned my lesson; moment into me thinking about it, he tried the exact same move, this time to the right. I hadn't figured out how to deliver the 'jackhammer' yet, so I just had to wing it. Harry placed his right foot forwards yet kept the weight back on his left foot. At the same time, I pretended to fall stupidly for the same trick of his, so I moved my upper body to the right to see where he would set up his strike. Harry's eyes glowed as he lined up his mark. He attempted to have a clean shot to my left arm, since I was supposed to move to the side. He threw out his coiled-up rag, and it sprang to life; I was waiting.

I saw it jump towards me, and Harry was surprised when it didn't hit the target. My left hand pulled the oily cloth from the air with such ferocity that he was left stunned. He had no defence and had nothing to strike me with. I threw out my own rag behind me and made this new grimy-covered one taught. The oil blackened my fingertips. I was the lion that had just buckled the knees of the gazelle. All that had to be done was finish off the prey. Harry's eyes glowed no longer. Now they seemed to hold a frightened bewildered glaze over top of them. He stepped back with nowhere to run. I tightened my grip and took a step forward. "No you don't, man, no you don't!" I made no reply. Lashing out, my first whip hit only air. A magnificent snapping sound resounded through the shop. The service bay doors opened at the same time. With Harry's back to the doors, he turned his head to see the intrusion, and I struck.

The rag was an inch or so shorter than the one I was using, which explained why the first attempt had been powerful yet failed to make contact. The second time I went to make contact, I delivered a solid and direct hit. Since Harry had his head turned, he lost his guard. His right thigh erupted into pain followed by the tail of the rag, which curved around to the back of the leg; that sure brought his head back to attention. Harry grabbed his leg and clenched his teeth together, "Cock-biter! Takin' down someone without a piece!" "All right, get outta the way! Bugger off," howled Berty as he came through the doors with the bike. "There yah go, rescued by the old papa-burger from Allen and Wright," I said. I tossed the oily rag into Harry's chest, "Here, as a keepsake for kickin' your butt." "Don't need that shit as a keepsake, got these fuckers right here!" He pointed towards one of the ships that had landed nicely on the side of his arm. "Hah," I threw back at him, "that won't even be gone by the next round." "Yah, well, you better remember that you still got a couple reds happenin' on your arms an' legs too. You remember those for next time." I put my fist out, and Harry gave it a quick pound. "All right, we got shit to do."

"So, Berty, looks as though you found yourself quite a nice little motorcycle outside, didn't you, fellow?" "Yah, sure did, 'n' it gits to go on *yer* bench! Ha-ha!" Albert started to laugh, but there was too much phlegm built up in his throat. He began to gag badly. Harry yelled from the bike he was working on. "You sick old man, get the fuck outside! You phlegm-fuck!" Berty scurried over to the garbage can and grabbed both sides. Great gobs of disgustingness flew from his mouth. He continued to gag and reel as bucket loads of discoloured substance dribbled and spewed in all directions. After the onslaught, he used the back of his sleeve to wipe off the remainder and then giggled as he walked back to his toolbox. This time he had a good laugh to himself and disclosed to Harry that it was one of the only ways that he could get back at us hooligans for jerkin' his chain all morning. "Yah, well you wanna know some a' the shit I put up with from you, boy?" Harry yelled back at him. "I don't even have enough paper to write down that much stuff." Berty scoffed in Harry's general direction and went back to what he was doing. "Get back to workin' on those bikes, you sleepyheads. I'm pickin' up all this damned slack here from you 'gobblers.'" "Berty, the only slack you're picking up are the ones that you left on the floor of the washroom." He scowled at me, "I don't wear slacks, biatch. I wear pants with long johns underneath." "Ahh, only kinda gathered that from the flaunting of your red jolly-jumper. Next, you'll be prancin' in front of the customers in that thing." Harry chimed in, "Dude, sat night after work, we'll put on a friggin' show. Berty's up on the stage, struttin' his moves. Think of all the old biddies Albert'll be cuddlin' with, hey? Rollin' up in the old GMC, taggin' tail, left right 'n' center." "I don't need none of that woman bullshit, you dorks, and I'm not going up front in my jumper. You boys have to suffer!" "We suffer enough, thanks, and thanks for that horrible breath of yours, and the constant shitting of yourself." Albert was getting all excited now, "Oh fuck you, you shit as much as anyone, *protein boy*!" "Listen, Prince Albert, if you took some protein powder once in a while, you might just end up weighing more than forty-five pounds. One gust of wind, and you'd topple right over." I took my airline off the wall mount and locked in the air gun. After uncoiling a few links, I moseyed over and gave him a big blast of air from the gun. "Oh, Berty, it's a *hurricane*, watch out, you're going to be blown ashore, Captain!" "Get off my ass, you brat! I'll tell you a joke about a 'blown ashore' boy." Harry walked over to listen to Albert's joke. "Well, Dad, we're all ready and waitin'." "All right, all right, gimme a sec, gotta remember the beginning, hold up." Albert looked up towards the ceiling for a second and counted out who knows what on his fingers. "Okay, so there's this ship . . ." "Oh, what kind of ship?" queried Harry. "Shut up, that's not the important part of the story!" "Fine," stammered Harry. "So there's this ship, a big ole boat, and it's got the skipper. So the skipper says to one of the deck boys, 'Hey, boy, you wanna see a ship with wheels?' The deck boy instantly stopped what he was doin' an' came over to the cap'n, 'Oh boy, that'd be great!' So the cap'n takes him below deck, 'n' he says to the boy, 'Okay, go over to the port hole over there an' look through it.' The boy goes over an' peers through the port hole.'" Harry interrupted the story again, "Come on, dude, yer takin' forever to tell this crap!" "You calm the fuck down! We're almost at the good part," Berty screeched back. "K then, get on with it." "Sooo, the boy's lookin through the port hole, 'This is great!' The cap'n drops his drawers and moves up behind the youngin'. Just as the boy starts to talk again, 'I've never seen a ship with *wheeeeeeels*,' the cap'n drops the kid's shorts and screws him. He keeps on screamin', 'Wheeeels,' as the cap'n holds 'im down!" Albert could barely contain himself as he finished telling the distasteful tale. Harry pointed at him, "You crazy cracker, that's nasty!" Albert opened his mouth and guffawed as loudly as possible. I waited till he was done with his hysterics and told him that he was a gross child molester that liked little boys. Then I walked back to my bench to start work on a motorcycle. Berty yelled at both of us as we went back to work, "I've never seen a ship with *wheeeels*, Cap'n!"

Harry walked over and turned up the stereo, "This'll drown you out, ya slimy toad!"

I don't really mind oldies rock. For instance, if CCR or some Zeppelin comes on the radio, it's pretty good. Then let's just say that it's been played ten hours a day, five days a week, for your entire life. Blaaaa, you begin to have a large hate towards oldies music. Every time you hear it, your body tenses up, and you wouldn't have a problem killing puppies or small infants. "Ahh, Harry, why don't we put on something edu-ma-cational, like the news?" He looked at me as if I had just murdered his sister. "The news is crap, man! The government controls the news. An' I don't need some piece o' shit politicians running bullshit through this head of mine!" Harry pointed towards his temple where a big throbbing vein was sitting, throbbing. "Whoa, easy girl! Take a quick step back and join me in reality land. There is a whole bunch of good things that the government does for us as well, besides filling our heads with garbage and propaganda. They also give people without jobs welfare to sit on their asses and collect cheques. In addition, they have safe injection sights for crackheads and other fucked-up junkies. That's only a small portion of where our taxpayer money goes. Lemme see, what else?" Harry's veins were pounding out from the side of his head. "Don't get me fuckin' started, man, I can't even go down the road playin' my tunes without gettin' pulled over by the fuzz!" I chortled to myself, since I knew that most of the circumstances in which he got pulled over and ticketed. "Prepare to be fucked by the long shaft of the law!" I said over to him, smiling in a deep authoritative tone. He waved a half-inch drive ratchet at me and ground his teeth together. "Hey, Harry, take a chill pill, come on! Remember, the news also tells you the weather, so you can tell if your family back home is safe, and if there is a dangerous situation in the Middle East. They let you become aware of it, so you can skip that on your next vacation. All of these useful things." He grumbled around for a bit and eventually agreed with me after I told him a few more actually helpful things that the media and news networks did for us, and the community, and the people! "That's all good 'n' fun, but we're still not playing that news on our system. This is a music-only zone, biatch!" "Okay then, how 'bout we strike up an old dealy-poo?" "Fine, no country or oldies, an' I'll play your music game," Harry said after pondering it for a minute. He then stroked his bristly chin and smirked a bit before heading over to the amp. "Fo-sho, he'll play the music game all right!" Harry flipped over the stations on the radio while shaking his head slowly. "Nope, nope, nope, this shits all bunk-dog." Then he hit it, our town's top-40 pop station. The right arm of his raised in triumph at his supposed success. "Bitches! Don't be cryin'." Urgg, this was more annoying than the previous crap. 'Bass, bass, bass, thump, thump, slam, slam, slam!' 'Yo, my bitches in da club we be bangin' on the dance flo'. Dem girls get hot fo slamin', dem hos day be ridin' one anotha'. I run mo ladays than ma drug supplia, yea yea. I wanna feel ya ride me, ho, ho. I wanna be inside ya! Bitches let's rock, ya bitches lets a roll. Get me 22s and we be dubbin' for sho.' And so forth and so forth. Okay, that isn't even a real song, even though I know it sounded good to you, I just made it up on the spot! That stuff all sounds the same anyways, at least at two in the morning, when you're annihilated, spanking a random chick's ass with one hand, and the other hand holding a double rum and Coke with a lime press, half drank, a quarter on the girl in front of you, and the other quarter warm and diluted from the ice.

I visualized the clock; "I'm guessing four thirty," I said to myself, "only one hour left to go," and after that was check-out time. Damn it, 3:37, two hours to go; two hours of this silly nonstop nonsense music. "Harry, this black-person music is killing me, and it's only on the second song!" "Ha-ha, you little slut, we're gonna drill this shit *way* into yer head, man! It'll be stuck in yer head forever, thinkin' the shit, dreamin' the shit! The next time were cruisin' in your ride, it's all you'll be playin'." "Oh, my future, thanks so much for that inspirational view of my future. My mind going to jelly from useless gangsta music and monotonous lyrics, and my internal organs as well becoming jelly from the constant bass. Guess I better invest in some SUBS for my car. No need to lighten my race car, when I can slow it down with a fifty-pound box and two fifteen-inch subs pounding away behind me." "Yah!" This got Harry all excited. "Now we're talkin'! In my old Hondas, I Dynamated (sound-deadening material) the whole interior. Like, twenty pounds of that stuff, so we could roll and bump to the Groove Armada. Man, I love that stuff!" "Urgg, yah . . . that will definitely be high on my priority list, Harry. Hey, did you know that one of the experiments the military did was testing the rate at how fast the internal organs of a human would disintegrate from low frequencies? I'm serious—it's actually pretty hazardous for you." Berty got wind of the argument and had to jump in. "What's good for the ears is that loud Folgers fart-can on the back o' that ride, boy! That car's loud as shit! Can hear 'er from six blocks away." I tilted my head over and looked at Berty. "You know that I wear earplugs whenever I drive my beautiful Betsy (my little riced-up race car). See those loud pipe noises are also high frequencies, and I block those out. It's those low vibrating frequencies that earplugs can't get rid of, so I don't have any sound problems whatsoever." "Then why can't you hear shit, hey?" Every time he said anything, it came out as a screech. "Albert, you tickly little guy, I didn't say I have always been 'all-knowing.' I will admit to you that in my younger days, my youth of gallivanting about, I did cruise around without earplugs and listened to loud music. But now as I am older and wiser, I have changed my ways and have turned over a new leaf. It's just too bad I am deaf now, since that leaf has been turned over." Albert's voice got even screechy-er this time when he spoke. "What about all those clubs and concerts you go to? Them speakers are three times the size of me!" "But, Tickles, I thought you were only three feet tall, which makes those speakers not so tall at all!" "Fuck you, squirt boy! I was twice your height when you started workin' here, and I was twice yer weight." "Um, Tickles, news flash for you," I closed my two fists in front of my face, then going towards him, opened the fingers quickly in front of his own, for a magical surprise. "I hope you remember that I was only fifteen when I started working here, so that means nothing so many years later. Know what I mean?" "Sure don't! All I know was that I was taller 'n' heavier!" "Come on 'oldy-locks,' I rarely go out, and when you're that drunk, you don't notice it's loud, so therefore, according to my calculations, that means it's not loud . . ." "Yer rank! That don't make fuckin' sense!" "Okay then, Tickles! It was kind of a joke, as to make you get confused." "Well, it didn't work, ya turd." "No . . . really? I thought it wasn't obvious!" "Don't you be gettin' smart with me, I'll grab one of them rags o' yours and make you bleed!" I laughed through my nose at him. "Yah, and I'm Brad Pitt. The only bleeding in this shop is from the haemorrhoids in your ass, haemorrhoid lover!" Albert, at this point, became upset. "Don't be bringin' my ass into this. The same will happen to you if you don't use mats to sit down with when yer on the concrete. It's the cold that gits ya. Didn't used to have 'em darn things. Jest since I welded up the pipeline in the rain a few years back. Ass in puddles, getting shocked an' shit. Now it's needin' weldin' again!" "How about . . . you just go on Hydro instead of having no power all the time and having to fix the dam of yours and those pipelines every weekend then!" His eyes lit up for a second, and his screeching stopped. "'Cause were off the grid!" With his right arm, he raised his fist triumphantly. "Ha-ha, the government can't track me!" I piped in and raised my arm as well. "Don't fuck with me, I'm the gingerbread man! Bert, if you don't ever have any power, you can't shower. Which is worse: smelling like crap, or the government knowing that you're having a bath? Think about it!" At that point, Harry was feeling left out from the battle of wit, and I was getting exasperated with Tickles. "Bert smells like Turd Island anyways, what does he care?" "Harry, that's only because he doesn't have power. He'd probably love water gushing out of his faucets." Albert stammered out, "I smell like flowers," at our insults, then stormed away to work on a bike. Harry spewed from his mouth, "Yah, you get back to work, smelly boy! I see you, I see you!"

I looked back again to the chronometer on the wall. To my chagrin, 3:48 is all the fun she held in store for me.

CHAPTER 6 — A Life Less Dismal

Crisp was the morning, and a chill hung in the air. Steam escaped my chapped lips, yet my feet continued forwards. With a gloved hand, I tugged at the scarf around my neck, bringing it over my nose. Around me on the ground was iced grass. It followed beside as I walked, each blade frozen in space and time. My gaze took in the abundance of green needles strewn this way and that in no particular fashion. As well, my feet took a liking to them. Stopping, one of my feet lifted and slowly stepped down atop the grass blades; what a sensation, for no one else at that moment would be sharing the same divine experience as me. A beautiful yet chilling-to-the-heart crunching sound was all that occurred. In slow motion, I started, each footfall breaking the backs of those slender life forms. With my head twisted back, I saw the carnage, which lay behind, perfectly shaped to my boots. The black soles were washed clean by the cold water, and they glistened in the morning sun. What a peaceful Saturday morning, one more day until the weekend and one more day until bliss and happiness.

I could almost make out the parking lot of the motorcycle shop. Around it lay other small businesses, and on the opposing side of the street were a few houses in need of repair. Twenty years previous, this was a condemned neighbourhood. Half of the apartments were those of drug dealers and the scum of the earth. Coke addicts once littered the streets, and garbage filled most of the lawns. All night, sirens would haunt those streets, putting the minds of the normal folk at unease. Then just five years ago, a tremendous program was put into motion by the city council; they were going to clean up their city. The main object was to make the streets safe for kids. The police were a big help (for once), and crime rates started to decrease. Special detective units came into play, and they eradicated many of the sources from which the drugs came from. In schools, drug awareness campaigns became more prominent, so the children would learn about the risks at a young age. On this same street, half a dozen houses were torn down, sidewalks and lamps were installed, and numerous shrubs and trees were planted to make it enjoyable to walk in the evenings. All the 'coked up' were removed and now resided behind bars, in programs, disappeared, or left for other cities.

I made my way across our parking lot. I turned the key in the lock and went inside. Trevor had already unlocked the stainless steel bars covering the front door and was busy in the corner cleaning the coffee machine. Diligently, he took apart the machine and every piece got inspected. He didn't even notice my entry, what a stealth

I was. I yelled out to him. Trevor jumped and dropped a red rubber stopper that was in his hand. It fell to the gray tiles below and rolled quickly underneath the nearest motorcycle. Turning his body to face me, he scrunched up his brows and balled a fist at me. Trevor did not say a word. On hands and knees, he crawled around on the floor in an attempt to acquire the stopper. It was further back than he could reach, and his arm was stretched to full length. He stuck out his tongue like a dog and gave it one more mighty effort but to no avail. I went around to the other side of the bikes in the showroom and managed to grab it. After giving me a quick thanks, he returned to cleaning. I escaped into the shop, but no one was in yet. As I unlocked the rear doors and began to roll out the service bikes, the other employees began to trickle in. I could hear when Gerald came in; his voice was bounding with enthusiasm, and he legitimately seemed excited to be here. Next in came Harry and Tickles. Harry probably parked his truck next to Tickles's rundown GMC in the lot across from our shop. It was a gravel lot, and almost every month, the owners would bring in new gravel to fill in the holes, those being made by the local 4x4 drivers who had never actually 4x4ed before, but thought that spinning your tyres and kicking up mud and dirt inside of the fender wells qualified them to be hard-core 4x4 drivers. As well as let them put dumb stickers of brands and organizations all over their windows and bumpers and go to all the meetings for the local clubs.

Albert, the silly old dog, had left the heaters in the shop on all night, but since I had to roll the bikes waiting for scheduling time and parts on order to the outside of out shop, the doors had to be kept open for approximately ten minutes; this being just enough time to let the cold miserable temperature from outside creep into the nice, toasty shop. Not only did this leave a smirk on my face but also excited me to know what kind of response he would have towards it. Of course, I had a good idea: he would be hungover. He would be tired. He would be grumpy. And best of all, he would be smelly. Nonetheless, I wanted to hear him say it. "Oh, Tickles, what brings you out to our Beemer shop at this hour of the morning? You would think a guy like you would be sleeping and enjoying their old age!" He was having troubles removing his tattered and dirt-embedded jean jacket with the fur collar. His frustration was evident without even setting eyes upon him. His stammering and muttering could most likely be heard from the showroom. Harry had big bags under his eyes and wore dark aviators to hide how red they were. He was currently at the freshly cleaned coffee machine ingesting caffeine. He was of no use for helping Albert out of his jacket. I felt obliged to help him and moved in to lend a hand. As I got within four feet of his hunched-over posture, a wave of intoxicating odours attempted to envelop me. I stumbled back and put a sleeve over my nose to stop myself from gagging.

Imagine being at the dump on the hottest day of the year, dropping off your bags of garbage. You have to remove yourself from the place quickly as it makes you want to throw up! Then throw old booze and musty unwashed clothes into the equation, and you have yourself one fantastic smell. That is what I breathed in that morning. If those smells could have had a colour, I'm guessing they would have a gross blend of brown, a putrid green, and tinges of bright red and yellows; similar to that of a guacamole with hot peppers.

I wanted to help the old man, but it was impossible because of his raunchy smell that made the distance completely impassable! "Albert, you smell like ass" was all that I could muster myself to say. He stopped his struggling and looked up at me. His haggard unshaven face accentuated his weary unloved gaze. "You really know how ta make friends in this place, hey?" was all he said. "No, no . . . I didn't mean in a bad way, well, yah it's bad, I just meant that I cannot help you out, and I even want to!" "How very fucking nice! So if I'm stuck in a ditch drowning in my own shit, you won't pull me out?" Now that was the best example before 9:00 a.m. that I have ever heard. "Tickles, you know that I would come to your aid in any way possible, but this isn't a life-threatening situation! Right now, you're just too drunk to get that skinny arm of yours from out of the coat sleeve. It is depressing, and because of that, I'm feeling emotions of sympathy towards you that I don't usually have! Herm Herm!" "What is Herm Herm gonna do for me?" His face became red and was starting to sweat as his heart rate was high, and there was now plenty of heat in his corner. I placed my hands on my hips and pushed back my shoulders. "Have you ever taken off your jacket before by yourself?" I questioned him. "No, I'm a newborn fucking prince for God's sake!" Such an angry man. "Why don't you stand up and just let your arms down to your sides, letting it drop to the floor? Evidently, the back of the chair is limiting your movability." Again, he stopped, this time exhausted and exasperated. The gears turned a few times and, without any vocal thanks or verbal abuse, did just that! But then of course, "Close the doors, you nitwit, there's a draft in here! Tryin' to heat the whole city?" Wow, finally, a little bit late, but I suppose he had other things on his mind. Yah, I suppose that's a bit of vocal abuse after all.

Harry came back into the shop with a hungover swagger. The kind where you know you're drunk, but think that other people don't notice, so you pretend you're not, and then everyone is good to go! He held a stir stick in one hand, stirring about the mixture of coffee that was in the other hand. His stirring hand stopped stirring, and he reached down to pull out his rolly shop chair from beneath his bench. Originally, I purchased the chair for him because he always used mine; and since it wasn't cheap, I didn't like other people using it. The one I purchased for him was rather cheap. As time went on, pieces of the chair broke off: first a few of the wheels broke off; these were two-and-a-half-inch wheels. We found a couple spares from a random project in a back room and welded them to the thin steel base; these wheels were three inches in diameter. As you can guess, it became unbalanced. Furthermore, they were louder than regular wheels, as their design was not for the same purpose. Another incident after these wheels were installed: Harry went flying across the floor in a moment of excitement for something, and it caught on a small divot in the concrete. He went in all directions, with hands and arms flailing wildly while the chair just smacked into the wall, breaking the seat from the base of the chair. This time, we welded L-bracket steel, which we strategically cut to hold on the seat. Besides the noisy wheels and occasional flip-overs, he never had a problem again.

"So, Hobbers," I pried, "how, ahh, did the evening go for you, little buddy?" His dark-tinted shades hid his drowsiness and red eyes still. He was just sitting there motionless, probably asleep; you just couldn't see his eyes. "Good," he finally answered, "it was real good." I nodded my head to agree with him, "I can see that since you're a great conversation piece this morning, we don't need to elaborate on what you got up to last night. How does after lunch sound?" He sat there, still not moving and just said, "Done," in a low crackly voice. I myself went to make some tea. With my vast selection of teas ,I took some Jasmine green and a regular Sencha, and mixed it 50/50 by placing a couple leaves of each in my tea strainer ball. Taking my time going to the showroom to the hot water dispenser/coffee maker, I perused over what was going on: lots and lots of new bikes, BMW bikes galore, a few trade-ins here and there, but mainly shiny new, yet to be ridden and enjoyed BMWs. Over in the corner, I saw them, the non-Beemers, the ugly trade-ins: the Triumphs, the Harleys, the scum, the abortions of motorcycles that don't even deserve a home. Every single time I had to have the displeasure of working on them or riding them, I was filled with discomfort. The thought of putting my leg over one, pushing my bottom onto the textured vinyl seat, and releasing the clutch made me cringe. At every street corner, I would try to be invisible, begging not to be seen. The notion that a friend or acquaintance would recognize me filled my bones through and through with dread. All right, that all might be excessive, but you have to believe me when I say that I'm just not as fond of them. I guess I'm just a stuck-up Beemer mechanic. As nothing else was interesting, I quickly looked over the clothes section. BMW makes so many different clothes that they call it a BMW 'lifestyle.' Not only can you dress yourself for any occasion but also any wives, lovers, or children that you might have as well. Half my closet was comprised of BMW clothes just because employee prices make the material only a little more mildly priced, instead of outrageously priced like the regular customers had to pay.

I filled up my stainless double-walled BMW mug with hot steaming water and made my way back to the *dungeon*. Harry had rolled out two bikes—what a hero. Albert was only now changing his pants—what a bunch of drunks. Taking the initiative, I then began rolling out the rest of them. Of course, the first happened to be a K1200LT, the biggest and heaviest of our fleet and even heavier than the large and in charge K1600 series. Eight million pounds of useless plastic and steel jumbled together to form something that resembled a bike. After getting it off the center stand, I had to manoeuvre her outside. Out the doors, onto the asphalt, past the two bikes Harry had rolled out, and into position to place it on the, *whoooa*, ice! Mother of mercy! Shit on my face! Heavy, heavy, heavy. Don't slip, don't slip, don't, don't. "Harry! Get out here! I'm gonna drop it!" I screamed. Both my feet were 'slippery-Suzy-ing' around, and I was losing my balance, and footing, and everything else that mattered at that moment in time in the world, or my world. I guess my screeching/manly yelling woke up Harry, for he ran like a bat out of hell when he heard me. "Coming!" he bellowed, and out of the doors he exploded. I suppose he knew that it was slippery and just forgot to mention it when he rolled out the two light bikes and skated around. Harry picked up speed while coming towards me, a lot of speed! Okay, he could not stop and ended up flat on his ass as quick as a gunshot. "Get up, you idiot I'm going to drop this piece!" He reoriented himself and got off the ground. Flipping and falling, he made his way to the other side of the K1200LT. Together we pulled the small truck onto her center stand, and by that time I had a litre of sweat dripping off of my forehead. Harry sat down on the ground; I did the same on the icy asphalt. Thirty seconds later, when the bottoms of our pants were noticeably wet, we got up. "Thanks, dude," I told him on our way back into the shop. "Sucks," I mentioned under my breath as I felt my ass; should have gotten up immediately as my boxer shorts underneath were also wet. That would be uncomfy for the rest of the day. Harry and I double-teamed the rest of the bikes in a nonsexual manner. On the last bike out of the shop, Harry piped up a quick "awe fuck, my ass" and sneered as he rubbed his own buttocks with disgust. Albert was outside having a smoke that minute and overheard Harry talking about his ass. A squeaky broken voice wailed out, sending smoke from his cigarette, and then steam from the cold into the air. "I knew you both were queers! Ha-ha, I'm working with faggots!" He continued giggling and then choked on some of his own spittle again, sending himself into a deep gagging and hacking fit that ended up with a bloody green and trickling trail sliding into the nearby drain. We both heard the first part and then, while watching the giggling coughing fit, laughed among ourselves; but at the finale, neither of us were expecting such a gross phlegm-bouyant globule of haemoglobin—sick! Harry himself gagged and shook his head violently to get the disturbing image out of his mind. This autumn, there were hardly any bikes to roll out, as not as many people were riding. Most of them were insurance jobs, go figure. I went over and finally closed the doors now that twenty dollars' worth of heated shop air had disappeared. Albert must have been preoccupied with our yelps and screams to remember that he was getting cold.

The sound of a single cylinder caught all three of our attentions. It was getting louder, and it was obvious that there was little in the way of baffling: A droning, blatting sound came down the alleyway to the shop. Two fast honks on the high-pitched horn came from the other side of the gate. "Fuck you!" Harry yelled at Dillen from our side of the gate. "It's locked, asshole," Albert joined in, "go around and open it yourself!" Dillen hit the kill switch and answered back after his noisy machine stopped, "Come on, guys, just let me in!" Albert flicked his smoke down the drain, which stated 'OUTLET TO STREAM' in bold letters on the grate, and curled his upper lip. The burning tobacco and orange embers turned to gray ash the second it hit the water. Its soggy lifeless form floated in full view. He jammed his hands deep into his black cotton work pants and took in a deep breath. Walking over to the gate, he hunched his shoulders and dropped his head while scuffing the rubber soles of his worked-in leather boots. The gate he wrestled with, and as it was made of steel and was *très* cold, it sometimes became stuck in its wood holster. 'Mumble, mumble, mumble' were the only distinguishable words exchanged between Dillen and Albert at the gate. Door swung open, and Dillen rolled his little BMW into the back lot. Oh, at the same time holding a mirror and a piece of headlight moulding in his right hand . . . Oh wait, why would he be doing that, you ask? Good news, good news. Harry and Albert both had smiles and expressed surprise when they saw this. I also wore a grin and a devious and malicious expression on my face. Dillen had on his helmet, so I wasn't able to see what kind of facial movements were going on; probably tearing up and ready to burst like the little bitch he was. Harry started randomly babbling about Dildo being a shitty rider and how he always crashed, where Albert was smirking and asking him how he managed to crash this time. I went around the bike while it was still being held to access the damage to make fun of him. The right-turn signal had been busted off, and the taillight was cracked and dangling down onto the rear wheel from its harness. Looking at the bike from the rear, the subframe also appeared to be bent, and that was only the half of it.

Trevor had heard the commotion and came to see the matter at hand. Through the back doors he came, of course putting his hoody on first. Trevor always had the proper equipment for the temperature and weather wherever he went: sunglasses, shorts, zip-ups, whatever was needed. His grin was quite evident. He never really bellowed or guffawed, but he did smile and give a quick sometimes witty remark here and there; the strong silent, yet not that tall type. He walked up to us and stood there for a moment not saying anything, just assessing the carnage. "At least you had your gear on this time," he said finally before turning and meandering back inside. Dillen removed his helmet at this time, and it was evident that a few tears had been shed as his eyes were a little puffed up, and his nose was a bit rosy. He had probably sat in the ditch for a few minutes and cried before going back on the road and facing any concerned onlookers that had happened to see his stupidity firsthand. Then, after letting a few of them sympathize towards his boo-boos, continued on to the impending hassling at our shop. Knowing that he was already hated for his personality and attitude, hopefully when mocked for his riding skills and being a crybaby, he would quit and never return; doubtful, yet hopeful all the while. "So what happened, son?" I inquired to the boy with the scraped-up riding gear and smashed-up motorcycle. Dillen did not want to look me in the eye. I was sneering at him still, and he was afraid to bubble up again; he looked at the ground instead. "I just had a little 'whoopsie-daisy' on the exit ramp . . ." His voice was faltering, and he said it at a barely audible volume ". . . but I'm not hurt real bad this time, just the leg." I kept on trying to get his gaze, but he wouldn't have it. I prodded a bit more into the situation, "Maybe you were going a bit too fast, hey?" After lowering my voice to make it sound like a mother soothing her child and eliminating the smirk, I asked again, "Do you think that perhaps the front slid out from you as it is cold and icy out this morning?" Dillen looked into my eyes and nodded his head up and down. By keeping up the nurturing motherly act for another minute, he decided to tell all and burst into song about his morning ditch-dig with his bike. All at once, the previous evening's late night was told about; then the woozy early morning; then the chap in the red Mustang on the highway looking out through his window at him, egging him on to race; then the race and passing cars on the shoulder, on his part at least, not the Mustangs; then Dillen's turnoff of the highway, a long off-camber turn winding back onto the main road. The best part about this corner is that the back half is shaded in the mornings, was icy as we had found out ourselves during the walk-in, and in the back lot rolling out bikes. Going around this corner, Dillen had been in race-mode mind-set and had had far too much speed. On a good warm day, no problem, but not this day. His body tucked over the right side of the bike, the tyres leaning up against the last bit of tread block that was left, a thin layer of cold frozen water between the rubber and the asphalt, and there is the good news, err, I mean the story. Dillen blubbered on a bit more about his taking *every effort* to keep the bike from going out from under him, trying to make himself sound like a sophisticated racer. I'm completely sure that in the split-second of 'Durr, look how far I can lean over' and 'What am I doing upside down?' he contemplated how he was going to crash. After that whole episode, the majority of us got bored with his story; and after the initial excitement of him laying his bike down, we remembered that he was still the pain in the ass he had always been. Trevor motioned for us to get back inside, as customers that had been waiting around could probably care less and just wanted to feed our diminishing Canadian economy a small bit more before it joined Europe.

My tea was cold, darn it! How was that going to warm up my chilled soul? Stinky Harry and Albert joined me inside, this time closing up the two large eggshell-white painted doors leading outside. Right afterwards, Dillen came through them but caught one of his backpack straps on the steel chain links, which we use to lock to the ceiling when we leave in the evenings. They tore at the shoulder strap, and with his forward motion, his body whirled sideways into the door, which he was caught on. The helmet in his hand smacked hard against the white plywood and marred the visor. Dillen let out an audibly aggravated squawk and stormed into the closet area for motorcycle jackets and such. "So angry!" he squawked again, throwing into the enclave his jacket. Harry laughed hysterically at Dillen and threw a few peanuts in his direction with no real intention of hitting him. They didn't, but Dillen ended up catching one. They were candied peanuts, tasty. He shoved it firmly into his mouth and chomped down on it. Seeing how he enjoyed it, Harry tossed a few more so that he could catch them.

Meanwhile, Tickles had been banging around in the machine room, digging up some chunks of metal for a project he was sure to tell us about in a few minutes. Harry's *almost*-helpful attitude towards Dillen was very unusual behaviour. Together we despised him and outwardly showed him. If we weren't putting garden hoses in his toolbox or letting the air out of his tyres, it was at least some verbal form of abuse, the kind you don't need imaginations for—the funnest kind, just simple words for simple put-downs. A kind 'fuck you' or 'eat shit' was all that was needed. But Harry, he was smiling, and feeding the stupid lemming! When Dillen went to the showroom, one of us was going to have to talk with Harry, and it wasn't going to be Albert. They giggled together before Harry went to push a few more of the bikes outside. Dillen strolled to the front with an immediate positive increase in his behaviour, a joyful one even. Harry came back in, and I laid into him in a somewhat quiet tone, "What the fuck is going on with you today, soldier?" His eyes still covered by the shades gave nothing away. His facial expressions didn't even seem to change. The second time I asked him, he decided to let us in on a giant secret, which he had been holding out from telling us. Well, in actuality's sake, he didn't tell us anything that we hadn't already thought of. "Just the usual, man," again, a motionless stance. The shop had heated up again, and most likely due to his guilty conscience as opposed to the heat in the shop, his cheeks picked up a bit of colour. Probably some nasty woman he had found at a party, with both of them dancing around high on some absurd drug. They had gone home together, fucked each other's brains out, and then drank and smoked until the sun came up. "Just in a kinda good, docile mood, buds. Don't get all crazy 'n' excited an' shit. No harm's done, I'll get my work done." "Okay, okay, that's all decent, but what about Dillen? Unless you're sleeping with him . . ." I started to laugh after saying this, as it was a pretty nasty visual, "Then there is no fucking way that you should be 'buddy-buddying' up to him like that. *Comprende, padre*?" Harry reached out and placed his right hand on my shoulder while still holding his peanut bag in his left. Then removing his hand off my shoulder, he raised it to his shades and proceeded to take them off. I was very, very surprised at what I saw: he had a nice shiner on his left eye. He grinned back at me face to face. "What the *fuck*?" was my initial response. Harry had a black eye. I had never seen him with one of these, and he didn't seem too upset about it either. I definitely had to find out what had happened the previous evening. "Dude! You've got a big-ass black eye!

And the rest of you is white. Don't leave me hangin' like this, man! Fill me in!" He kept the grin and just walked away while putting the shades back on. I raised my hands above my head in a 'what the shit' fashion but got nothing more. Harry was going to play the old poker player and not turn over his cards—that bastard.

Berty had been sneakily watching and listening to the confrontation. He moseyed over to me and grabbed my bicep, dragging me to the battery room. I didn't have any interest in going with him, but he acted as if it was important. "You see that, son?" He whispered hurriedly, "there's word 'round the shop that Harry's been into the drugs." At hearing this from Berty, I attempted to leave, but he grabbed onto my arm again and squeezed me back to face him. "Hear he's sellin'." "Bert, this is bullshit." I kept my voice low. "You and I both know he's into taking whatever drug finds its way into his hand or pocket or friend's hand, but come on!" This time, I spoke in a Bert-you're-so-full-of-shit tone. This pissed him right off, "Listen up, you little shit disturber, I've been 'round this block more times than we c'n both count, an' in that time, dem drugs ruled ma life, so I know 'xactly what I'm sayin' here." Albert's countryish hick voice, whenever he talked in a serious manner, always made me laugh or smile. I was trying my hardest, as hard as possible, to keep myself from breaking down. He was being serious! The damned fool! I didn't want to break this serious moment of his. Gosh, it was funny though. With my molars, I bit the inside of my cheek to keep away the incoming smile, the imminent smirk. Albert went on for at least three more agonizing minutes about past drug experiences, waking up with strippers and losing his friends in his youth. It was heavy stuff, and he could have written a pretty good memoir with his jibber-jabber. I'm not much for drugs, even recreational usage; but to me, it sounded not to bad: not having a care in the world, parties, women, cocaine, acid trips, more women (I would make sure to get to know them before the drugs kicked in to make sure she didn't look too bad), crashing cars on long weekend benders, good times! Instead, a life of work with an old drunk, occasional boozing, not really many women, and a few friends that were as bad at hitting a pool cue as I was.

Albert trailed off, and it seemed an okay time for me to end the talk and get back to something else. I peered over Bert's shoulder and checked up on the 'Harry-machine.' He was reading a magazine and seemed harmless, not really looking like a drug dealer as Albert had been proposing. My gaze switched back to Bert, but Bert also appeared harmless. Maybe I was the problem child here: too trusting and far too honest; just a simple optimist with a bright exterior. After our fantastic talk, we moved out of the battery room, thank God! The battery acid smelt like farting men, and the gasses would easily put holes in my shirt if it didn't get washed.

Trevor slipped into the shop and showed us the list of the day's bikes: some blah de blah to work on followed by a bit of ho-hum. He left with no particular entrance or exit, which reminded me of a diligent secretary. I'm sure that Trevor would love being referred to as that. I was going to confront Albert again in a less-isolated and closed space, but he had disappeared somewhere. Catching Harry's eye, I walked over and tried again to discover the reasons for his secrecy. "Jest can't get enough?" he quickly jabbed at me. "Just gotta help you get all those built-up secrets off your chest!" I jested back at him. "All right, well, let's put it like this: I don't want those little gay boys up in the front finding out about this or Bert for that matter." "All right, no troubles by me!"

I leaned in so as he didn't have to talk loudly. "The other night," I interrupted with "last night." "Yes, *fuck*! You wanna hear this shit or not? One-time deal here, 'brosef'!" For a moment, he actually seemed irritated, but the chance to tell some juicy gossip about himself quickly covered that up—dirty gossip actually.

"So after work, same ole same ole, nothin' fancy. Cruised back to my pad where my roomy is smokin' a jay, like he does twenty other times in the day. Grab a quick shower, some cheap-shit food, then call up some buds to go out. You know how it is: throw on a nice shirt and shoes, an' I'm on my way after a few drinks." "Sooo, you had a few drinks before you went out? Very economical of you." Harry and I had a habit of drinking and driving. Not generally accepted as acceptable behaviour, but life went on, and the sun kept on setting. Harry seemed to get into more trouble when he was behind the wheel though; all those damned cops loved to hassle him—they just loved it. "Head down to the best waterin' hole in town, and my buds already got a booth. Meet up, get a pitcher or four, an' start shootin' the shit; good times, good times. This place is got a low lightin' an' chill-shesh music, none of that gay-ass pop shit. We're talkin' like nice, East Coast lounge-fest stuff—real music. Like we're having the usual midweekday blast. There's three of us, and these are great guys. Anyways, 'cross the way are these ladies. I'm not talkin' derogatory bitches either. We're talkin' sweet, fine, lovely ladies. These girls are the ones that you move mountains an' shit for. Know what I'm saying? Like the three of us are pretty sportin', we're talkin' not bums on the street. Those fine pieces of *ass*!" Harry used his hand to make a triumphant ass-grabbing gesture. He also made a hungry 'grrr-ing' sound to emphasize the point. "At this hour, we've got a couple of drinks in our bloated bellies. We're checkin' out the scenery, and it looks like they're also havin' a few bevvies. And it also looks like them fine biddies are checkin' out our scenery. Guess how many are at their table, you just guess." I gave him the satisfaction of guessing and saying seven, about two for the each of the boys, but one would have to deal with a third. "Naw, man!" He seemed confused that I had guessed the wrong amount of girls. Why ask me in the first place if it was a rhetorical guess? Don't lead me on like that! "I pick up a little courage to get a little chitchat happenin', 'n' they move over to our table!" Harry was so giddy when he said this, like it was his first time hitting on some hot girl. "The *consuelas* sit with us, there's the three: two blondes and a brunette. These blondes turned out dirtayyy too. Fuckin' short-ass skirts, almost bust a nut eye'n' up their legs, oh god! But the brunette had a medium-length skirt with a big slit down the side, and the most godlylike legs and body and face and everything!" Harry raised his hands to the ceiling, and he looked towards the heavens and kissed the air. "At that moment 'n time, changed my way from being an atheist to being a God-fearing man. We're talkin' it up with them, an' I just can't stop staring. Tits from Titus! Not that he's got 'em, but just sayin', goes well with a low-cut navy blue top. They'd been drinkin' gin tonics an' some other girly shit. They'd just finished up some big-ass exam for some fancy course I immediately forgot. But anyways, blabbin' away, my buds are gettin' along well with the blondes, so we're all right, talkin' to each other. They were practically gettin' their dicks sucked at the table! Those two were fuckin' hot, and them peaches so fucking wet at the table! John, after about twenty minutes, gets up, leaves me thirty bucks for drinks, and splits with one of the chicks. Before they get to his car, they most likely shagged twice. Two couples left at the table, right? Reliable

Jeff and myself. Now, Jeff's not as much of a ladies' man, so this morning, he texted me and told me that he did not get any action whatsoever, but she wanted to 'hang out' some other time during the week. Back to me, way better story! This brunette, found out her name's Juliette, fuckin' hot eh? She's doin' some accounting gig on the side, don't really care, boring shit really. We 'stroll' back to my truck, 'n' I've almost got a big 'rod-on' for the dame right then! I'm half cooked from the drinks, she is too, but we're both rarin' to go. Know what I mean?" He says it without giving me time to respond this once. "In the truck, turn on some heavy drum 'n' bass tunes, s'all sweet though, the girls lovin' it, tryin' to get me off in the truck. She wants to take me back to her place. Perfect! I don't wanna bring her back to my shit-hole anyways, weed smell everywhere and trash from my filthy roommate. Decent place she's got too: high-end shit, must be a good accountant or rich folks, whatever! Like slobbering dogs, we're goin' at it. I'm fuckin' laying into her, and she's going fuckin' wild. Not a heavy moaner, but like the best high-pitched woman noise I've ever heard—beautiful, fuckin' beautiful. Still drunk, we finish round one then go outside an' smoke a couple cigarettes she had lyin' around. Now listen here: this Juliette broad is what I would call fucking amazing. Not one of those clingy bitches but a strong dependent woman." "Sounds like a treat!" I mentioned while he took a breath. "Round two, we pick up right where we left off, every fuckin' position you could ever dream up or find in some Kama Sutra fuckin' book. She is damn good!" Harry stopped for a second and looked dreamily into the distance. I motioned for him to continue, and he started again. "After the second time, I'm tired, drunk, sweaty, and fucked." He laughed when saying 'fucked.' "Literally, and we go to sleep, with her head on my chest, warm tits pressed up against me."

"Eight o'clock, knock, knock, knock. Takes a second for me to recognize what the noise is 'cause I'm still cruisin' in 'dozy-land.' I tap Juliette on the shoulder, an' she mumbles a little something and doesn't want to wake up. Knock happens again, this time she opens her eyes, and then a big fuckin' look of urgency hits her. Slowly, she says, 'Oh shit,' nice an' drawn out to tell me something is not right. Then it hits me that it's her fuckin' man! So I quickly push her to the side of me and look right into her eyes. 'You've got a boyfriend, don't you?' She bites her lip and nods her head. Right then, I gotta get outta there. I ask her what the fuck he's doing here in the a.m. She tells me they always go for breakfast in the morning, but the drinks, her friends, the sex made her forget. Two seconds later, I'm lookin' fer my pants!" Now I could not stop laughing. Here is Harry, the drunken womanizer that he is, finding himself in a precarious position. I'm loving every second. "The dude calls out her name as I'm throwin' on my shirt. I try to find another way out, but she's only got the one door! Tell her to quickly throw on a shirt or somin', so what's she do? She grabs the blanket and wraps it around her. Come on! She yells back to fuckin' 'boy toy,' 'Coming, Tomas.' What kind a name is Tomas? We go into the living room where the door is, an' the blinds aren't down. Bad, bad, bad. Tomas was lookin' through the window already and sees me! At that point, it all went to hell: he starts pounding on the door and swearing like a baboon to both of us. The chick's already yelling apologies and 'so sorrys' back but unable to be heard under his bellows. What's she do next? Goes and unlocks the door! I start to think of the consequences a second too late. Doors open, girl's pushed out of the way and trips over her own leg to the floor, with the blanket opening up, revealing her amazing naked body. This Tomas guy is no fuckin' slouch. He sees his girl, 'n' then he sees me. My eyes go wide as they can, and he catches up to me in four steps! Before I can even raise my hands, he lays a big fist right in my face." Harry's telling me about this dirty cheating girl and getting beaten up by her big boyfriend, and he's almost crying because he finds it as funny as I do! "I stumble back, and he follows. Now, I can't even hear what he's saying, but he's saying a lot. Maybe five or six more heavy fists hit me in the face or stomach before I can get outta there. I don't even have any goddamn shoes on, so I'm runnin' out to my truck in my socks! Best thing I did the night before? Parked around the block, since all the visitor's parking was full. At that point, I was running for my life, but I reached the truck and started her up in record time. Slammed it in reverse and gunned 'er! He was like, right on my heels, so I could hear him while I ran to the truck. He tried the door handles and was screaming at me and tryin' to get in. No fucking thanks, man! He was huge! Yeah, so I ahh, drove home, changed my socks, dropped on some shoes, and came to hang out with you kids for the day. Nice fuckin' shoes I lost too."

CHAPTER 7 – Oil Spills

"**D**amnit, you fucking piece of fucking shit. I fucking hate when that happens!" Harry bellowed this through the chasms of the shop. I peered underneath the bike sitting on my bench and watched as transmission oil seeped down the side of the bike on Harry's bench, all the way over to the edge . . . and then poured eagerly onto the floor. The small piece of curved plastic used for draining oil had become dislodged from its advantageous position and now lay underneath the center stand covered in the thick residue of 75W90 weight hypoid gear oil, with the oil drain basin residing only inches away from catching the oily fiasco. I laughed out loud to him mainly because with Harry, dropping the tranny oil on the floor had become a common occurrence. It amused me greatly whenever it happened as most minor dilemmas as such had started to do the same in recent years. "It's not fucking funny, you jerk," he exclaimed whilst he began cleaning it with some previously dirtied rags. "These damned trannies are a stupid-ass design." The rags began to soak up the HGO, and I decided helping him would probably help my day along. A bad start to a morning usually turns into a bad rest of the day. When Harry gets bitchy, he whines and moans about other random useless things all day, and then everybody else gets into a similar mind-set, and it all goes to hell in a short time span.

Both of us had managed to control the situation by the time Albert sauntered into the back. He held a small doughnut in his right hand, which he was using as a stir stick for the 'stool softener' in his left. The dirty fingernails dug slightly into the thin circumference of the Styrofoam cup, and the steam rising from the beany liquid moistened his hand as he continued to stir. As he walked over to see what the two mechanics were doing so close to the floor, coffee dribbled over the rim of his cup. He kept on walking and dribbling for about two metres before he came to a halt towering over us. "Hah! What are ya dorks done now?" He cackled through the yellow mismatch of teeth protruding from between his thin withered lips. "Need to spend bit more time workin' on the bikes instead o' the floor." My gaze and curled lip both met him at the same time. I then released a yell, "Bert, you get back to work! 'Dorothy' here dumped his load all over the floor, and I'm helping him clean it up, and get your own rag to clean all that shit up that you've been dropping on the ground. This place is a dump already, don't make it worse for all of us." Albert's gloating over us had diminished greatly after that statement.

He placed his coffee up on the seat of the nearest bike, leaving a ring at the bottom. Using both his grubby mittens, he forced the soaked donut into his face. After, he began chomping noisily while smacking his lips. His pointer finger moved over his face pushing small pieces of sugary dough into the abyss of his throat. When most of the remnants had been removed from our presence, he hastily grabbed the steaming cup of Joe off of the textured seat and downed half of it before letting out an exaggerated belch and then a sigh. The smell wave hit Harry and me square in the face, and the feeling was of warmth, death, and vulgarity—in other words, gross. Both of us hollered out obscenities and coughed a few times in an attempt to relieve ourselves of the nausea. "You big piece of shit," I called out through gulps of air. Bert had receded over to his workstation, and with his arm resting on a nearby shelf, he slouched his body and continued cackling to himself. Where is the humour? It is just plain sick not amusing, or at least it shouldn't be amusing, that is for sure. Harry and I kept our voices low as we devised a comeback scenario for the old man—a fiery one.

After lunch, Albert leaves for no one's enjoyment but his one, a giant 'bomb' in our shop's lavatory. Yes, we have a personal one for the men of the service department; and yes, we do not have a fan to release the deadly gases into the atmosphere. Instead, they circulate in the shop as there is a reasonably sized gap, as previously mentioned, about the door. Since there is no air entering or dispersing to the outside, it hangs like smog at nose level in the shop for thirty minutes *every* time he does it. That means about three or more times per day, arrg!

Whenever we can, the attempt is made to literally *make* him go up front and use those washrooms. For one, they are glamorous and spacious, with nice lotions and excellent lighting to accommodate the most finical individual. They also have fans! Today, when Bert wanted to use our facility in the back, we were going to bomb him. But that was after lunch, and there was still work to be done.

I chucked the extra oily rags into special red containers to eliminate spontaneous combustion, as if it ever happened! Then I carried on up to the showroom to grab a tea. The day had been too up and down so far, and I needed a bit of relaxation. Now I cannot say a mug of green Sencha tea never hit the spot because it did. Casually, I strolled through the maze of new motorcycles for sale in the showroom and then opened up the pleather-bound book with service work for the day: boring, boring, I mulled over the work to be done, a very bland day at that. "Oh well," I said to myself, "might as well go on the Internet for a while 'n' see if anybody tagged the photos I recently put up." This would be more useful than what I had been doing anyhow. There was an oil truck coming today to take away our used drums and it was the most exciting thing to happen unfortunately.

Lunch went quickly without any major arguments or quarrels. Peter, the fuzzy dog of Gerald, had ventured into the back and grovelled for some left-over steaks or anything else with a meaty substance. He was such a sissy dog though. The smallest noise or movement, and he would scamper away to the nearest opening. Albert fed Peter a length of pepperoni he had bought at the local grocers. I knew the next day, Margaret was going to come waltzing downstairs from her humble abode to ream Albert out for stinking up her condominium. He had done the same a month previous, and Margaret's car had become a stench-mobile. Was she pleased after the drive home?

Doubtful to say the least. At least Dillen had taken the day off due to his being 'sick.' In reality, he was hungover and was too big of a wimp to admit it. Knowing him, his dorky little bike would have been run into the ground anyways. Rack up another crash for the bugger. The next time he crashes, I think he deserves a gold star.

My lunch consisted of some banana-flavoured dessert tofu. Most of the audience reading this will cringe at the thought of tofu. Afterwards, I entertained myself with some chunky soup. I do not know what to say about that one, just that at one and a half grams of sodium per can, how are they legally allowed to sell that shit? And why do I buy it? Then I take my salary into account, and I remember. My cheese bun and royal Gala apple made up for it. In a small way, it was better than a fast-food restaurant. We put our garbage away and pretty soon thereafter got back to work. Harry even put on Albert's favourite radio station at a low volume to keep the restless minds from wandering.

Duane rushed into the back almost as fast as when his food has arrived at lunchtime! This time he had a different agenda. "Guys of the service department, the oil truck is here. They are ready to pick up the drums." "Holy shit," I said to myself, "the world is going to end, and we shall all burn together in a fiery pit of used motor oil." No wonder the company loses so many customers when you have a 'whack job,' like Duane doubling as the general manager who freaks out at the least important of issues. "Thanks, Duane," I said out loud. He appeared all bold and confident that he had delivered the message unto us lemmings in the back.

Hmm, as this day was slow with plenty of free time, moving the bikes and taking the oil jugs to the parking lot up front was in the least of my interests. Plus, I was still working on a bike, meaning I needed to 'schmooze' the workload onto someone else instead. I knew just the right victim—good ole Bert. He was sitting over by his bench with a thumb up his rear. "Hey, Bert," I hollered. "Yah, what do ya want," he called back. "What are you doing right now?" "Fuck-all, like usual, just sittin' here doin nothin'," he grumbled. "How would you like a very special important job that only a man of your great stature could handle? Think you could be up for something like that?" I lured him in with the smooth tone of my voice. "Sure, whad I gotta do?" His voice hesitated as he let the words out. "Oh, just a light job of moving the oils around front with Forky. I'll even move the bikes outta the way, since I am such a nice guy." I grinned out at him, and he knew I was being the biggest jerk ever. I just hate moving the barrels, that is all. Albert scuttled outside through the dual-opening doors of our service entrance. A moment later, the forklift could be heard sputtering to life. Its dull roar overpowered the quiet music playing in the background. After a few moments, I took the liberty to go outside and reposition the motorcycles outside in the service bay. Those are the bikes either waiting for parts, service, or pickup.

The paved area outside the doors is petite. It was once a large area where you could roll your car through and work on late into the night, but not anymore. The ever-so-small showroom got the expansion instead, leaving barely enough room to even get new bikes and service work into the shop. At that time, we had a wide variety of bikes outside to get placed on benches: K75 BMWs, two of them; a Yamaha VTX1800, what a horrible beast it was; also an F650CS 'street carver' along with a K1200LT (like always). I strolled back over to my lift after moving those bikes and closing up the service doors.

Grabbing my brake clean bottle and a few rags, I began to wipe down my wrenches and place them back in my toolbox. At that time, Harry was still ho-humming around doing the bare minimum. Why not, right? Might as well slack off when you can. All of a sudden, the service-to-shop door flew open abruptly, and Trevor ran through. "You guys! There is a slight bit of a problem up there!" He said all of this in an urgent tone and pointed to the parking lot up front. "Bert seems to have created an oil spill in the parking lot, and he looks as though he could use a hand. Would you both mind?" I hmmed softly under my breath and wondered what Bert could have done and how he could have gotten oil all over the place. Probably when the truck came in, his spout for sucking out the oil left some residual oil on the ground that had not gotten wiped up. Trevor was most likely making a bigger deal about this than needed, those silly overreactors. I glanced over at Harry and rolled my eyes at him. This was supposed to be the slow and boring day and not the wildly adventurous type of day it was turning into. Harry hung his jaw down low and rocked his head back and forth in some strange primal type movement. I got the gist of it though 'cause I felt the same. I guess the bikes were going to have to wait to be finished today as a little clean-up session was in progress! The rag bin was full of new and fresh rags, so I went over and picked out a bunch. Harry and I trudged up to the front in search of the supposed spill.

As soon as we both got through the service department door, my jaw dropped. "Mother Teresa," I exclaimed. Harry followed suite with a quick "What the fuck." Looking through the showroom's glass doors, you could see the parking lot, or to be more specific, what was covering it. The entire lot seemed to be lathered in a thick layer of used oil. There was the oil truck in the entrance, but instead of the regular 'sucker-upper-truck,' the company had brought the barrel exchange unit. The deck was roughly seven feet off the ground.

What usually happens is the representative of the oil company will exchange an empty barrel and oil-filter barrel for a customer's full barrel and full oil-filter barrel. I suppose Albert decided to keep our barrel and share it with everyone instead. The barrels were overturned and spilling out godforsaken amounts onto the asphalt. With the forklift, he has lifted the special oil-retaining palette, which carried the two barrels the seven feet into the air right near to the deck. The representative had planned on removing the barrels one by one and replacing them with the empty barrels—bad idea. When rolling the first barrel off of the palette, the side became extremely light, about 205 litres of oil lighter! This action caused the other side of the crate to suddenly become unbalanced. This flipped over the palette, which knocked the second barrel onto the ground. In the same motion, this tipped over the barrel that was being rolled off, and a catastrophe ensued.

Albert and the truck driver were both cleaning up the mess as fast as they could manage, but two people were just not enough. We rushed through the doors to access how we could help first, since there was no shortage of cleaning that needed to be done. By the time I got outside, my boots had already received a thick deposit of black poo all over them. From his truck, the oil-remover rep had pulled out a couple ginormous plastic bags containing absorbing fabric made specifically for such circumstances. Let us just say that they were not enough.

After we had been working diligently for a couple minutes, Gerald, Margaret, and one of our financially 'respected' customers strolled into the lot from their lunch. Their expressions were those of people genuinely in shock. For the bosses, it was due to the fact that their business was slightly under a wash of a gross substance with a lot of employees putting man hours into a completely unsuspected circumstance. For the customer, his brand-new expensive car was in the lot depreciating at the very moment he was looking at it. "Oh god! What has become of my fabulous machine?" the customer wailed while approaching his ride. "There's a quarter of a million dollars resting on those tyres, and, and I cannot even drive her to safety. That cumbersome truck of yours is in the way!" He grabbed the hair at his temples and pulled it tight over the scrunched-up eyes underneath. Gerald immediately began to take action even though he himself had only just learnt of the pickle we were in.

With the fabric soaking up large quantities of the oil, Albert righted up the oil filter barrel, so we could place them back inside. The barrel filled up quickly as we worked on after lunch break. The lot was going to have a nice oily coat when done unless there was a chemical we could buy that would completely remove the layer inside the asphalt without damaging the asphalt. Harry piped up, since he is not really the quiet type. "Yo, dude, I know the perfect stuff, man. I was like working back in Ottawa, and like some buds and I were changin' out this pan gasket—a favour for 'im. So like we dumped the oil out, but when we lifted the car up more, all the shit spilt on the floor! Oh right, so I bought some cleaning agent at the local Can-tyre near my house. Craziest shit ever! Took like every drop out of the concrete, not even fuckin' jokes!" "Do you think they sell the same product here?" I asked. "Dude! Lemme get my truck, cruise down, and check it out! Take like two seconds!" Harry said all of this very excitedly and ran off. "I guess I'll just keep cleaning this up then."

So Gerald ran hurriedly up to the customer, hands in a doggy-paddle position, and his high-pitched voice immediately babbling reassurance to him. "Oh sir!" He began in an overexaggerated tone that he speaks in. "Oh, I am so sorry about all this. I know it looks really bad, but have no concern! If there is so much as the tiniest scratch by the time they're finished, my insurance will cover it, and there is absolutely nothing to worry about!" The customer looked over at the whimpering mass in front of him, and for a moment, it looked as though he was going to let him have it, verbally. It would have been awesome for that to happen, but it never does—darn. "Gerald," he started in a Southern drawl, which suited his huge physique well, "is this how you run your business?" He pointed down at the short man. "I don't think that anybody bringin' in their bike for service or a purchase would like what you have going on at this place. Do you know how it looks from my perspective? Let me tell you! It looks real bad! There is a huge truck," he emphasized with his grotesquely huge hands, "and there is crap all over the lot, and you've got half of your staff out here. To top all of that off, I cannot even leave, since you have me blocked into your parking lot!" At this point, Gerald's lips were quivering, and his pose kind of reminded me of a scared little mouse (always a mouse). "I can see that sir, but I don't even know how it happened! I got here at just the same time as you did!" Gerald said all this while shrinking further into the ground. "Fine, I will leave this establishment, view some shops, and if this dump isn't cleaned up in the next hour, and I cannot leave, my garage will hold one less German motorcycle. And yes, I mean one of the motorcycles I purchased off you, just to clarify."

The customer lifted his head and marched away, leaving Gerald to babble incoherently in his wake.

Meanwhile, back in fiasco area number one, the mess was getting slightly contained. The oil representative had handed over a few extra empty barrels, which were redundant as we now had plenty of empty barrels! Forky got rolled into her parking spot in the back to give more cleaning room, and some of the bikes that weren't sitting in oil were rolled back into the showroom. "Harry should be back any minute now," I yelled over to Bert. "Yah, well, he shouldn't 'ave left anyways, since we gots shit to do 'ere without 'im runnin' around on some other planet of 'is!" He almost spat those words at me in his grouchy tone of voice. "Are you going off on another tangent right now, Berts? Like usual?" "Whatever the fuck you want to call it!" he hurled back at me. Hah, maybe dumping a whole barrel of oil on the ground leaves some people in a bad mood. Whatever though, Bert doesn't screw up that often, and he always lets us have it. A few minutes passed, and Harry returned in his shiny truck. As he got out, he carried a jug of cleaner in each hand. He grinned as he walked towards us, "I love this shit!" He held the container up into the air and yelled more praise for us to hear, "We're gonna be back in business in no time!"

We helped the oil rep gather his supplies and then sent him on his way. The massive-sized orange cones Dillen bought at the department store the other week got thrown in front of the shop. The thought of one of our customers riding into the parking lot on two wheels right now was not a good one. They would probably agree as well. Now we had the chance to see if this magical blue cleaner would live up to the hype. The idea behind it was to pour it on the spill, mix in with water, since the concentration was high, and then scrub. We had a large spill and decided that brooms would act as our scrubbers. Not any intellectual work going on today, just good ole-fashioned physical labour. Harry connected our two hoses from the back and let the asphalt have it. The water came out in beautiful clear droplets. As soon as it touched the ground, the colour turned into brown and became a clouded mixture of pollution ready to accelerate down the storm drain . . . leading out to a stream. Yes, it is supposedly biodegradable and safe for drains, but still, no matter how you phrase it, it is filth going down the drain to the fishes. Our shop did have special filters installed in the drains before this happened, and hopefully that is enough to keep the safety inspectors off our backs.

Scrubbing was hard, and as soon as the truck left, so did everybody else. Harry and I continued on into the afternoon, and no one even came out to thank us or offer any assistance. Two hours later, Gerald came strutting up to us; and over the noise of the hose and scrubbing, he started talking in a fast-paced, obviously agitated type of voice. "You guys," he stuttered, "I cannot afford to pay both of you as much as I do to be cleaners! There are bikes to be worked on, and this is how our shop makes money!" I stopped sweeping, letting the water flow unhindered to the drain. "Gerald," I said slowly, "it is very dangerous having this much oil in our parking lot. I don't want to endanger the lives of our customers, since they would probably file lawsuits. Those lawsuits would cost considerably more than a few hours of work from Harry and me." Gerald's expression was gloomy. He knew that my comment was true. I stated it with enough patience and emphasis on the correct words to get my point across. "Fine," he wanted to yell at me but kept himself reserved. "You get this done as soon as humanely possible and work harder if you have to. This kind of nonsense has to stop." "Oh, and just so you know, Gerald, if any of the showroom staff had helped a little, this could have been done a lot sooner, but it is just the two of us here working," I pointed to Harry and then back at myself in defence. He mumbled something incomprehensible to me and turned away from us. Harry looked at me and shook his head. If he had talked to Gerald instead of me, it would have turned into a verbal argument—no questions about that. He doesn't try to think things through when he talks; he and Gerald always have quarrels over the simplest things. In addition, they both are great at overreacting.

The rest of the cleaning went quietly and uneventfully. The remaining oil on the ground was removed, and some of the old oil leaks underneath were removed. After we finished the job, Harry rolled up the hoses, and I went about cleaning the used jugs and brooms. I got into the shop and trudged my soaked footwear over to the bench. The socks inside had become drenched, as there were some large holes in the bottom of the boots. It felt very nice to remove them. All the toes and the bottom of my feet had the prune effect going on. The only exception being that they were white and gooey, but had a beautiful texture to them. I let out a groan and an urgg. Tomorrow there was going to be some blisters all over these feet—how exciting. I was going to be limping around like a dork, and the boys in the back would have a riot with their joking. Albert was ho-humming over by the tyre machine whilst changing a front Metzeler Z8 on an R1200R wheel. He was replacing the Dunlop tyre that had come on the bike from stock. In the '08 and '09 production year, BMW had started putting Continental Conti-RoadAttack and Dunlop tyres on the R1200R series, as well as putting Conti-TrailAttacks on the R1200GS line-up. The Conti's are amazing tyres if you warm them up before going on a hard ride.

"Hey, sport, get o'er here and gimme a hand," he babbled. "These Z8s got real tough sidewalls, an' I can't ged id over the second half of the rim." Albert, you could put gently, was not that strong, and he needed a lot of physical help. Over in our coverall closet, I grabbed a fresh pair of socks, quickly strapped them, and then stuck some old DC shoes onto my feet. "Bert," I protested as I walked over to the red machine, "why you gotta use so much tyre lube? That crap gets all over the place!" He gave me a sour look and retorted back, "I'll use some lube on you in a minute if you don't gimme a hand somin' quick!" Grabbing the lever on the tyre machine and rotating the foot switch, the tyre struggled for a second and then with a loud 'bong' popped on the side of the rim. Still holding the machine, I tilted my head back and gave Bert a look, "All right, you 'meadow muffin,' (his term for a hippie chick) get over here and finish your *wheeeeel!*" Hunched over, he jumbled his way towards the machine and gave a quick thanks. After pushing past me, he grabbed the wheel still held by the plastic jaws of the red device and, using his left foot, pressed the foot release lever, so he could remove it. Off our nitrogen machine, Albert took the hose and bent over the wheel. The nitrogen filled the expanse of rubber and slammed both beads into their appropriate grooves. The green gooey tyre lube flew off the sidewalls and hit Bert with a 'splat' directly in the face. "Bah!" he said while spitting the goo off his lips. It continued to drip down his spectacles and, with the back of his hand, wiped part of it off. A green smear stuck to the lenses, and I chuckled loudly from behind him. He spat out some obscene words at me as he grabbed one of the pink shop towels to wipe himself down. "Hmmm, wonder who it was that said you had a bit too much tyre lube on there?" I questioned Berty. "You can never have too much lube for anything!" he shot back at me. "I'm talking about tyre lube, you tool!" Albert started to grumble and ignored my last comment as he set the pressure for the tyre. "Five thirty come on, time fer a beer already." Bert growled from under his breath. Harry came into the back with an iced tea and a piece of Biscotti. "Dum de dum, oh, what am I going to do today? Oh, I don't know, maybe I'll just dump all of our oil onto the ground outside, yeah, that sounds like fun!" He turned around to find that Albert had been outside washing the wheel. "Darn, he didn't even hear me! What the heck?" Berty came back into the shop with sleeves soaking and rolling the wet wheel over to his pink towel to dry it off before placing it on the balancer. Everybody seemed to be soaked in something today!

These pink towels we buy are from the local thrift store that we pass by on our way to the grocery store. Harry and I, a few times per year, head into the store to buy our shop new towels. The peculiar thing about our visits is that they only ever seem to have pink towels! Does that make sense to you? Not to me. I suppose all the old ladies that peruse through those bins every day pick out the good colours. In addition, for the shop, they accentuate the masculinity aspect of motorcycles nicely . . .

After toodling around with the bike on my bench, I finished up, rolled 'er up front, and began lockin' down the shop. Harry put on his duds, Albert put on his normally filthy duds, and I put on my motorbike gear; time to do a little night riding on the old R1150R.

CHAPTER **8** — Dreams and Reality

Cold, cold, cold outside once again on the forklift. Her iron and steel exterior was coated in white from the nights falling snow. Shivering even with a dirtied-up work coat, my grubby hands turned the right combination of the lock holding the industrial metal chain for the engine compartment. The seat and propane cylinder were mounted together, and I pushed the subframe, holding them to a forty-five-degree position, before placing a random piece of two-by-four under the side to allow entry without being decapitated. Whenever my teeth are chattering, two hundred pounds of thick steel is the last thing I need on my head; a toque would be preferred. Underneath the black leather work boots that were dutifully insulated, countless leaves layered the ice, planting them in such a way that whenever I stood, balancing was key; otherwise, I would slide and do the splits. Not one for gymnastics, I doubt that it would go over well. The purpose of all this was to get Forky running. As mean as the temperature outside was, two bikes were still on their way to the shop today. Forky was the only way off that truck for them.

She had let me down in the past many times. Most of those times were due to failed battery, failed ignition switch, or fouled plugs. All those had been rectified with good results. Nowadays, she had on constantly a battery tender, plug-in block heater, and a waterproof ignition switch. This morning, I had no clue as to why she wouldn't start. Being made in 1953 had nothing to do with that. The old relic had piles of years left in her; she only had 12,000 hours on her blue body and propane engine. I checked over all the systems again: lots of amps from the battery, and it should have had, since it was replaced last year. And it was the size of a small tank. I looked over the connectors of the ignition switch: a little green, but that was usual. Then the old jumper wire was attempted: A nice hearty spark but still no turnover. I let out a disgruntled curse; not even a noise from the engine bay. Absolutely nothing to tell me she was even alive. That's why I was sliding around with the heavy compartment open, sorting through the rat's nest of mismatched coloured wires that were hated with a passion—electrical, not my forte. Random ones overlaid with other random ones poorly installed maybe twenty or so years ago, worse! But the cap and rotor looked good, and the plugs and wires seemed decent, even though it would have turned over whether they worked or not. Carefully walking over the ice-covered leaves and asphalt, I made my way through the poorly painted shop doors to grab my multimeter.

Inside was just as I had envisioned: old Berty with a few straggly hairs, grey, and protruding from under the brim of a firefighter's ball cap. Even though it was black, he still got it filthy. He was sitting on the nice suede barstool Harry and I had picked up the other week and was in front of the computer plugging away at different sights to find new gen sets to run his place. He had ten up at his place already, but all had been bought used. All were nonfunctioning at the time. "Oooh, another of those little generators to light up your life?" He grumbled back at me but didn't turn his head. Still dressed in his home attire, Albert had a Styrofoam cup in his left hand, which rested on the counter, and it was nine o'clock on the dot. The coffee was half drank and most likely his second cup.

Of course the service bikes were still inside. It's unusually agreed upon that if the up-front staff actually tells us that shipped bikes are coming, which—whom are we kidding, ourselves?—they rarely do, that the forklift will be moved to the parking lot first, and then the bikes can be rolled out. This morning, no one but me would dream or rolling them out as they might fall on their hiney.

The only other thing that could possibly cause the old bag to not start was something to do with the starter, which had never acted up before. It had been rainy and icy lately, and she hadn't been used in a while. I mentioned my troubles to Albert. Taking his hands off the mouse and his other off the keyboard, he swizzled on the spinning bar stool and lifted his eyes up to mine. "Ya check the baddery?" He squawked. I told him yes and mentioned the other parts I had been over. "How do you feel about the old starter-mobile?" "Back in the day, we'd git froz'n ones all the time!" "Frozen starter motors? From rust or ice or what?" "From ice. The conden-something turns to ice." "The condensation?" "Whad I jest say?" "Pretty sure you said conden-something." "Whadever! Go fix the thing already! It has got six wires for the whole thing!" "Well, Berty, the six wires appear to be just fine. What say you about a heat gun? That fix 'er up?" Albert was watching his Internet page again. "Naw, you gotta use the fire! The torch!" I bellowed out a laugh in his direction. "Okay, you help me roll the oxyacetylene outside, and we'll torch Forky all right!" "You idiot!" he squabbled again, "Jest use the propane one! The oxyacetylene's too big!" He hadn't gotten the joke. Not that he got any of mine for that matter. He only got his own jokes, which everybody, including all of the customers, had heard a hundred times. "Well, Bert, you stud, I'm heading outside then, good little chat." As I continued out of the shop doors, his 'grumble grumble' was barely audible. I had managed to escape him though, the most important of details. The cold had momentarily been forgotten but now was being remembered. Of the two propane canisters we had, I chose the fullest, with a light blue paint colour and a brass nozzle to let the flames escape.

The starter was ginormous compared to my car's little starter or any of the BMW starters I had been used to. I surprised myself, since the forklift starter motor had never been noticed before. Its big black hulking exterior was a matte finish. An aluminum label from the '50s was coated in oversprayed paint and grime from the leaks around the engine and tranny. There were no numbers or words on the label anymore, for they had all flaked or fallen onto the floor of some extinct warehouse in who knows which province. Modern forklifts were electric and painted yellow so that they could be seen by careless passersby. They also had seatbelts, which are a novelty item if you ask me. The back-up buzzers, the lights, the horns, and other useful trinkets I would not mind to have though. One time, a spur of the moment idea was to get a license to drive a forklift. I found out that I was not allowed to take the test, as our forklift didn't pass any of the safety requirements needed! But I have yet to see the forklift police, so the operations continue.

At the end of the starter solenoid was a copper cap. Its finish was full and lustreless, a lot like a shiny new penny! Ramming the torch upside down (the only possible way to fit it into the compartment and the reason for the full one being chosen), the flames smothered the starter. Lots of *fire*! More fire! More fire! After thirty seconds, I turned it off. Even when the engine bay cover was in the forty-five-degree position, you were still able to start the old girl. The line to the propane tank had ten unnecessary extra feet, so you could have the propane on a trolley beside the forklift if you really wanted. I hit the switch and got a 'wurg' out of her. Beautiful! Something was happening, and I referred to it as success. Starting the torch again, it got rammed home near the starter. Thin blue flames turned into big red and yellow lapping waves that covered the black surface and burnt off some of the cheap overspray from years gone past. If thirty seconds got a bit of a turnover, another minute or so would get an 'apple'-turnover for sure! Or just a start . . . I hoped. By that time I decided to check its progress, the thin copper cap had turned red-hot and seemed to be melting along with a few dangling wires, a few of the six. Feeling a wee bit nervous with all of the melting occurring and the impending bikes needing forklift action, I decided to turn the torch off. The seething solenoid reverted its colour back to a somewhat normal one, and I hoped all was well inside the brutish unit. It should be, for it was made in a better, more industrious time then what we are used to nowadays—made of strong metal from strong people, like Mother Russia! From the satellite race to the Cold War era of nuclear weapons and espionage, where every little communist that was in the States was suspected of selling to or working for, the Russians. This time she turned over, and I was ecstatic. Pressing down the button again and holding it down got her to start. Revving the engine, she sputtered and farted but warmed up quickly. I cheered to myself and ran back inside the shop with my little box of tools and multimeter. They got tossed onto the desk in the corner, and then it was back outside for me. Forky was purring now. The heavy lid got closed up, creaking as she went, but the sound was not minded. The steel chain was thrust back through the welded-on rungs, and the combination lock, sticky from being in the open weather its whole life, was hastily placed between the links of the chain—locked and loaded!

Old Forky lifted up the forks, the extension cords for the block heater and the battery charger were disconnected, and all systems were a go. Then she got stuck on the ice, the dumb brute! From swearing continuously for the duration of getting a snow shovel and picking away at the ice until she was free, I was breathless. Forky rolled happily through the back gate after this though. The snow in the front parking lot had been cleared by a few of *us* early this morning, so I parked her in position on the wet asphalt for when the transporter arrived.

Going through the showroom, nothing much was happening, and not many customers were expected today. Coffee was being had all around, and the slush and muddy water from my boots laid waste to the clean tiled floor. All of their expressions were that of a scowl. With the cold nasty weather and nothing really to do but reread magazines and talk to one another like they did anyhow, they were all moody; not that I wanted to talk to them in the first place!

In the shop now at 9:15 a.m., the day was just flying by. I took a rusty flat-blade screwdriver and gouged out my eyes, then I reconsidered because of the time and place. We had a few rear ends from R259 and K2X style bikes (R1150 and R1200 models) that had to be rebuilt before sale, and we called them our winter projects. Unfortunately, they stayed winter projects, since no one ever rebuilt them. They lived past the tyre machine in the spare tyre-storage room, which was cold and damp with the bearings and shells rusting away. Ten were counted on the first shelf, and the lower shelf had old trannies covering it. These were warranty transmissions waiting to be destroyed from the early K1200S/R bikes that sucked balls. The shelves for the tyres and miscellaneous bike parts had been one of last year's winter projects . . . how exciting. One of the newer silver R1200GS ones was eventually picked from the pile, taken back into the workplace, and laid on one of our pink shop towels. The selection of the towels was always so vivid, and I just loved the hard-core pink—anything to brighten the workplace. Now don't you go calling them flamboyant either, for that is just rude! To do with the rear ends though, I did not have any sort of interest in measuring any sort of small clearance or backlash this morning—the story of my work life!

Harry had bicycled in this morning, in the slush. He had arrived chilled and pissed (angry), like the rest of us, well, of course not I! Passing cars kept on showering him with muddy water that had found its way down his back, and for the past hour, he had been sitting quietly at his workstation with a box of assorted electrical motors, switches, and wires by his side. Deep in his own activity, Harry was always building little devices: Flashing LEDs, buzzers, zappers, and his love for stereo equipment always kept him busy. He also enjoyed buying speakers, installing decks in friend's vehicles, and constructing sub boxes for extra bass. This morning, he mentioned he might be making seat warmers for his truck. A few weeks back, Harry had found a few sets of used heated grips and took it upon himself to deconstruct them to obtain the heating elements. When laid out, they are very similar looking to the heating elements for car mirrors. After removing these from the grip assemblies, his next step was to install long enough wires to exit the seat and make its way to a switched power relay. In his assorted box, I saw around seven relays with different blade layouts and options of how many switched power sources to have. He chose a blue one, a good colour in my book. Moving in to see the quality of his soldering, I compared his soldering to mine. Obviously, the smoke of the Flux burning off was strong for my eyes, but I was pretty confident that mine were better. I prided myself in my soldering/shrink-tubing work. Harry moved his head and looked up, "What's happenin', dude?" His straight black hair was a bit greasy, and his nose had a bit of a drip. This he wiped off on a nearby rag that he had been placing the soldering gun on to remove the extra solder. It was a nice place to wipe a soggy nose, right on the lead and tin, the healthy choice. My reply was a nonchalant shrug and, at the same time, a "not much, just cruisin' around." This meant not wanting to take apart rear ends, waiting for the transport truck to arrive with some uncrating, and PDI work to do (predelivery inspection). I had not even thought about the possibility that with the weather being the little bitch she was lately, that the truck might not be able to come out to us. What a horrible feeling! That rear end might have to be taken apart today. The only other way that time could be wasted was on the computer, except Albert was on it researching gen sets and used dump trucks for sale. Fail. I made a tea up front instead.

Slow winter season days depressed the crap out of me. Getting paid to be lazy, great if you're working on personal junk; but it seemed the second that a project of mine would be brought out to play with, the ole boss would make an appearance, and no one other than myself took the scolding. The scrags in the showroom, their favourite thing to do, was rat me out on such occasions. Them, with their spines of jellyfish and loyal to the idea that if they ratted me out, the boss would think more highly of them and therefore want to increase their pay. Or it could just be the mutual hatred between them and me. The former sounded less personal from my perspective and more from theirs. I scuttled back to the domain of real motorheads, not the sissy motorheads. Then the truck showed up. Big Duane bustled his way into the back. How was it that he was sweating? Going ten steps from the counter he had been holding down from escaping to walking through to where we were lounging did not make it acceptable to start sweating! "The truck's here! Someone has to move the forklift. The bikes are here!" Duane liked to repeat things over and over again, and with a pompous air about himself as though he was king shit. Most times when talking to you, Duane expected to be treated like royalty. Well, two words for you, Duane: go fuck yourself! It may have been three words, but I was nice and did not say it to his face this time.

Our driver for the truck company wiped his boots aggressively on the blue and black mat in front of the main glass doors. His grin was from ear to ear. He was a shorter fellow, maybe Italian, and I could never remember his name. He usually received a hearty welcome, and we shared a short conversation before I got to business. Any outsiders received into our world were greatly appreciated, and I tried to be as hospitable to them as possible. He hadn't covered up his head with the thinning hair. From our coffee machine, two presses gave him a strong black cup; and beside the machine, he grabbed a few Timbits to help warm the body. I went up to him and inquired how many bikes were in his truck. Supposedly two were on the way, Duane had told us earlier. It turned out that only one had made its way to the shop this morning, an LT. It was a K1200LT, a light truck. It was actually an older model that had been sitting in a warehouse, and it had been the last year of production for the 4-cylinder. Now they had to make way for the new gunship, or flagship, the K1600GTL finally after years of production and research being done. So this K1200LT on the truck was only available in black and still only the brick motor from the past thirty years of K-bikes: a 1.2-litre laid on its side, pushing blue, no matter how new or decrepit. The 1.6-litre, with its F1 technology inspired valve train, like the K12K13S, (not the same, but both being influenced by the technological advances) made heaps more torque and had bucket loads of new technology in the electronics department.

I put my dirty work coat back on, and a toque, and also some leather work gloves, yellow and beginning to fall apart, but still warmer than bare skin. She roared to life almost instantly, as she barely had enough time to cool down. Our truck operator opened up his door, revealing the mighty brute. The last new, crated one to come to this shop. I just about needed a moment to shed a tear, but then decided it was not worth it; just a motorcycle, just a cruising laid-back touring motorcycle, nothing special or memorable in that. No tears would be shed for this one. It didn't even have a single piece of carbon fibre on her! I let out a deep breath, and a billow of steam escaped from in-between my semi-white teeth. The heavy steel fork extensions clanked and clanged on the small forks. Matting the accelerator, she began to move. It was a lot of noise and commotion with little result. We were used to each other. The wheels are made of rubber because if they were made of air, in car yards and dock yards, nails and shards of metal would be penetrating into them all day long, expensive for flat repairs. I had run over doors, printers, and countless times used her to smash TVs and monitors for computers, a good girl. Plunging ahead to the truck, I brought the forks up and moved them underneath the crate. A few of the structural wood cross-braces were broken, and the forks dug into them. It pushed the crate further back along the wooden deck of the truck. "Come on, bitch!" I yelled at the crate. The forklift had to be driven back and the forks realigned. Instead of parallel to the ground, they were moved to a fifteen-degree angle with the fronts of the heavy steel forks almost digging into the deck. This way, with the forks moving under the crate, the broken cross-braces were pushed up and out of the way instead of being directly in the way. The friction of the steel against the wood made a horrible squeaking that was amplified by the cavelike truck. The tips protruded out the end of the crate, but the front of the crate was up against the hydraulic arms. Ready to lift! Yah, baby! An initial strain on the hydraulics, which made the revs die down a bit, slowed the journey. The new LT was heavy as fuck, like they always were, especially when people dropped them, which they did a lot, and especially in parking lots at slow speeds because people always misjudged how heavy they really were. Reading the VIN tag says it's about 800–900 pounds. The newest K12LTs had hydraulic center stands to go along with all the other extravagant accessories. It went nicely with the reverser though . . . a good touch for weak people that were generally older.

She grunted and strained under the effort. LTs came in steel contraptions as their weight designated them unsuitable for conventional wooden crates, and for some reason, the warehouse wanted extra caution for once. Forky lowered the bike and drove through the tiny alleyway to the back lot after a six-point turn. Oversized crate for an oversized bike. Just about a foot wider than regular crates as you couldn't remove the bag lids of the LTs without excessive bolt 'undoing' and unwiring of the central locking system; in other words, a bitch, one giant bitch. She lumbered through that alleyway narrowly like usual, avoiding the air-conditioner unit that hung out of the showroom wall.

The old boss of the place when renovating, as an afterthought, threw the air conditioner into the wall. It takes even more room out of that tiny little passage for the bikes and forklift. The old boss would smash into the air-conditioner unit with the forks, and because of that, all of the fins were dented and mangled. Then someone had attempted to realign those aluminum fins with a flat-blade screwdriver, which is impossible, so it looked even worse; in turn, it was an abortion of an air-conditioner unit. Puddles in our little passageway had turned to ice. With my weight and momentum, it meant nothing. The ice was powerless, and it got ploughed right the fuck over. It would be so much fun to light the forklift on fire and drive it off of a bridge, I thought dreamily to myself. Of course it was a dumb idea, as there weren't any bridges within a ten-mile radius of the shop, and you can't drive the old blue girl on the road legally. Legally . . . laws and rules are for cops to try and enforce and for little sissy bitches to live under. Driving the forklift would just take all day to get to the bridge and was not really worth the effort in the end.

The metal crate holding the bike was taken off of the wooden crates underneath. This makes it much easier to roll the K1200LT off the metal crate so as not to damage the belly pan. It is only plastic, yet the three pieces of painted plastic on the K1200LT add up to roughly $1,100 Canadian. As this was dumb as well as expensive, it was a good idea not to scrape them up even if the company would foot the bill. That would mean less of a bonus at the end of the year. As the precaution . . . I took out the wooden crate, simple. Next step for uncrating: the Saran Wrap, a four-foot-high roll of industrial-sized packing Saran Wrap. The crate had four pillars, four round tubes of steel that fit into the bottom of the crate, and are pinned so as not to fall out. Around these metal poles they use the wrap. Layering it six times, it is believed to be protective enough that the bike will remain unharmed; so far so good. For years, we have been receiving them with nine out of every ten being undamaged and not one being damaged from the shipping company, not on an LT at least. One of our first R1200GS bikes back in 2005 (2004 being the introduction in Canada late in the year) was on its way to the shop, and the truck flipped over. Even under those circumstances, the bike, with its fully wooden crated assembly, only needed a few cosmetic pieces to put of the showroom floor!

Hanging from the middle of the bike above the seat via more of the wrap were the goodies: the windshield, the mirrors, etc. In a separate box altogether came the top box with assembly required. With a nice long razor blade, the Saran was cut and then dumped carelessly in our green bin. Others came outside to look at the bike after the delivery driver had been thanked by me, graciously because now there was real work to be done. They inspected the bike as though they had designed it, going over the styling, the accessories, sooooo knowledgeable. "Get out of the way! Some of us want to get this thing uncrated today!" That was me yelling at them after five minutes. They moved their fat bodies to the side and kept on a murmur between themselves about the bike; useless turds, good for drinking coffee and incessant blabbing. On our gas tank shelf, I placed the windshield. There wasn't enough clearance for the cardboard box holding the black top box, so it was put on the floor. Some of the bikes were still inside, so there wasn't much floor space. With the over 300 feet of the cling wrap in length alone now removed, the bike looked decent. No scratches in the paint, no gouges from the warehouse forklifts, and no missing pieces. This was going to be as easy as pie. Outside just had to be finished up, and then back into the warm domain I could go. White tie straps hold down the bike to the dark-brown painted steel frame. The suspension would be heavily compressed, as this made the bike sturdier and also lowered the height, which probably helped on shipping costs. Instead of four stacked high in the container ships, maybe five would be able to fit—money, honey, money. When these white straps were released, i.e., cut, that compressed suspension suddenly became uncompressed, and at a very quick rate, at an 'if you're not paying attention, the bike will rodeo-star you into onto the ground' quick rate, A 'hell-o' quick rate.

Surprisingly, I chose to do this for all of the bikes, as the lemmings of the shop could not be trusted as they were always too drunk or disorderly. I got Trevor with his handy pocketknife to cut the two rear straps, since they only affected the rear shock; then the middle two going from the metal crate to the metal subframe on the motorcycle. Trevor was far too light to hold onto the motorcycle. He would put up a good fight but just wouldn't be able to hold on! I jumped up on the crate and then onto the LT. The bike had the new soft-touch style seats, so I sunk in. "All right, Trevs, you ready for this?" "Yah, I'll pull on the handlebars to help." "Sounds good. She's gonna wanna fly!" Trevor was ready to cut the front strap on the left-hand side, which would uncompress the shock and want to send the bike careening over the right side of the crate. My right foot was braced against the metal wall of the crate. It had a small lip at least, big enough to position my foot against. The strap was banjo-string tight. The bike tried to heave me off, yet I stood my ground. Trevs ran over to the right side and started sawing away at the last strap with his knife. Together we positioned the bike level. Built into the crate was a little ramp, a convenient BMW design. We struggled to roll her down without the brakes. There is a coating on the brakes, and brake clean must be used to remove this coating. If you pump the brake lever with the coating still on, it gets all over the brake pads and will initially prolong the amount of time for braking. It is not a huge amount, but it won't stop you as fast, so we roll them off the ramp without the brakes. With Trevor pulling from the tail end of the bike, I was left on the top balancing. Once on the ground, she got rolled into the corner—clean-up time.

Using Forky, the metal crate was lifted onto the roof of the tyre storage area. It was flat, and we used it as storage for big flat objects that took up too much space. These metal crates were somewhat flat and big and took up way too much room. On the roof was a mixture of snow and small branches and leaves. The metal crate crushed them, and its little square feet sat firmly on the torch-on, which is all the roof consisted of on the shop addition. After turning the forklift around, she got rolled back into her home and back over the spot where she had gotten previously stuck. Turned off the propane, lowered the forks, plugged in the charger and block heater, then let the propane left in the line get used up before turning off all the ignition switches. Well, turning off the two ignition switches and then getting parked for another week or so until the next bike showed up. Now it was time to finally roll the bikes out for the morning. It was eleven o'clock.

There were not too many bikes left in the shop; people just poorly parked them, so they took up a lot of room. One had been waiting for parts for the better part of two months. Almost every day, the customer would call, but we are not in control of how fast Deutschland decides to make the pieces; we just order them. Usually, the customers call the service department, then they in turn page the mechanic working on the bike, who in turn gets pissed off at the service 'manager', a.k.a. douche bag Dillen. It was a vicious cycle.

No more ice on the concrete for the rolled-out bikes, so we teamed up, and it took but a minute. My bench got the light truck. First, Trevor took the rear ends and the towels off my bench. We joined forces to roll her onto my red Snap-on bench. With the battery disconnected, the electric center stand and integrated braking system are nonfunctional. Albert came over, and with a man on one side and an old man on the other side, we managed to lift her onto the stand. Break time! We all got hot drinks for our *huge* efforts and a job well done. In the shop, Harry was testing his latest creation. He had rigged up a battery and then attached testing cables with alligator clips and an inline fuse to the positive. After hooking up another lead from the relay 'switched positive' to the batteries positive terminal, he sat there waiting for the element to heat up. Albert and I came back while Trevor stayed up front. With drinks in hand, we watched Harry grin as his contraption took flight, or rather the heating strips warmed up. "Show time, boys, time to install these bitches and heat up some ass!" His enthusiasm was a lot more than the rest of us for obvious reasons; Harry Houdini was getting heated seats. Meanwhile, Bert's seats were filthy and literally falling apart in his truck, and mine were also filthy and coming apart and lacked heating elements and were as comfortable as sitting on an old 7 Up crate. Harry made us all have a gander and express how excited we were—very. He was also thinking about bicycling home to get his vehicle and installing them in the afternoon. He did so and went to work on the truck. Dillen was in charge of the batteries in the shop, so of course, the gray gel cell batteries for the K-series weren't charged. My hassling made him run off in a whimper to the battery room and start filling the empty lead-acid ones and charge the gel cell and AGMs. With little black latex-free gloves on my hands and brake-clean-doused paper towels, I went about cleaning the brake discs. One time, Harry was spinning the rear wheel on a similar light truck and put his hand through the moving wheel to get at the disc. Needless to say, he squashed his thumb between the caliper and one of the silver painted spokes. Endless swearing and cursing came out of his mouth. His thumb was red and swollen and then turned purple. Extremely funny, not for him, but Albert and I had an amazing laugh. Most of the time, when Harry hurt himself at work, which was frequently—more than normal people, that was for sure—he'd run outside with a hammer and smash our wooden crate pile. This time, his thumb was in too much pain, so the swearing and kicking of things had to suffice.

I cleaned the discs and took out all of the brake caliper bolts to Loctite them. Then I torqued the engine oil drain plug and the oil filter cover bolts, which only the old 'flying brick' motors had. The center-stand mount was actually covering one of the oil filter cover bolts, and motorcycles from the States would come to the shop, and we would find that this same bolt was always stripped or cross-threaded. Mechanics in the States are paid piecework instead of an hourly or salary wage. I went to work on installing the top box. The liner was removed, and I found the bolts and installed all the appropriate wires, including the ones for the speakers, trunk lights, and other garbage that is entirely unnecessary. By that time, since the gel cells come 80-percent charged from the warehouse, she was good to go. The battery had its terminals gently brushed with a file for the freshest contacts possible before being washed, since gases from the lead acid batteries in the battery room get everywhere. The LTs come with batteries, so it was swapped out for a fully charged unit. I found the keys and alarms fobs to turn her on. The needles on the dash swung fully to the max and then returned to the stops, while the whole dash lit up in red. At the same time that the ABS servo-assist motor performed the system test, the HID Xenon low-beam began to heat up, covering Albert's toolbox with an incredibly bright blue light. I threw a portable BMW charger into the bike's onboard socket for all the power being expended. Next, it was decided that she would obtain a windshield, a freaking expensive windshield and one huge piece of clear plastic just dying to be scratched. Four tiny bolts hold it on, and cheap steel brackets clasp the fake chrome plastic trim panels overtop. These are installed for a flush, clean, aerodynamic appearance. I went and got Trevor to hold the windshield as I installed the bolts. He always seemed to enjoy helping out with the bikes, and it is probably due to his bicycle mechanic-ing past. Since he was stuck in the showroom doing paperwork and helping customers pick out matching coloured helmets for their bikes, this was a lovely change. I never get a lovely change, probably where the constant feelings of killing myself come from . . . Anyways, the German air, which always smells *über alles* came out of the tyres, and nitrogen was shot into them instead. Airplanes have been using it for forever, so something must be behind the reason. As air consists mainly of nitrogen already, the other 22 or so percent is comprised of mostly oxygen and a few other random gases. With nitrogen, the molecules are larger, so pressure isn't lost through the rubber as fast. Oxygen loves to sneak through those cords in the tyres. In addition, it does not heat up, like oxygen, so the tyres stay cooler and regulate the temperature better, preserving tyre life, and saving the customer dollars on tyres. Our shop puts it in for free, and some customers come by for top-ups every once in a while. It seems to make them happy. Torqued the trim panels, and the rear end drain and fill plugs; easy-peasy. Then these fill/drain plugs were marked with my trademark red nail polish for antitampering. The right rider foot peg bracket has to be removed to check the tranny oil levels and to be properly torqued. Checking it is a hassle, and by the time lunch had come around, Albert and Harry bundled up and ventured out to buy fettuccini at the nearby grocery store. I made some chicken sandwiches that had been squished together into one ziplock bag. The bread was compressed into millimetre slabs of wheat. As a side, Campbell's Clam Chowder—'souper' tasty . . . Harry burnt the shit out of his tongue 'cause he left it in the microwave for four minutes and then tried to engulf it right away. Berty cut his pasta into cat-sized bites and used his signature spoon to eat it. He grinned a menacing lack-of-tooth grin and asked about the sammies. "Just delightful: a little bit of pesto, nice whole grain bread, warm delicious soup. What could make a lunch be any better?" He cackled his usual cackle. "Think you wanna bit o' my noodle?" "Umm, I'll pass on your 'noodle,' but if you're offering fettuccini, I wouldn't mind." "Sick fuck, what I said, not the sick shit you think all the time!" "So does that mean fettuccini for me?" My retort sounded sarcastic, and I didn't get any noodles for lunch. The chowder and chicken seemed to suffice anyhow. The mood was still dull, and during lunch, there wasn't much conversation; no one had anything to talk about, and we sat around, eating and lounging, trying to make the day go by faster. As I didn't care to test ride the K1200LT today due to the fact that on shoddy parts of road black ice could be hit, there wasn't much else to be done to finish the predelivery inspection. There was definitely no way that the rear end was getting put back on the bench no matter what anybody said. Well, it could get put back on the bench, but there was a low chance of it being worked on.

Harry managed to polish off the pasta, cringing with every bite. He was drinking cold water now because it was 'soothing.' A nap would be nice; it would hit the spot. A little half-hour nap. A quick climb up into the warranty area, move a few boxes of wheels that weren't round that we kept replacing, and use a bundled-up towel as a pillow—perfect. How could it be done with the boys not noticing? Not that they would care, but still. For over an hour, we sat around doing nothing. Lunch break was only thirty minutes, but what would anyone do about it? They could send us home, but that is the dream of all the mechanics on slow miserable days. I cleaned up the bowl and washed and put away my spoon. I also didn't keep and reuse the plastic bag for the sandwiches; my mother would be appalled at the wasteful lifestyle that was being lived by her son. After lunch, Albert went up front to get another 'stool softener,' as he referred to it. I watched him open and go through the door. Harry's cell phone went off, and after talking for only a moment, he went outside. It must have been highly personal. I sat thinking for a second and then went into action. Quickly, the ladder got pulled out of storage and opened up underneath the warranty area. It was on level two, meaning, the attic overtop the machine room with an opening cut for an entry. Clambering up there, I chucked on the fluorescent tube switch (light switch) and began moving crap to clear an area. I worked the fastest I had all day. Boxes of ESA struts (electronic suspension adjust for R12GSA and R12RT bikes that had failed), headlights that the metallic reflector inside flopped up and down, and K13GT saddle bag locks that stuck had to be moved. Luckily, a towel was covering a few rocker box covers in the corner, which would do perfectly. She lay out nicely over the eggshell-white painted plywood that acted as the floor. Stretching out felt so good! Then Albert came back. "Where'd e'r'body go?" he exclaimed. That fucker. That party pooper. "Come onn, gurls, show yerselves." Albert wanted some company to do nothing with, and Harry was still outside talking on the phone. My lids were so heavy. How did they weigh so much? I don't even remember the next thing that he said; I was out of it. Kind of ridiculous, as I had literally just fallen asleep at work, again, and on purpose . . .

A wooden lawn chair covered in one long cushion. All the timber was a brilliant white, so its type could not be distinguished. Peaceful was the best word to describe the scenario. There was my body, yes, it was me, so why was I in third person? I was looking at myself sprawled out on the chair. My lips were set in a smile, and my eyes were covered in dark shades, and closed. There was a beautiful soothing breeze caressing my skin. The skin was quite white itself, and the air movement was able to cool it. 'I hope I'm wearing sunscreen', I thought to myself, since it would be an even yet horrible burn if prolonged exposure occurred. Next to the played-out body was a small square table with four legs. It was for drinks. There were a few empty bottles standing, and one full bottle still perspiring. It appeared chilled and delicious. He was wearing long boarding shorts, and the pattern was that of hibiscus flowers, black and made of thin polyester with large red flowers. Underneath his lawn chair was sand in a small amount of shade. The rest of the beach was blinding. I had to squint just looking around. Racoon eyes are what 'lawn chair' boy was going to acquire and a nice white band where his wristwatch was attached. Behind me, or him, depending on how I looked at it, were palms. Oh how I love palms: piles of them, strong rough trunks, unmoving with the breeze gently lifting and lowering the branches and leaves. It was sure a shame that I was asleep. There was some sort of tournament going on, a sports tournament, a volleyball tournament, with girls, many of them. Oh yes, there were many, and I was looking at myself asleep, while they were getting hot and sweaty in their sexy little bikinis playing with one another. What an idiot, why didn't he wake up? He could go talk to them, make a few . . . friends. Wake up, you tool, wake up! For a moment, the image disappeared. The girls kicking up hot white sand hitting the ball to one another turned into a white screen. It seemed to soften to a white and black wall. Another second passed, and the beautiful bathing-suit-clad girls returned. This time, one was walking towards me. I was still on the lawn chair but appeared to be not as docile. I watched him move his arms and bring his hands up to his face. Rubbing the face, he also took off the glasses. He turned his head in the direction of the girls. She appeared about five foot seven inches and had magical tanned white skin. Her hair was a soft and straight brown and was in a ponytail. Some of the hair wasn't long enough for the hair elastic and swept across her face. And her smile . . . I was mesmerised, and so was my figure on the chair. I wasn't actually sure if I was mesmerised or if his mesmerisation was just being felt by me; a strange sensation. Her bikini was white, and everything on this beach seemed that way. She also had flowers on the outfit, but I wasn't sure of the kind. I made a witty remark about the matching swimwear—or he made the remark, not sure. She stopped three feet from me and giggled while brushing the amazing hair behind her ear, her left ear. What an adorable creature! I looked on at myself proudly, and then I asked her if she would like to sit with me and take in a drink. When she smiled again, I watched myself almost die with anxiety. For a brief moment, she didn't say anything and just held her gaze with my own, showing me sparkling teeth and luscious rosy lips. Then she nodded and, with a quick yes and a spring in her step, moved in front of my chair to the one right next to it. He asked her what kind of drink she usually enjoyed. Whatever I was having, but I couldn't remember! In my head, I got worried. Shit, don't mess this up! Then I let out a smirk, of course it was beer. The table beside me was overcrowded with them. He asked her how she felt about beer. If I like it, then she liked it, she responded. Oh my gosh, what an angel sent down from heaven for me! He hoped that the moment would never end. Bliss, bliss, bliss. He turned back to the palms behind him. Two waiters were close. He flicked his fingers, and one came immediately. The waiter's accent was foreign and perhaps from Asia? His skin was dark, and his hair was jet black. His attire was very clean and consisted of a pressed long-sleeved white shirt and a graphite tie with diagonal interchanging yellow and grey stripes, not very big stripes though. He also wore dark pants. His belt buckle was chromed, and the band was made from leather, but it held no brand name—classy. His shoes could not be seen as they were too close to the chair. "Yessir, wha can I gye for you?" I chuckled under my breath, what a surreal moment. "Two of the same, thank you." "Vewy good, sir, wom moment." I looked back at the girl, and she looked dreamily into my eyes, or was it the other way around? He hadn't got a burn yet, and his 'defined' body tensed for a second as he leaned in to get closer. He mentioned something about her beauty, but I couldn't quite catch it. Why couldn't I catch it? I thought it was me! All she seemed to do was smile, but this time, her cheeks flushed. I think I love this girl! I thought in my head, or his head. The beers came briefly after, and the old ones were cleared away. I still had a spare one but offered her the freshest. Thanking him, she pushed the hair once again behind her ear. It only seemed to fall on the left over the high cheek bones and cute button nose and ridiculously adorable eyes, blue eyes. She tilted her head back and let the golden liquid flow down her thin infatuating throat. I took an immense gulp of my beer. Finishing a third gulp, he looked back at her; and they shared a laugh, a genuine laugh, the kind that makes you feel so good inside. That was one of the best moments he had ever had. They sat facing each other talking and laughing. She giggled at his jokes, and she understood them. The jokes were witty and cynical, and she chided with him about it. The volleyball was forgotten by her, and he loved every second of it. They polished off the beers, his one for every two of hers, and he ordered another round. The beer was a pale ale, and it went down easy. As they waited for the drinks, he took her piano-player-like fingers into his hands. Their chairs were close, and their feet in the sand brushed against one another. She looked down at the toes and then back up again at him. Her painted toenails were partially covered by the tiny grains from the sand. Attached to her feet were elegant smooth legs. They were long and not heavily tanned, just heavenly. He wanted to bring her closer to him. He was longing to reach in with his lips and kiss her, but only softly at first, for she might be fragile. She seemed to be saying something, but he couldn't distinguish what. He saw lips and them moving, but couldn't hear them. A black flash appeared, blocking out everything. "No, no, no," I told myself, "take me back!" Then she was back: her eyes were closed, and he could see the accenting eye shadow. Her beautiful face was slowly coming towards him. Her lips were luscious and were begging to be enjoyed by him. She was moving so slowly towards him he had time to look around him. Why in the heck did he want to look around? He was in a room, and they were sitting on the bed, or he was lying on the bed, and she was over top of him and on her knees straddling him, and her palms were on the sheets. He was surprised: it was a queen-size bed with an enormous amount of pillows. He looked back at her as she leaned in, and their lips touched. It was amazing! Their warm wet tongues flicked in and out of each other's mouths. His hands grasped her sides, and he squeezed her rib cage. She squealed and pulled away from him, becoming breathless. "I want you on top!" she said quickly and in her dreamy voice. I grinned wildly and threw her down on the bed. She squealed with pleasure and wondered why he hadn't undone her top while she was straddling him. Too many testosterone-filled thoughts at once. He leaned into her and, at the same time, kissed her neck feverously. Her oohs and aahs were creating a triumphant impression. To please is a pleasurable feeling. With a flash, she undid his belt and the button and zip. He was busy groping her breasts with one hand, while the other became entangled in her hair. He was kissing her neck and ears to help. For a second, she struggled to pull off his flowered shorts. Pulling off the boxers and shorts got them momentarily caught, and he stopped what he was doing to use one of his hands to pull them off of each leg. "That's better," he told her. She agreed and gave him a puppy-dog face. "Why do you get to be the only one naked?" Her soft sweet voice questioned him. He gasped and offered apologies. He was throbbing with desire and pulled off the small bikini that kept her only minimally covered. "How inappropriate of you!" I bellowed in a moment of mock seriousness, "Taking advantage of me like this!" Her face contorted into a bewildered and scared look, but his grin came back, and she punched him in the shoulder. Every inch of her body was perfect. The only blemish was the man on top. He looked down at her smooth body and almost melted. They came together as one body, and they continued breathlessly—what an incredible journey. Then she started talking. At first, he couldn't hear, but then the words became discernible. "You've got to wake up, you've got to wake up." Her words were getting louder now. He was having the time of his life, and they were both loving it. Why would he want to wake up? He felt so good inside of her, and his sweat was dripping uncontrollably down onto her already-perspiring body. Her upper body was off the bed in an arch, and her head was positioned almost to the point of looking back against the wall as she writhed in enjoyment. "You've got to wake up. You've got to wake up." She kept on hassling him. "No, no, *no*," he said incessantly. "Wake up, you slut!" I opened my eyes, and it hit me like a two-by-four. Albert was standing on the ladder, yelling in my face. I looked down at my pants and saw that I had a huge boner. Could have been worse? I looked back at Bert and saw that his yellow teeth had formed into a smile. I groaned with disgust—back to work.

CHAPTER **9** — Roadside

Another morning; they seemed to happen every day. This one was more joyous than the others as a few of the local troublemakers were out. They were picking up a roadside, a broken-down motorcycle. Our shop had no truck for picking them up, so Albert was driving his own with Dillen riding shotgun. He was the muscles of the operation, or the retard of the operation, I wasn't sure yet which. Either way, I didn't care because he wasn't at the shop. Harry and I had the whole place to ourselves to do with as we pleased. It was nice to have a bit of peace for once. A moment of peace is a perfect time to think about war and chaos. When we first opened that morning, a few distributors happened to stop by to show off the upcoming year's products. They also dropped off some stickers. I love stickers, Harry loves stickers, and Dillen's toolbox was soon going to love stickers. We had already accumulated two big stacks of them. "Hey, Tiger-toucher, what kind a shits goin' on in your head?" Harry had a different way of asking questions compared to the masses. He was already rummaging through his bottom toolbox drawer full of rubbish, which also contained a bunch of dirty shit and more random stickers. I did not yet know what was on his mind. "Well, my fellow, biatch, I say we pummel Dillen's face with an axe! But first, let's cover his fuckin' toolbox with stickers. And not the kind that are easy to come off. Know what I'm sayin'?" He waved his right arm at me and pulled off our 'Wucked' sign—pinky finger and thumb splayed open, hand going back and forth, and the arm moving forward and backwards. This had been created by a few friends earlier in the year and was spreading just like wild fire all over our workplaces. "Wucked, dude, lets ged id on!" We both grabbed our stickers and, giggling like little Catholic schoolgirl sluts, tiptoed (for no apparent reason) over to his toolbox. Within arm's reach of his cheap-quality contraption for holding his paper plates and plastic spoons, which he called tools, a voice rang out through the shop. Shit. We looked at each other and then at the direction of the voice. It was Gerald. He appeared oblivious, which was a momentary relief. Harry immediately kept on walking out through the big motorcycle entrance doors out the back of the shop. "Where's he off to?" Gerald said in his fast high-pitched voice. He was walking through the sales-to-shop door and over towards me as he said this. I propped my head over to my right shoulder to acknowledge him and put an 'I'm semibusy, but I know you're the boss, so what's up' look. "Oh, Harry?" While I talked, I attempted to stuff the stickers into one of the back pockets of my overalls and made it appear as though it was an adjustment to relieve an itch or a bunched-up piece of cloth. "He just popped outside to wash a bike, I think." I hesitated with my last remark, and Gerald knew something was going on, or at least he knew that I was full of shit about something. "You busy?" he asked. "Oh, well, you know, just finishing up a few jobs, nothing fancy. Would you like a hand with something?" Even though Gerald knew there was wool being pulled over his eyes of a suspicious activity afoot, because of my lousy ability to lie or deceive, it came out that he did need a hand up in the front with a service question from a customer in the showroom. Sticker fun was over!

Whenever there is a job or a customer to deal with, the fun is always over. Up front, it was the same ole same ole: just a dude, a regular Joe overfilling the oil on an ancient '90s R1100RS, the queen of rubber-mounted handlebars; retro baby. And the story goes: guy drops his oil but doesn't change the filter 'cause it cost more (turd). Then he reuses the old crush washer for the drain plug, which isn't that big of a deal. He torques it with his Joe Blow torque wrench that was $35 Canadian at the local whatever store. Still no big deal. He doesn't have the manual for the quantity, since he bought the bike used. He reckons it would take the same amount as a car due to its large displacement. Then his problems start. She should take with a new filter approximately 3.65–3.75 litres; good times for all. Unfortunately, he left the old filter on the bike, which has 0.25 litres in it and another 0.15 sitting above it in the crankcase. He also never noticed it had an oil window. But anyways, he rams four litres down her left-hand cylinder oil-fill hole. So far, she'll run, but maybe you won't have to top up the oil as often and I would give you a scolding. Furthermore, and here is the fun part, the owner started up the bike and tried to eliminate the ticking sound, a.k.a. the rocker arm noise, which you cannot eliminate on the old oil-head boxer motors. He thought more oil would help. He put in another two litres . . . gasp! That's 6.35 litres in a crankcase that holds, guess what, not that much oil! Sucks. For the record, he didn't have the bike at our shop. He had left it at home, as he did not feel safe riding to the shop with clouds of blue smoke pouring incessantly out of her single exhaust can. It was difficult not to laugh; seriously! Usually, it is useless questions like 'Is it okay to ride my tyres down to the cords?' or 'If I get a few litres of diesel in my tank, will the bike still be fine to run?' But this was good; this was brilliant; this was hilarious. The serious issue with overfilling the oil on most BMW motorcycles is that the seals in the engine have too much pressure on them and are literally blown out of the engine. I told him if there wasn't oil underneath the bike when he got back home, all he might have to do is drain those extra litres out, swap out the plugs, clean out the airbox, and then ride the bike to heat up and burn away the oil sitting in the exhaust. He decided to have our shop do the work, which was fine. I booked him into the schedule for the following day, and with our telephone, he called a tow-truck company for the following morning to pick up his beast. This was all good and dandy, right until he asked if warranty would cover the repairs. Excuse me, sir? This is a 1996 motorcycle. Not even a two times extended aftermarket warranty would cover that. What a stupid question. It pissed me off that the dork would even think of asking that, and I started to go into a grumpy mood. The customer blabbed about some other random crap for a couple minutes, and then pretending to have urgent work lined up, I snuck through the door, going back into the shop. Surprisingly, Harry *had* washed a bike when I was with the customer.

I peered into Gerald's office to make sure he was engrossed in paperwork, which he was. Whatever happened to the days when a man could get up early in the morning, plough the fields, toil in the dirt, and that was the way to feed a family, with none of this paperwork mumbo jumbo.

With fresh socks, Harry seemed sprightly again. They had been drenched from the bike washing. I mentioned the imbecile, excuse me, customer, to Harry, and we shared a laugh. So many retarded customers, probably too many to count. We returned to the toolbox and began liberally applying stickers. At first, we put them over the drawers, so they would be difficult to open, but then we went into a frenzy. Stickers went here, stickers went there, and stickers went everywhere. For some reason, we had bundles of garbage stickers, in the sense that they had warnings for proper grounds, cautions on how to turn on a light switch, I don't know, crap. They were perfect for the job. Cheap enough that they weren't made of high-quality materials: paper tops that made them leave most of themselves behind when being removed. Dillen was going to ball his eyes out. I loved it, every second. His toolbox after five minutes went from black to mainly white with little flecks of colour here and there. Just before Harry and I had finished, the door from the front opened again. This time, I scurried outside and left Harry to whomever it was that was entering into our domain. After a few minutes of useless sweeping of the back lot, I popped my head through the shop doors and checked in with Harry Houdini. "Yo, dog, what's a happenin'?" He was at his bench, making a midmorning sandwich. "Oh, ya know! A bit a this, a bit a that!" "So who came into the shop when I headed out?" Harry stopped preparing his food and turned to face me. He put his elbows on his desk without squishing the food. "Was the boss man, mate. Want to have a chat with the lot of us. He's just bin crunchin' numbers, and he didn't seem happy." "Well, I've got some cheery news. Look over there, son." I pointed at our handiwork on Dildo's tool chest. It was beautiful and a fine job done by us. Together we laughed and admired our schoolboy antics. Harry polished off his sandwich, and it got me thinking about food.

Bert and Dillen arrived back quickly thereafter. The roadside must not have been that far away. Albert hobbled to the back and yelled for someone to help take the bike off his truck. I raised my hand and mockingly yelped, "Pick me, pick me!" He glared at me and motioned to get my ass on to the bike. He was out of control! Scrambling past the stainless-steel showroom counters and over the blue tiles, I noticed that Mr. Oil-Overfill was still babbling away absentmindedly to the next employee he had found—good luck to him. Dillen was up front, brownnosing with one of our rich customers, just pumping out the lies to impress him. For all I knew (which wasn't much), it was probably working. Walking at a medium pace, I called out to him as though he was a dog, or rather a bitch. He got told for his ass to get in-gear and hold the bike on the truck steady, as I was about to lower her down to the asphalt level. Dillen gave me one of his regular dumbfounded expressions and apologized to the customer for the need of his help, the cheeky bugger. Albert's truck was not a tall truck, just a regular height—4x4s are a cunt to load bikes onto and to take off. With the ramp already in place, I hopped onto the deck and studied the bike as Dillen undid the tie-down straps. She was an oldie: a gorgeous relic of a bike, the infamous R100GS; a beauty to some and a beast to others. She was a teal green/blue colour but faded. She rolled down easily onto the ramp, and since she was very light, it could be done by myself. "Okay, now that I've done all the hard work, run back there like a good boy and open the gate, since it's not going to open itself." Looking glum and oppressed by the constant nagging and hassling, he mopped through to the back and opened the gate. He walked through the showroom and out the parts door, so he didn't have a chance to see his box. She rolled into the back lot, and the owner followed. He carried all his heavy traveling bags and planted them down in the shop: sleeping bag, tent, and his box of tools, which obviously hadn't helped. We made small talk: he was from the States, had two kids and was divorced, and was riding across North America to 'find' himself. Story of my life minus the riding around North America and making a family . . . then we chatted about his bike. The past couple days of his trip, it had been cold; and from Montana and up into Canada, she was beginning to have hard starts. His policy was camping, no hotels or motels; and the less civilization, the better. That was most likely why he smelt like an old camel. On his back was a twenty- or thirty-year-old canvas Belstaff jacket. It was once a dark canvas with sharp lines and a crisp new look. Now it appeared to be an old potato sack, lovely. The boots looked the same, the pants looked the same. I suppose it was the general overall appearance of all his equipment. The few mornings he had been riding in Alberta and British Columbia, he was getting jump starts when he stopped for petrol, which I found depressing to hear. This morning, with his tent outside the ferry terminal, he had slept. Motorcycles are put onto the ferries first, and this time, he rolled his bike onto the boat. I had a good chuckle. The lucky part for him was that when it docked, he had a ramp to roll down. An hour and a half later, the ole brute rolled down that ramp, and the faithful push start/downhill roll took over. It would have been a kick in the teeth if it had been flat land. Cruising along the highway, the battery was so dead that when he slowed for a stoplight, she died, and no way was she gonna start again. A cell phone call later, and Albert-o showed up with the convoy. It was such an amazing story that I needed caffeine to stay awake. Why hadn't the customer had the bike fixed in Alberta when he knew it was acting up? Sounded like a regular cheap-ass. I didn't want to ask if he was aware of the prices for electrical parts on old Beemers. My kind emotions kicked in, and I left it alone; it was a job for someone else.

Berty came back from parking his truck. It sounded as though he and the customer were just regular pals from birth the way they got along. I guess it helps when you have three grown-up dudes confined together in a smallish truck, swapping body heat. Albert's bench was free, so after jump-starting the bike off a spare battery and testing the charging system with a multimeter, we threw it up onto the bench. They continued on chatting for what seemed like eternity, but in reality was only twenty minutes. I couldn't take it; either they were going senile or I was. They talked about the most useless things. If only I had my music player handy, then I could drown them out! Alas, it was no use, so I went up front. Talking to Trevor about his mountain biking would be more interesting. For fun, we sometimes got him to give us the mountain-bike tip of the week: some useful tidbit about manoeuvring down hills at break-neck speeds. Today, he was occupied talking to a certain customer who still hadn't left! Well, I certainly did not want a part of that conversation, nor one with Duane or Dillen. In addition, Gerald was supposedly with his panties in a bunch, so that was out of the question. He usually had a good story about old rock music or a Vietnam War movie from his past. I stayed clear of him today. "Fine," I told myself, "I'll have a goddamned tea. I'll just do it!" In the back of the shop, the bum buddies were jabbering away about something to do with wrestling. Almost running with my tea mug, I made it back to the hot-water machine in one piece. It was a beautiful Japan Sencha, which turned out to be an excellent idea. I dawdled around looking at the BMW T-shirts and accessories. Should I buy an aftermarket exhaust for my Beemer? Perhaps an HID headlight kit instead. Naw, these were all overrated and only make a small amount of difference. Plus, they were ridiculously overpriced.

He was showing Bert a few bottles of whiskey that were magically appearing from a saddle bag. Then he opened one and took a swig. What the hell was wrong with him? With the cuff of his jacket, he then wiped his chin right before offering Bert a midday pick-me-up. He declined after a moment of hesitation. His eyes seemed to long for the bottle, and his alcoholism wanted to grab the bottle by the neck and chug it down halfway. Then he brushed the thought away and waved his hand in a disappearing manner—perfect timing. Gerald had noticed we had all returned to our workstations and decided to have that 'word' with us that he had mentioned to the 'dirt-diggler' Harry a little while ago. Hah, that would be horrifying to think about his reactions and the consequences that would follow: Gerald walking in on Bert with his mouth on a whiskey bottle. Anyways, he nonchalantly walked in without notice and without making a sound. In his spare time, he must have been turning doorknobs and walking through them, for he was quieter than a mouse; or in a former life, he had been a mouse. Either way, he 'schooshed' away the customer and led him up front to the coffee machine. The older fellow with his creased brow took the message and grabbed a book out of one of the rucksacks before venturing away. "Now that I have you all in the shop for once, there is something I'd like to talk about." Gerald had clasped his hands together, and it was evident that this 'one of many' confrontation got him extremely anxious. He was sweating profusely and was putting words together in his sentences wrong. We (the shop as an entity) grasped the seriousness of the moment and paid attention; this being one of the very few times recorded in the shop's history. "As you are all very aware, as a retired accountant that ran an extremely successful business for over twenty years, I am aware of all that goes on in this business. He emphasized his 'business' heavily. "Every evening, contrary to popular belief, Margaret and I are upstairs doing paperwork and crunching numbers. The problem is that those numbers lately have not been adding up." For a moment, he stopped talking. Then he moved his head slowly to look each of us straight in the eyes, one by one. How uncomfortable is that? Gerald was building his confidence up the more he took charge and kept on talking. Bert was starting up his little grumbling noises, which prompted a louder onslaught from Gerald. "As you all know very well, the inventory here may not be as perfectly categorized and organized as a large automotive company, but we do have a small idea of what we have through our records. I also know what we don't have!" He broke off again from the speech and did the stare. An awkward silence trailed behind the eyes. "The big item we are lacking is oil, gentlemen!" Harry knew this was coming. He turned his head and murmured something about it being hard to keep track of the oil when we put in different amounts than we charge the customers. Gerald was unimpressed. "Listen up! The customers are entitled to any oil from the bottle that is not needed for the oil changes. If there were any discrepancies, we could have a bitter lawsuit on our hands. This is not under discussion! For the record, in our inventory, we would then have more oil not less, which is not the case in hand. The problem is that there is less oil in the system than the company should have. This does not go over well with me! The hardest thing to do is for me to come out and say this, and I really don't want to. This is a business based upon trust. It is a business that has a small staff. I do not want to say that this company has a thief. I do not want to point fingers at anyone. If you are the person that has been taking the oil, I ask you to stop this instant, or I will confront you! Furthermore, if you have not stopped, and I do have to confront you, you will not be welcome here—period. You will not be employed in this company any longer, and I won't ever want you on the premises again." Gerald had over exerted himself and looked exhausted. The only thing Gerald said after all those comments was that the oil was not the only item he meant. He did not want any problems with the inventory, but of course, he meant from employees abusing the system. Small discrepancies, which were genuine mistakes, would always happen, since humans were involved, with input from machines being secondary. Gerald mentioned this point last, and with a final "thank you for your time, gentlemen," he returned up front.

For a few minutes, us mechanics did not say a word to one another. A bit dumbfounded and slightly shocked by Gerald actually speaking out at us, what was to be said? After we had been back on the job for a few minutes and had time to let his speech sink into out thick skulls, Harry decided to have an argue and let off a piece of his mind. "Yeah, so I've been thinkin'. He was just totally unfair to us a minute ago, hey? That's what I think." He sounded very upset. Under the circumstances, I most likely would be too if I had been found out for taking things that did not belong to me. Okay, not exactly found out per say, but being told finally that you had been found out and had known for quite some time about it. "Gerald has no friggin' right to come at us like that. We're the fuckin' blood at this shop! Without us, this place would be shut down for good." "So Harry," bringing myself into the conversation by mistake, "are you saying that because we do a good job, that it's okay to take without paying?—stuff from the shop, I mean." Now Harry was getting all wound up and furious. "Hells no! That is not what I'm sayin'! We get paid shit here, put in all this overtime, 'n' I'm sayin' he should understand that! The old boss would give you cash bonuses, cash for all the hard work and extra time. But what does little ole Gerald give us? Huh? How 'bout a good kick in the teeth? Does that feel good? Nah, didn't think so, 'cause that's what you get every morning when you get into work, a nice fuckin' kick." "But Hobbers, I thought what I just said was 'Is it okay to take what isn't yours,' and you said no and contradicted yourself by somewhat admitting to it." "What? Nah, I didn't say nothin' contradicting. I've . . . never taken anything!" Albert at this time cracked up before carrying on with his R100. At least the American customer had not tried to get into the shop while this mutiny was taking place. "I just don't see him reaming out those fags up front. We're always laid with the blame game, while those sorry little bitches, fuckin' good-for-nothin' cunts, do nothin' all day up there and jus' brownnose their way outta everythin'. It pisses me right the fuck off!" Harry had a point: the other staff did get away with everything. They did constantly come in late, do nothing but hold down the counter, drink coffee, and watch YouTube videos all day. Unfortunately, that point was irrelevant for the time being. Abusing their privileges of having free time in-between talking to customers was one thing; stealing from the business was something entirely different. I quickly paraphrased this to Harry, but he was still upset. It was probably best he did not go have another 'conversation' with Gerald today, as both were in excited positions. Gerald would most likely, just guessing, come out of the situation better off.

Albert had not said much lately, so I looked over his way to check on him and make sure he hadn't been 'chugging away' on the R100 owner's alcohol stash. He wasn't, and I knew he wouldn't be, but I checked anyways. I could see that he had removed the side panels from before to get jumpers to the battery, which was currently disconnected. Afterwards, the front cover had been removed to access the charging system. Unfortunately, the amount of garbage in the way of that cover was highly annoying: crossbars, horns, dirt and grime, tool tubes. Since it was the old 'shit beater' that it was, every bolt was corroded, cross-threaded, broken, or just hard to reach. In the small conscience that I had, I believe that I momentarily pitied him. At first, when I was rolling the bike off the truck, it had looked far better than it was turning out to be. At least he wasn't struggling; at least not with this particular job. I'm sure that just getting up and coming to this horrific place was its own struggle—the thought of never ending, the thought of slavery. Michael Trent Reznor writes songs, cynical as they are, about 'Happiness in Slavery.' Coming back here day after day, it is yet to be found. For the record, the lead singer wrote most of his songs under the influence of alcohol and drugs. *Nine Inch Nails* could not be the amazing band, spanning over twenty years today, without that past. Bert appeared to be at some sort of peace or equilibrium with the world. If he did not raise a hand of defiance or speak out, the world would let him slowly deteriorate and pass away unnoticed. As a rebel-rouser and a troublemaker, I'd rather go out with a bang or a brilliant explosion, filling the universe with a blinding light, and then gone forever. Sort of like a supernova without all of the light-years intervening. Dillen then walked in.

It was not a particularly pleasant day outside, for we had been experiencing an on/off of showers. It was also cold, somewhat dreary, and we had had plenty of ice and snow over the previous weeks. Still, as inside the temperature was quite roomy, it was not overly uncomfortable. Now that the roadside bike had been picked up, dropped off, and started to have a diagnosis and be worked on, Dillen had no reason now to go outside. He had put on shorts: thin summer shorts that almost covered the knees. We often made fun of his attire. It was uncoordinated, and the colours usually clashed. Of course, we said that his mother bought all this for him. Later we found out that she did! She also cut his hair on a monthly basis. After that, the joke seemed rather pathetic: to be joked at that you cannot buy and dress yourself with clothes is slightly childish, and among friends, you don't say such things. Among co-workers, it has to be said, especially about him, even if it was childish! His shorts were red, they had some emblem splashed across the left leg: Billabong, or Board World; something you would wear while surfing, not at a highly established motorcycle dealership. But that was my opinion, for my clothes at that moment were dirty; but at least I had reason for it, being a mechanic and all, and they did not clash. He had on a collared shirt made of thick cotton. Dillen never 'did' his hair, and as it was a dirty blonde, not to thick. It just kind of sat on his head, like a bowl, with no style, no contrast, just dull, just hair.

He opened the door noisily and tromped in with his black sneakers. On his face he wore a half-witted smile. It was kind of a dreamy lost-in-wonderland smile. We all knew he did not take part in any drug usage, so it must have been due to the part in him that was mentally deficient, the part that was not always there. As he came in, he initially addressed Bert. I suppose since they spent an hour or so together in his truck this morning, Dillen thought they had developed a sort of special bond that would bring them together through the hard times, a shoulder to rest on and an individual to stay up with and share feelings with. Gay if you ask me, but we already knew he was, so it made no difference. "Oh hey, Alberto!" His tone was so . . . happy? I wasn't one to exhibit similar happy emotions, since most of the time, when other people showed off those traits openly like that, it disgusted me, especially when it was not an attractive young lady expressing them around me. Dillen seemed to skip over to Albert's bench, maybe even a frolic. Tra la la! Tra la la! His body suggested this as he frolicked over. "Sooo, how is that old Beemer going Berty-boy?" What a gay boy. One of our old parts girls used to call him this, and after that moment, everybody called him that! She used to put 'bear' after everyone's name as well. Luckily for her, she was very sweet, and it fit her personality to make up cuddly names for people. No one else but her would put 'bear' after my name though. Berty-boy/Berty-bear was not so lucky. Albert seemed to shy away whenever there were confrontations. He never wanted to speak up or speak his mind. Happiness in Slavery! He was truckin' away on the R100, giving it his all, and he didn't need any distractions! Dillen is an annoying distraction. "Jest tryin' ta fix this beast, that's all." Dillen nodded in agreement and kept on his dozy smiley face. For some reason, his facial expression today reminded me of a cartoon character, but I couldn't put my finger on which it was. Then I remembered: "Ah yes," I said to myself, "It was Goofy, the dog." I was somewhat sure he was a dog . . . His face cracked me up and, at the same time, frustrated the shit outta me. To entertain myself and Harry who was also watching the little 'tweed-curtain' boy, I called out to him. On my face was the most (don't hate me for using this expression) Down-syndrome face that could possibly be mustered by someone who was not. As Dillen turned around, all he heard was "Ba Durr, Ba Durr!" Harry started killing himself laughing, and a huge grin spread upon my face. I clapped my hands with satisfaction. Only a small part of Dillen's smile disappeared. He began to turn his head back to Albert, but his eyes fell short on his toolbox. Harry and I had forgotten about the toolbox until just then.

Dillen's jaw dropped, and his mouth spread wide open. He appeared momentarily astounded. At first, he stammered but couldn't find any words. Following his eyes was great! It brought back the good memories from the morning. Harry who was initially laughing from the 'Down-syndrome' expression just kept on going. He had turned hysterical. Together Harry and I bawled for a minute straight. Dillen's little smile had finally disappeared. He ran over to the box and held either side with his hands. "What the shit, guys!" His eyes looked straight into mine, and his sadness was very apparent. They were also glazed over as he started to whimper. The laughing quickly subsided because he had actually started to shed tears over our sticker job. Dillen attempted to open one of the drawers, but the attempt was fruitless. Then he made a gesture to tear off a few of the stickers, but like I said, they were cheap! Most of the sticker was left in place with the top portion ripping off. "How could you do this to me?" His voice sounded as though we had chained him to the floor and were beating his ribs and stomach with my polycarbonate boots and causing internal bleeding (oh how I wish!). Without pulling himself together, he ran outside through the large twin doors. Silent, Harry and I smirked at each other. "What a little bitch," he said in a half whisper. I turned and hollered at Bert, "Hey, Berty-boy, did you get a load of what just happened?" He didn't look pleased, about as pleased as he usually was when we pulled some amazing prank he wished that he could have dreamed up. "Yer on a short leash from the boss man, 'n' you go 'n' do that? Dem shits gonna hit the fan, man!" "Oh, wrinkly old man, always thinking negatively! This is a time to be happy and optimistic. Harry and I worked hard this morning to get that desired effect, and we pulled it off. You should be proud." "I'm not proud of you. Yer a shit disturber. "Come on, Dad! Tell me you're proud!" "Shut up an' let me work on this clunker! Leave me out of your prank business." With that, Albert ignored my other pestering comments and worked in a huff for the next hour. Hobbers was still in good spirits, so we looked at pictures of hot chicks on the Internet for a while. Recently, we had found a super good site that was all image based (just artsy pictures with clean stylish outfits and a bit of photoshopping in excellent poses). These were the best kind of computer wallpapers, and the staged shots probably take an hour or longer to set up. We didn't hear anything from Dillen for a good amount of time. We made a few jokes about his whimpering and thought he would be outside with a soother. After a great deal of time wondering, Dillen reappeared inside the shop very quietly. His eyes were slightly puffed, and his nose appeared to be a slight shade of rouge. His head he kept low so as not to gaze into any eyes that might be looking about. Bert peered over and stared until Dillen looked up, depressing. He looked like a wounded kitten, not like a guy that had a few stickers thrown on his toolbox, what a little girl! Way to be a man, moping around, licking his wounds. Dillen started to peel off the easy stickers. With his fingernails, he tore up a few more of the hard ones. A cheesy grin spread across his face as he managed to eradicate most of them. In his head, he was probably saying to himself, "I'm doing it! I'm doing it! Now they will all look up to me as I did not cry in front of them. I'm so proud of myself, and my daddy will be proud when I go home and tell him about this tonight. What a big man I am. Only moments ago, I was a little dyke." I may have embellished a little there but only to get the point across. Sick of his whiny childlike glee at destroying my hard work, I went and made a sandwich.

What a bloody good sandwich: whole grain bread, cervelat salami, strong white cheddar, and not to forget about the lettuce, tomato, salt and pepper. Also a slew of sauces I loved: mayonnaise, Dijon mustard, and sweet onion. Amazing, and one of the most beautiful sandwiches to set foot in this shop. I was literally beside myself. Cervelat and Gypsy salamis were my absolute favourites for sammies. Snack meat was either Landjaeger (mmm, Landjaeger), Mennonite sausage, or beef jerky. The joys of not being a vegetarian! If they only knew what was being missed. All those taste-bud opportunities just thrown out the window—a total waste.

Albert had been giving my sandwich looks—the kind where he looks at the sandwich, and his eyes almost pop out of his head, and his lips constantly being licked, and his whole body on a tilt in the direction of the sandwich. What a cheeky bugger he was. I told him there was only enough for one sandwich. Furthermore, he got told about the 'earlier in the day' events, and he said that he was not proud of me. With my pointer finger on the hand not holding the sandwich, I traced an invisible tear running down my cheek. "Boohoo, Berty" This I cackled malevolently towards him. Bert stopped his lip licking and replaced it with a snarly look. All worked up 'cause he never brought spare food with him, sucks. A lesson a day keeps the boredom away, just not the hunger. He went on grumbling whilst working on the antiquated R-bike. He had just got to the diode board.

With the petrol tank off and the front cover removed, the bike itself was not very big or complicated. Compared to today's standards of BMW, the frame was crude, made of steel, and only in the shape of small round tubes. Today's frames were made of alloys, aluminums, and composites. They had honeycomb oval-internals welded to square shapes and were bolted to subframes and strengthening bars and links; übercomplicated in comparison. I suppose everything was complicated nowadays though with the special 'brain boxes' and ignition-immobilizers for antitheft. There were also crazy emissions to make the exhausts spew out gum drops instead of hydrocarbons. Even the BMW motorcycles had crash safety features, as all the wheels and structural components bended in because of soft materials. They were supposed to when a crash or accident occurred, so as not to injure the rider as much. In reality, they were just cutting costs and needed an 'out.' The ultimate riding machine! Also the ultimate pain-in-the-ass machine when doing insurance claims; everything was bent or broken, and nothing ever survived.

With nothing much to do in the afternoon except for random services and tune-ups, I started digging around in the spare-parts room. It was a tiny eight-foot-long room and only four feet wide. The ceiling was accommodating but just barely, and it was definitely not a two-person room. If you could fit through the entranceway (which two employees could not), then you immediately became cramped. Little cardboard boxes lined the cheap particle board shelves on either side of the room. I wasn't sure what was to be found today. I hoped for something interesting. Minding my own business, which I never usually do, something of interest came into my possession. It was electronic, very expensive, and seemed to be in nice shape. Originally, the part may have been installed and then found to not fix the problem, removed and then put on the shelf as a 'used' part. Cooly-dooly! I replaced some of the small containers back onto the shelf and tidied up some nuts and bolts that were hanging out on the floor. My body had to be squeezed through the small opening in the side of the wall commonly referred to as a door. Berty was going to have a party in his pants when he set eyes on my new baby. I called out his name, but there was no response. He couldn't still be mad at me, I thought to myself, It was just a fuckin' sandwich. I dwelt on the food for a second again—damn, that was a fine snack. Where was Berty? Harry peered up at me from whatever he was doing, "Yo, man, he's checkin' out up front, probs cruisin' with R-bike buddy." He read my mind. He was most likely with the crazy divorced drunkard that had no money. I didn't want to show the American the part yet, not until we had tested it and arranged a price. In addition, Harry would have to work double time, since he knew we had the part in stock, and the job could be finished today. And . . . the customer wouldn't have to pay for a hotel for the night, which could blow the whole budget for the trip!

I sauntered into the showroom after placing the brown cardboard box with the diode board on my desk. From left to right, I swept my gaze over the customers: a few hooligans with backwards hats were talking loudly to Trevor about dirt-bike jumps and other intellectually stimulating things. I caught his eye, and he appeared to say, "help me, I want to die." Just had to break that look, as there was nothing a lowly mechanic like me could do. In the far-left corner underneath the skylight was a couple. They were old, not old, but older, and were discussing which gloves their daughter would like for her birthday. They had picked up the biggest and manliest-appearing pair of gloves and were even considering them! What kind of parents were these? Obviously they had been damaged as children, mentally, that is. Shaking my head, I kept peering about looking for the slacker. A few more customers, a few more fellow employees, and few more, oh, and there was little tiny Albert. And yes, I had assumed right, he was talking to the American, and yes, he appeared somewhat under the influence, not of love, but of alcohol. They were having a good laugh and didn't seem to be giving a hoot—what a lovely couple. Almost as lovely as Dillen frolicking around in the shop earlier. A pity I was the only one to see it. All of Bert's grinning and laughing stopped the second he saw me. For but a second, he had slipped away from this motorcycle world and into another, a joyous happy place where he was not tormented. Now his tormentor had come and was standing before him. "Bert." The American himself had not noticed that he had stopped laughing, for on his face was still a large grin, and chuckles were escaping his lungs. He noticed Bert's gaze and followed it. Suddenly, he as well stopped laughing and went expressionless. "May I talk to you in private?" The American became a bit uncomfortable in the awkward moment and excused himself. Bert's grumpy self had returned. He was back in the real world again of flesh and blood. "Wa da yah want?" Bert barked at me. "Let's just go in the back for two seconds where I'm gonna show you something totally sweet, and then we can talk about it, okay?" Albert looked back to where the American had decided to sit down and gave him a quick flip with his hand. I took it as an old-person wave. Someone not able to lift the whole arm, just flicks his wrist, which lifts up the hand, and you've got your wave. Good time to take notes for saving energy, for one day I would become old and senile, and morbid. They always tell you to learn when you're young, and the lessons keep on givin' till you die. Not that I believed the saying, but it sounded good at least. We walked to the shop unhindered by the customers. I closed the door, and Albert turned on me, rather than to me. "Can't you stop botherin' me for two seconds? You don't care at all that I was talkin' to that dude, do ya?" "Now, Berty, take it easy! This time my excuse is valid. I don't just bother you for any reason. Most of the time, it is for my personal pleasure!" My comment and following smirk got precedent over my actual reason for bringing him back here. He was becoming rather agitated, and the frustration began to grow on his face at a rapid pace. After this, he attempted to get verbal with me by referring to me as 'a little slut' and a 'dumb little conspirator.' Those marked the height of his intellectual creativity, and soon he could not carry on with the insults. Most of the time, after four or five, he would begin to repeat the first comments. He would forget that he had said them and, thinking that they were brand-new insults, that they would offend me. How wrong he was. "Anyways, Albert, this is more exciting than your random banterings towards me." He did not look amused. "I've got something on my desk, something you'd like to see." I walked him over. He had a sombre expression on his face, a face of defeat. Languidly, I picked up the cardboard box and held it out to him, keeping my distance so that my arms were fully outstretched. "Merry Christmastime, my darling." Albert's moods were changing from sad to mad and back again rather consistently. He took the box. Actually, he grabbed the box and began opening it, meanwhile grumbling how his time was always being wasted by me. Grumble, grumble, and grumble. After what seemed like an eternity, he figured out the folds in the cardboard top. A thin smile spread upon his lips. "Good job," he said to me quickly as if he didn't want to say it but had to. This was of course the most likely case. "I don't know if it works, but it looks clean. None of the diodes are black or crusty. It could be new. Looks new. Think you should give it a whirl, and it'll save your pal a bundle." "I'll do it right now!" "All were gonna do was wait for the parts. Gunna tell buds the news!" "Just hold on a quick second, sugar-tits! Let's talk money. They're like five bills new, an' I think it's pretty new. What do you think?" "He don't gots no money. He's broker than me!" "Okay, Berty, this is still a business, right? We gotta charge him something. This place doesn't run fer free. Two hundred. That is way less than half, sound good?" "What? Two hundred? That's piles!" "Bert, what the shit?" I raised my arms up in despair, "Over five bills new, five bills! We were orderin' in a brand spankin' new one for him anyways. This way, he doesn't have to rent a hotel, where he saves a hundred or so. He also saves food money!" At this point, I was showing him my fingers and counting off each one. "The new one he has to pay for shipping and install time! This is a win-win situation for all of us." "How ya figure fer all of us?" Albert cut in. "Umm, well, I just explained how he wins," I said in a mocking manner. "But we win as well: the shop gets rid of a part that's been sittin' around, makes shelf space, makes money off of noninventory parts, which the company doesn't have to claim as a sale. Since the part was probably new to begin with and chucked in the back, when inventory was counted, and it wasn't there, it got written off and is tax-free, baby!" He nodded his head up and down in an exaggerated manner and dopily said, "Okay, okay, one fifty!" I just stopped and shook my head. "You are such a turd." "Hah." "Go tell yer bum buddy he can have the part for $200, but he owes you a case of Lucky, right?" This bantering was astronomical! I wanted to help the business from crumbling, and Bert wanted to make long-lasting relationships with the 'broke-ass.' "Fine, $200. He'll probably drink half the beer before it gets here anyways, and it'll be warm piss-water. Costs extra to cool dem beers." "That's the spirit, old boy! Get up there and tell 'im how to git-er-done." He ignored the comment of mine where I was talking like a redneck to a redneck. But honestly, come on: he lived in a pallet shack in the woods, on many, many acres, with his parents. He made his own electricity and owned several shotguns for 'whatever needs to be shot.' That's pretty hick redneck if you ask me. He walked up front without another word and shut the door behind him to make sure that he wasn't followed. Don't worry, old Bert, I thought to myself, I don't consider myself a follower. Now that was all true, yet at the same time, I did not consider myself a leader. I suppose that meant that I did not know at the time what that made me, perhaps a doer? Does that fit under the same category? Not being swayed by people's thoughts or opinions and, at the same time, not wanting others to really do the same by my hand (except Albert). Maybe just to be, that is enough in life.

Neither Harry nor I had seen 'whiny-boy' lately. And it would be rather unfortunate if he mentioned the incident to Gerald. I was pretty sure he hadn't, as Gerald had not stormed into the shop, offering out any death threats or firing remarks; the firing remarks being likely and more his personality. Death threats didn't seem to be his 'thing.' He was, under all our thick layers of complaining towards the company, a somewhat-good boss. My resume did not have many other bosses to compare to, but there were a few. You always heard about friends and family members and the stories of their co-workers and bosses. Gerald, compared to some, was an outstanding citizen. The funny thing was that even after his justified outbreak earlier in the day, I still thought so. Honest and trustworthy people just do that to you, I guess.

Wrinkly Albert came through the shop after five or so minutes. Harry asked how his sales pitch went. Albert responded by telling us that he and the American had agreed on $150 and some beers. "Bwa? But when you was back here, like twooo seconds ago, you agreed to $200 and beers!" Harry looked over at me and tossed his hands up in the air, a popular motion for the day. "Yah, well, I felt bad for the guy," he mentioned very discreetly and quietly. "Woulda been the same for anyone goin' up there tryin' to sell used shit to customers." "Ahh, don't think so, bud," Harry interjected. "Dude, I'm like king salesman. Probs could a got the guy to pay big dollar for that part. Diode board? Those don't come cheap." "Well, it's a bit late fer that!" Bert stammered. "Told 'im I'm tryin' to 'ave 'er done by closin' time." All things considered, we still had no idea if the part was any good. This got mentioned immediately after it was thought of. He made it sound as though I had asked him if two and two were four. Furthermore, he went as far as to sound exasperated. "Of course I told 'im the part might not work. What do I look like, an idiot?" After that, he glared at us both. "Don't you answer that! You're both a bunch of jerks." Bert was implying that we did think he was an idiot, which was a ridiculous idea, since he was so kindhearted and friendly . . .

"Bert, get to work on that bike." I had to be stern with him as his mind wandered on occasions. "You've only got a few hours to finish up that beaut, so you'd better get on it." "If I didn't have to explain myself fer every goddamned thing I did, he'd be rollin' out the door right now!" Not bad for an oldie. "Albert, for someone as old as yourself, that was actually a pretty decent retort, so proud of ya!" Muttering under his breath, all I could hear him say was "When I get outta here, the shits gonna hit the fan." Most likely unlikely. Albert got right to work. For the rest of the afternoon, no one bothered him. By the same token, Dillen did not bother us.

With this in mind, Albert did finish the old R-bike before the day was over with moments to spare. The American did pay the bill and was happy that the work was completed. The price even at the reduced rate made him break out in sweats when handing us his credit card. The beer received by Bert was warm as expected. The customer also took one of them to congratulate Bert in a toast as expected. They were Lucky Lager, which was a mild consolation since that was Bert's favourite. Dillen, on the other hand, did not even show his face in the shop for the rest of the day. Instead, his father showed up the next day with iced cappuccinos for all the employees. What? Oh, but he did stay in Gerald's office for a large part of the morning. Hmm, coincidences like that don't happen every day, do they? Nah, I'm just a doubtful, pessimistic person, that's all. Best to just think about sandwiches. Good night.

CHAPTER 10 — Bikes and Tea

Drizzle; the sky was dark and overcast. During the night, there was a constant downpour over the shop. For the moment, it had subsided, but water was still all over the floor. We were used to the holes in the roof. No matter how many attempts were made at fixing them, either they made their way through the inadequate patch jobs or found new entrances. The early morning was a mess with the running around of people trying to find misplaced tubs and buckets. It was one o'clock now, and we had just finished up lunch.

The three mechanics of the shop: me, normal; Albert, with his boots unlaced; Harry, boots laced with feet on the cheap, black, pleather-covered foldable table with thin, inexpensive tubes of mild steel for legs and numerous holes in the top from knife 'incidents.' In the middle was a red plastic wash bucket collecting drops. Bert had thrown a towel in the bottom to stop the splatter; smart boy he was. "I'm so full right now," Harry patted his swollen belly. "I hear that, but at least my food-baby is only half the size of yours," I mentioned, patting my own stomach. "Beer will fix you up properly. Follow my lead, son," Bert groaned as well, leaning back against his toolbox. "I'll never eat food again!" I wailed to no one in particular. "Until you do it again tomorrow," Albert belched out at me. "Berty, you seriously just burped out that sentence to me, you vile pig." He threw a malicious grin my way and then helped himself to a mouthful of the gross-looking concoction in his bowl. It appeared mutative: a brown and creamy frothy liquid. He used a large Pyrex-branded bowl with a glass handle for all his food and drinks. What he had in there today, I wasn't sure of. "K, dude, lowdown on the bucket of puke, what is it?" "Don't you talk 'bout this beautiful drink an' how it looks." What a dork. "Just tell me what it is." Bert wanted to play the smart-ass card today, it seemed. "It's my favourite: chocolate milk 'n' coke." His simple explanation almost made me spew whatever I had for lunch all over that 'nice' pleather table. "You sick *fuck*! No wonder your head's not on straight when you're drinkin' that shit!" He immediately became defensive, "You've never even tried it! Sayin' yer all cultured 'n' travelled 'n' stuff." Harry piped up and agreed with me. Bert began to sulk.

We all heard the door open, and through it walked our Snap-on tool representative. Two steps in, and a giant droplet plonked right onto his hair-diminished head. His initial smile went immediately to a scowl. "What in the blazes?" Bringing his head up to search for the instigator of the cold wet feeling adorning his noggin, he received another droplet on his nose. From our relaxed positions on the pleather table, we watched with glee the happenings by the door. "It's called a leak, Herr. Snap-along, perhaps you've heard of them." Mr. Snap-on was hurriedly clambering through the maze of buckets by the shop door to avoid another onslaught from the ceiling. "Good day, fellows!" His facial expressions had changed back to a happy one—bring on the customers!

Over the many years of working in this dealership, many Snap-on reps have walked through the doors, with all of them leaving just after a year or two. It was kind of sad and hard to build up a lasting and trusting relationship under these conditions. Nonetheless, he was still a friendly fellow. "What does your bag of tricks have in store for us today?" I pondered to him out loud. "Well, I am glad you asked!" He cheerily exclaimed. He opened his large industrial-style satchel and tossed us each that month's flyer. "New toys for the boys!" Harry didn't usually buy any new tools, so he just briefly glazed over the coloured pages of promos and on-sale items. "Mr. Albert," referring to tiny Berty, "I've noticed how your ratchets have been getting outdated." Harry chimed in by adding that they went perfectly well with Bert. Mr. Snap-on, with his five feet eleven inches height, a mediocre build, and slightly greying hair (what was left), gave a small smirk towards the implication that Albert was outdated. His voice was neither shrill nor bassy but an in-between baritone. I suppose it was a good medium? With his nongrimy fingers (he sold tools but did not use them), he pulled out a long-handled chrome ratchet. "Forget what Harry thinks, this is a new 3/8th drive eighty-tooth ratchet. They have been out for a little while and are the highest quality in the industry." He handed the tool over to Bert whose eyes were gleaming. "Give it a try . . ." Those four persuasive words were all it took. Like usual, he was taken in: hook, line, and sinker. "Purdy smooth." Mr. Snap-on nodded, "Much stronger than our older models, and it feels like silk. Here, try the eighty-tooth with a socket on the end." Out of the magic bag, he took out a seventeen-millimetre socket and fixed it to the ratchet's head. "Remind me a' butter," Bert thought out loud. "Clicketty click click," said the ratchet to Albert. "I'll take it!" He yelled out of excitement at this newly discovered toy to add to the excess in his overflowing toolbox. "Umm, don't you want to know how much it is?" Harry asked referring to the cost. "What does it matter?" He responded bitterly towards Harry, "I wan' it." Harry laughed from his outstretched lounge position. "Whadever works for you, budday!" Mr. Snap-on grinned as he listened to our back-and-forth squabbling. No matter what our argument with Bert, he always had a sale. Every time he stepped foot through the door, he met his quota for the day.

All three of us piled inside his truck where the ceiling, dashboard, and all the walls were covered in tools. Just like a chick going to an outlet mall, it was a fantasy world with new and shiny things to touch: Red rubber handles on needle-nose pliers, glistening chrome on unused extension sets and sockets, etc. Whoever said Christmas doesn't come every two weeks was wrong. Berty ended up buying the 3/8th drive ratchet, along with a new dead-blow plastic hammer. Inside of the head is filled with sand to inhibit the rebound of the hammer after impact. This makes for less effort on the user, as the energy from the swing is firmly planted against the impacted area. Hence the term dead-blow 'cause it stops dead. I also 'caved' and bought a new 1/4 drive ratchet, which had forty teeth, or something close to that. It just meant that I had more butter-smooth. Furthermore, I bought a new pick set. It had new rubber handles and included a straight pick, ninety-degree pick, circular-ended pick, and a pokey one that curled slightly at the end for getting into hard-to-reach places (best description of my pick set for you). We left the truck content with our purchases, and Mr. Snap-on drove away content with his sales.

On the benches were some nasty bikes to work on. Harry had a Suzuki Marauder for a tune-up/service, which had been living in a bush for many years and was trailered in, as it was currently uninsured. My bench had a gorgeous example of a mid-1990s R1100RT that had been involved in an accident, and our provincial insurance company needed an estimate on the damage. They wanted a write-up of the labour costs and parts, etc. Lastly, Berty's bench had a slightly newer R1150RT. It was the pinnacle of early 2000s road touring machines. It was in for servicing of the valves, throttle synchronization, and an annual service. Taking off the damned bodywork from both the RT bikes took up all the space we had in the shop—useless bodywork.

The owners of the motor bicycles being serviced were a little cold and wet after their rides through the drizzle. They had to run off to the local coffee shops to warm up, leaving the showroom fairly empty. On my way to get my third cup of green tea for the day, I checked out what they were doing—okay, what Trevor had been doing. The rest were doing their usual. Trevor was cleaning the inside of the windows. He was not the tallest man in our known universe, so he had a stool for help. It was a three-foot-tall white stool that unfolded. He was using our no-name window cleaner and for drying had small balls of newspaper. For some reason unbeknownst to me, newspapers did not leave smudge marks when drying windows. My old boss had shown me this many years before. Years later, I found out that everybody else in the industry knew about it as well. "What issue you got, Trevs?" His look was somewhat puzzled for a brief moment as he stared at me. His initial response was that he didn't have any issues. I raised my eyebrows and stared at the newspaper a little longer before it clicked into his head. He unrifled the ball in his hand and answered back, "Nov. 2009." I kept on walking, but before I took my tea into the shop, I told him it was a classic issue, and he should save it in his memoirs.

Once in the shop, Harry attempted to belittle me by mocking my joy of tea, but to no avail. I loved the tea, and the tea loved me. When he arrived at eight thirty-five this morning, he had brought in a broken BB handgun with the thoughts of fixing it. After a few hours, he decided it would be more cost efficient to buy a new one, as the parts needed were those of strange-sized springs and pieces of plastic. Most were not even available separately. Beside his ruined handgun were CO_2 cartridges, many of them. A brilliant idea popped suddenly into my head: rockets. How I loved rockets. "Hair ball, wanna use those outside, wink wink?" "What choo talkin' bout, Willis? You takin' drugs?" "What? No, I am not taking drugs. Do you want to make some rockets out of those CO_2 cartridges?" "Oh, why didn't you just say that? Silly fool." "I have no idea how, but let's just have a whirlybird at it." Harry shook his head at me, "I ain't havin' any fuckin' whirlybirds. If we gonna make rockets, let's make rockets!"

For the better part of an hour, we threw around ideas and designs, most of them failing terribly. With scotch tape and tiny fins cut out from plastic parts-boxes, the cartridges took shape. A few we spray-bombed black to appear 'authentic,' whatever that means, since they're three inches long! For the platform, okay, there was no platform. Instead, we used a sheet of wood, and the rocket was just placed on this board. NASA was probably going to come 'round soon asking for ideas. The next major achievement in this whole ordeal was the firing mechanism. This consisted of a nail and a hammer. Let me repeat that: a nail and a hammer. It was not going to travel far as the diagnostic/navigation computers we were going to install were on backorder . . .

The first one fired away with a 'poof.' It landed in the neighbour's yard not ten feet away. At least it had managed to get over the fence. So the ramp idea sucked. Brainstorm, brainstorm. Okay, new idea. I went and rummaged about in the scrap metal bins that lived in the machine room under the drill press and right next to the fridge. What a dumb place to put a fridge, next to dirt, grime, dust, and metal shavings. Anyways, from that accumulation of assorted crap, I found a new ramp. It was a piece of steel in a vee shape, approximately two and a half feet long—just perfect. The launcher of destiny! Harry also got excited over the discovery and congratulated me in finding it. My eyes creased, and my mouth moved into a wicked smile. "Show time, take two!" While the metal was being acquired, Hobbers had been adding longer stabilizing fins to the next CO2 cartridge—I mean, rocket . . . This time with the new and improved launch platform, the anxiety had built quite a bit, and we were just about to launch. Albert came through the doors into the shop's back lot. Always interrupting! Nobody ever gave the misbehaving hooligans a moment of free time to destroy, create, or fool around! Bert began mentioning the customers to us. Then he began huffing and puffing about his 'respectable' image we always put to shame. Then he began going off about our job security right up until Harry interrupted him. "Yo, Bert-ski! Why you gotta be messin'? Just watch the show, man, you'll love it, promise." For a moment, he mulled it over, and then his grouchy face appeared the moment before he told Harry to 'fuck off.' He then turned about face and stormed back into his dark little domain. Harry faced me and shrugged, "Always screwin' with our shit." Albert did have a legit reason for bitching at us, but he never stopped bitching; what a bitch. We set up the platform for the next flight. Then we went over the preflight check: we have a rocket, check; we have a platform (cheap ramp), check; we have a nail and hammer, check; good to go. I positioned the ramp at a near-vertical level. "Oh boy, oh boy!" Harry said excitedly while he placed the cartridge at the bottom of the launch ramp. The moment of triumph and exhilaration was going to commence. Bert could be seen peaking from around the door. Old doom and gloom did want a piece of the action! The old wolf wanted to huff and puff and also see the rocket launch. I pretended not to notice him so that he could stay grouchy afterwards. This time it was great: a tiny shooting beacon in the light of the day. The rocket went up, up, and up! Then it hit a huge cedar tree and became lost from view. No troubles, she was flawless and elegant; and for a few minutes, there was a good 'whooping' session. After the ascent, Berty had scuttled indoors. He was probably smiling and laughing at our accomplishment. Harry and I both agreed that our last rocket was the best, so we left it at that and returned to working in the shop. The whole rest of the day, I planned on renting October Sky, a rocket movie based on a true story. It featured Jake Gyllenhaal and is a must-see movie. Since it came out in theatres when I was younger, a few tears were probably shed.

Damned insurance claims! The whole front subframe was constructed from thintubed steel. Its face was of a thin ABS-made plastic. This plastic has a small amount of bend, but once it is pushed over its limits, the chances of gluing it back together are almost impossible. The steel tubes were mangled sideways, and the face was ground down so that no amount of Bondo and paint would fix it. Ca-ching!

The story was this: rain involved with wet leaves and driving at night. That was the story. My story, which was kept to myself was this: bald tyres mixed with rain and mixed with wet leaves and driving at night. Those cheap cunts, getting parts replaced under insurance because they are . . . such cheap cunts! Grrr. One of the mirrors was not to be found, and one of the bag brackets was busted up so badly that it could not even stay on. Other damages consisted of trim panels, other fairing brackets, and foot pegs. I laughed and showed Albert the bag with small amounts of 'weed' in the bottom. This was found in the broken-off bag, and he chuckled as well. When the pieces had been categorized and written down onto a blank white sheet of paper on my clipboard, the next step involved the joyous task of pricing everything out. An ICBC job took generally an hour or so to get a full price list. Add all the time of the estimate and the labour costs together, and you had a grand total. This was handed to the up-front staff, whose job it was to contact the insurance company; now the problems start. For some reason, every time the list was handed to Duane and two minutes had passed, most of the information would disappear! All the parts ordered arrived were in the wrong colour or for completely different bikes! Of course, if it was brought up at one of our general meetings that were extremely dysfunctional and rarely happened, I was considered the 'black sheep' of the flock. They all looked at me with their scornful glares—in Dillen's case, a brownnosing, never-say-anything-bad-about-another-person glare. This was the kind where he wished he could approach people or talk to them as straight faced or as bluntly as I did. He pushed up his nose and crinkled it; what a dork. One of the reasons we never became friends.

Duane was a completely different matter. You would think that being a fat and useless slob was enough! Add the never-on-time quality, memory of a sieve, and the armpits and breath smelling like shit, and you might have the meal deal. To the employees in the shop, all this was evident. To the employees in the front, as well as the bosses, he was a knowledgeable gentleman, as well as intuitive and helpful. My attempts were in despair and always in vain. For this reason, insurance jobs hung around the shop for literally weeks longer than required. Customers also appreciated this . . .

On Albert's bench, the R1150RT service was slowly coming along. My insurance assessment was done for now, so I asked if he would appreciate a helping hand. There were a couple of working hours left in the day, and the customer would most likely love to go home before the darkness crept over the wet dreary earth. Bert mentioned that he would be delighted (not his actual words) if I were to help him out. "Okay, Berts," I said whilst wiping a bit of wheel-bearing grease from my black latex-free work gloves (I had no idea how grease got on my hands, since I had been writing part numbers on paper while working on the computer). "What do you need done?" He grinned that toothless grin of his. When he talked, it went right inside my head and made me feel gross. It was as though he was trying to lure a baby to candy in the back of his windowless van. It started as a small whisper and was much too friendly. "You may do the valves." I glared at him and mentioned to his face that he was a 'dirty fucker.' Obviously, he loved it and broke off in a loud guffaw. After his fit had subsided, he spat out from that gaping toothless mouth, "You asked for it!" Oh god, this place was killing me from the inside out. I would definitely die before my thirtieth birthday, and maybe it was for the best.

Valves, the year of 2010 saw BMW boxer motorcycles with 'race-inspired' hemispherical shims for them. They were easy peasy to check and adjust. The older models of even a few years ago seemed pathetic! They were time consuming, underpowered; why couldn't they have brought out a dual-overhead cam model back in the '70s like every other bike in the universe? Whatever, they kept me employed. The fun part of me only having to do the valves and sync was that I had the opportunity to watch Harry suffer as he worked, or attempted to work, on the Marauder.

The bush it had been living under had treated it poorly. Cheap chrome seemed to be peeling from places that I wasn't aware had chrome. Harry looked like he was struggling to undo every crusty bolt. When he dumped the oil, tar seemed to appear. It was nice and thick, extremely black; and since it was so cold, an ounce per minute escaped from the crank case. It hadn't been possible to start the bike, since the battery was dead as well. The whole time he cursed and swore at the machine. In the same circumstances, I would easily have done the same; shitty Japanese bikes sucked to work on.

The valves were a breeze, and the rocker arms didn't need any adjustment, which was unusual for an R259 series bike. She had eighty thousand kilometres on her fine silver body. I noticed that the fuel filter and alternator belt could use a change. Both of these should be done every forty thousand kilometres. I mentioned this, and he shrugged his shoulders at me. "Not my problem," he whined while carrying on with whatever he was doing. "Bert you slut, those are part of a safety check!" He sneered at me before asking for help to look up the service history in the computer. Together we found out that the fuel filter had been replaced a few months previous when the customer had dropped in for a tyre change. "Well, that's a bloody hassle that we don't have to deal with," he mumbled over my shoulder looking at the screen. "But you still gotta change the alt belt," I chimed in. "Yah, but I don't gots to replace the fuel filter. That's like an hour I save. "Albert, did you just say Yahbut?" He looked at me with a blank yet always grouchy look on his face. Now was not time for antics. I just told him 'never mind' and started to look up the part number for the alt belt in our computerized inventory. "So it looks like it's either a '779' belt or an '841.' We've got both in stock, but it depends on what year the bike was made in." "I already gave you the VIN (vehicle identification number)." This number gives both the year and country of origin of production. "Yes, well, that particular bike was made in between two months of production, so she could be either of the belts. Just pull off the front cover and check the number on the belt. Since you already removed the bodywork, and it's got the R259 exhaust instead of the R251s (R1100 series excluding the R1100S), it's just four tiny Allen-head bolts, no dice!" "I'll show you no dice, you do-gooder!" "Wow, Bert, I'm truly ballin' my eyes out from your obscene criticising remark. You're just *so* mean to me!" I threw him both the belts and told him to get on with it. When he wasted time, he knew how to waste time.

Harry interrupted our silly charade by cursing loudly from his corner of the shop. All that could be heard was "You dirty cum-guzzling, piece of dog-licking, ass-fucking, cock-biting, motherfucking cunt!" The rest became drowned out in his smashing and hammering. It was kind of a run-on sentence, so it was definitely not worth listening to . . .

My only other job on Albert's horrible boxer was the synchronization of the throttle bodies. I laughed whenever a customer asked for me to 'synch his carbs.' Didn't anybody know the difference between a set of carburetors and a set of throttle bodies these days? I guess not 'cause they carry on asking me to this day. Berty seemed to have trouble installing the new belt. As strength was not one of his high points, I was not particularly surprised that he was struggling. On the boxer models before the introduction of the K2X models tensioning the alternator belts was a two-man job. Elastomer belts are now used, which use a tool to stretch the belt over the pulleys as I already explained. This eliminates any over- or undertightening, which could accelerate the wear of the belts. In the end, I tightened the nuts for the alternator, whilst Bert tensioned the belt. It was a great team effort!

The throttle cables were old and well used. BMW recommends replacement of the cables every forty thousand kilometres; no one had replaced them at that time. Instead, since the rest of the motorcycle begins to deteriorate, they are neglected and never thought about until it's written on a repair order as a cause for poor performance and surging. They always disagree until the customer eventually replaces them. Today the synchronization was a hassle. The worn cables and butterfly pivots in the throttle bodies were making the two-cylinder's vacuum pressures fluctuate. This sucked to adjust. Note to the BMW boxer model owners: always leave a few millimetres of slack on the cables. Do this at the handlebar adjustment as well as on the throttle body mounts. Without this clearance, both the cables and throttle bodies will wear exponentially faster.

After a few minutes of attempted synching, she began to overheat, which raised the idle. Bert brought out our large fan and placed it in front of the wheel. He was getting impatient as the day was carrying forward and the bodywork needed to be bolted back on—the largest part of the service. The sprinkling of rain was infuriating. Not only was I sweating in my overalls because the bike was overheating, but the humidity was also atrocious. After the levels on our synchronizing machine were able to be brought to within ten millibars of both cylinders, my temper was almost at its peak. I slapped on my jacket and helmet and threw on the front seat of the bike. I wanted the test ride to be over as soon as possible and get the damned bike out of my life. The boxer had the usual surge at 3000 rpm, but it had already been mentioned in the service history. I ignored it and instead made sure that the tyres and steering worked well. I also made sure that there was no unusual transmission or rear-end whines. There weren't, and as soon as I arrived back to the shop Bert hurriedly started to bolt back on the bodywork. I had to get in his way to put the synch caps back on the brass protrusions (rubber sealing caps for the throttle bodies). The oil level after five minutes of sitting (proper BMW procedure) was perfect; 'props' to Albert. Even with broken clips and missing bolts, which we replaced, the panels went on fairly quickly and without disturbances. Harry had taken his Suzuki outside when I had ridden away. He seemed to be in a similar huff with his bike. The customer wanted the bike right away and kept on hassling. Harry's impatience, combined with the customer's, was making the matter worse. I was glad to have dealt with my annoying bike, and I felt his frustration. Our shop boy cleaned up the R1150RT before she went to the front parking lot. It was slightly pointless as the gentle rain would cover the bike once again with dirt and grime, but it looked good after a large exchange of money took place—kept them happy. Away she went up front.

My bench still had the insurance job, but it wouldn't have any progress today. Albert's job was finished, which became both our jobs near the end. Lastly, Harry, after his continuous verbal battle, came to an end with his project. He was ecstatic to be finished, and I was not surprised. After locking up the doors, the three of us found our feet on the pleather four-legged table, watchin' the water drip into the buckets.

CHAPTER **11** — The Days of Our Lives

Albert's new helmet looked out of place; it looked as though there was a duck on his head. A few weeks previous, he had ordered a new one from our BMW catalogue, but the pictures did it no justice. The helmet was our 'top-of-the-line' endure-style helmet for the 'off-road' market people, or someone that looked at magazines and thought they were. It was graphite-grey with a large matte black-coloured stripe down the center that was three inches wide. On the top was a large plastic sun visor that doubled as an aileron when landing jumbo jets. The visor was interesting: it was tinted and, like snowboarding goggles, was convex. This is a great gimmick about depth perception, with concave instead of flat visors and the human eye. The 'beak' was the amusing part, as it stuck out and quacked at you. In the first few hours of him owning it, the beak fell off from faulty glue. I had a good laugh, but the others were all upset as over two dozen of them had been ordered. On Bert's head, the padding on the inside fit very well, but the exterior seemed exorbitantly large in comparison. At the end of the matter, I still thought that he looked like a duck and a 'quack.'

That morning, all hell broke loose: Duane was at the doctors for one of his unpopular diseases, so he wouldn't be around for the day; Harry, he had a snivelling cold, coughing and hacking all over place; Berty had had a flat tyre yet only called us after he had fixed it and was back on track some two hours after the fact; the bosses had to fly to see family in some other province, so the staff was almost nonexistent! A skeleton crew, as some might call it; they were always the bones of the operation . . .

Due to his nasal congestion, sore throat, and runny nose, Harry had barely said a word to anyone. In the shop, it was rather peaceful again. We were all very worried initially about poor Berty, but after calling his home line and cell number three times, there was not much that any of us could do without sending out a search party. Just wait it out and hope for the best was everybody's advice. Before he eventually turned up at 11:48, I had already rolled three bikes off my bench. Harry was close behind with two of his own. What a team! Harry and I, since Berty wasn't present, had put *Rage against the Machine* onto our stereo, which blasted us with motivational lyrics. Tracks such as 'Calm Like a Bomb' and 'How I Could Just Kill a Man' pounded out of the speakers and begged us constantly to be turned up. We caved to the temptation for a while, but disgruntled looks from the showroom quieted our enthusiasm, mildly. Then the disgruntled look from moody Albert when he decided to show up made us turn it off completely. Oh well, a few moments of 'Rage' is better than none.

His faded and fraying blue jean-jacket was coated in a thick layer of filth and mud; it seemed to stick to the shirt underneath and peeled off, like it was a layer of skin. This raised his undershirt, exposing his extremely white and hairy belly. I yelled out that his epidermis was showing. His mood was not that of a sprightly elf, much closer to some despicable creature from *Lord of the Rings*—seething, festering, and with eyes of cruelty, and a different kind of rage from what had been listened to earlier. After the long battle of him and his coat (which happened more often than naught), he put on his work-duds and, while clomping up front to grab a cup-a-Joe, sprayed balls and clumps of dirt from his boots all over the shop floor. Moments later, he reappeared with no 'Joe.' I questioned him on his coffee whereabouts, and in a subdued manner, he mentioned that the machine was out of order. My reply pertained to his lack of knowledge on how to use the machine. I tried to say this in the least offensive way possible. Surprisingly, his response was not overly angry towards me. He told me that he had been using the same machine for his drinks before I had finished high school. I found it to be a very valid point. A few minutes later, after sneaking from the shop to the showroom, I wanted a reassurance on the matter. The red light from the machine glowed ominously in all directions, and no one shared in its vicinity. My approach was from the side with my stainless-steel mug faithfully in hand. I removed the bottom tray from the machine that catches excess coffee. My mug was too large to fit under the hot-water dispenser with the tray in place. The button was pushed for the water, and steam poured up and out of the mug as the hot water poured in. At least the hot water part of the machine worked. Coffee was unimportant to me; tea on the other hand was. Gloating was contemplated to me as the tiles got walked on back to the shop, but then I reconsidered; Albert's mood might send him over the edge, and it was possible he would attack me with a weapon, like a torque wrench or piece of pipe. Of course he could be fended off, since he was weak, didn't have experience handling weapons, and would become breathless as his heart rate increased. I was able to gently mention that the water still poured freely from the black-finished coffee machine if he wanted to consider having some of my specialty teas. What a gentleman I was; or so I thought. He declined my generous offer, which did not surprise me in the least. He seemed very peeved as well by the fact that Harry was sick. Even though Albert smoked too much of everything and drank too much, he did take many vitamins and, for the most part, ate a variety of healthy foods. He hated and loathed sick people and, under his breath, usually whined and complained about Duane. "He's always tryin' to infect us," he would tell me in a whisper. "Disease-ridden dog 'e is" was another one, barely audible except for me and Harry to hear. There was absolutely nothing that could be done about the 'sick-os' that frequented the shop and were also employees of the shop. For the most part, I just agreed with him and tried not to add any insightful comments of my own. They were rhetorical statements anyways and didn't need to be dwelt on. Today, to make for lighter conversation, I brought up the topic of his truck. To Albert, this was not a light conversation piece as I found out soon thereafter. Going on his uneven muddy drive is where the tyre blew out, making for an unpleasant start to the day; hence why his clothes looked like they were sewn together with dirt. His father, the old coot, couldn't help either, for he was not just old but a wee-bit senile as well. Lumbering along the winding muddy path between the trees, water had created a triumphant river right across the road. This in turn had swept away the mud and dirt, leaving behind rocks and stones. As some of the rocks had never seen daylight in their life, they were not smooth and polished but hard and sharp. Grinding through the gears with water swishing to and fro on the windshield between the cracked and weathered wiper blades caused a bit of a distraction, and he became unaware of the sharpened tyre destroyers. He ploughed right over them, smashing and crashing until the truck did not move quite the same. Right away, due to the large 'bang' that was heard, he knew what had happened. His left hand gently splayed over the steering wheel center, while his right hand landed on the ignition keys. He swore loudly to no one in particular. The Alice Cooper tape stopped playing the same second he turned off the key. Sitting for only a quick second, he heard the raindrops on the roof pitter-pattering and saw steam wistfully rising from the heated hood before him. A bad morning had just turned into shit. His already-muddy boots hit the waterbed and let up a giant splash. He didn't care because right now he hated everything: the birds, his clothes, his lack of cornflakes for breakfast, everything. By just turning his face down the trail, he found it was his left rear tyre that had blown out. There was a nice-sized gash in the sidewall that could not have been fixed with a whole rubber plant at his disposal. For a moment, Albert thought that a tear had come to his eye, and he was finally going to break down. He had felt this day coming for years, and now it was upon him. But no, he realized bitterly that it was cold water, and it had to be from all the moisture that had broken free from the sky to come lay hate and abuse onto his already tormented soul. Back to angry self! Again he swore, and this time, he kicked the tyre. Kneeling down, he made sure that the ground beneath could hold a jack for lifting the damned machine. "Yes," he grunted to the truck, "she'll hold ya." In the truck bed tied to the side was the spare filled with air and full of life and tread just begging to be installed. The fun part was the nice soggy position in which he lay to lift up the truck and having to use the cold damp tools for removing and reinstalling the tyres.

After his joyous time in doing the swap, thinking that he was on his way again, he jumped into the cab and started 'er up. The tunes came blaring into his eardrums, and cheering up was an inviting possibility—that is, until he made it up to the highway. Almost forgetting that after work, he had to renew his eye-drop prescription, he hurriedly reached for his fanny pack to check for the bottle. He rummaged around trying to find it while he waited for a change in traffic. In all his kafuffle getting out of the house that morning and missing breakfast, he had forgotten to grab the sack! Albert's head was reeling, and this situation was making him see red. First, being late out the door with his stomach growling; second, getting the darned flat tyre out in the shit weather; third, he now had to go back down the couple of miles of driveway back to the house, grab the sack, and possibly get another hole in a tyre. That was his only spare! And fourth, he was almost out of gas! He pounded his fists in an exasperated gesture in an attempt to fix the situation. He turned the truck around in a heat of rage (key word of the day) and barrelled back from whence he came. Puddles sprayed up all around the wheel wells and onto the windshield. The wipers worked overtime, and the humidity from being wet, working hard, and being furious made him sweat and feel like 400 degrees Kelvin. After a few minutes of hammering back through the way he had just come, he found himself emitting a continuous yell. Once he realized it, he decided it felt good and continued to yell. Not even words, just a solid voice penetrating the tension-filled space inside his truck and overpowering the music. He didn't even bother to check his watch, for of course he was late, and nothing could be done about it. Getting to the drive, he parked quickly, leaving the truck running. He then stormed inside. Albert's 'pop' approached, complaining that he was wasting gas leaving the vehicle running. Bert growled back, "We're all going to hell anyways, quicken it up!" Albert and his folks that he looked after had a very loving relationship. After grabbing his prescriptions he went back out in a huff. In the rain, he lit up a smoke and took note that it was the first one of the day. Perhaps this was the reason for the flustered self; perhaps not. At the same time as the good feeling of nicotine and formaldehyde hit his lungs, the impending feeling of early death also took hold. He looked at the smoke and flicked it in an annoyed manner into a puddle that was being riddled with raindrops. "Fuck you, surgeon general's warning," he muttered bitterly. "I hope you get run over by a bus." Placing the crumpled pack of cigarettes back in his fanny, he zipped it back up (he had previously unzipped it) and jumped up onto the worn and foam-missing seat of his truck. The initial heat in the running vehicle was overwhelming, but since his adrenaline from the drive back to the house had worn off somewhat, he didn't mind. This time, going up the rugged semicleared pathway to the highway, he took extra care. Not only did he use care and drive slowly past the washed-out sections, but he stopped and moved several of the sharpest stones to the bottom of the ditch where they could not trouble him later on in the dark after work. Back up by the highway, the early morning traffic had died down; and without further ado, he was on his way to work. Down the twisty winding roads he went. Unclean water from trucks and trailers coated the already-dirtied sides of his GMC. The heater pumped dry heat from the cabin vents and kept the windshield condensation-free. Barrelling along (yet again), he didn't even notice that a car coming the other way was partially in his lane and out of control in the rain. Work, and to get to it, was his only objective, never mind almost being hit by passing cars. Another twenty minutes, and his truck shut off across from the shop. He stayed in the cab for a few good minutes to make sure his attitude was in check. Then he walked into the shop, and his foul look made me turn down my *Rage against the Machine* playing on the stereo.

The bike lined up next for my bench I generously donated to Bert instead. An old K100 with a coolant flush, water-pump rebuild, and a valve check. Fun, fun! Best to let him have all of that fun, as there was more-exciting bodywork to do. I think it was the K100LT but couldn't be bothered to look, since it was far too ugly. Looking at the service schedule for the day, not much else was taking place; the busy morning had consumed all the bikes. But an R1200R naked roadster, a less-expensive version of the RT and GS, needed an LED flashing taillight installed. It was a half-hour job that I let go on long after lunch just because I could. Later, Harry and I took our staple guns and shot rounds off at each other. Pretending to be WWI biplanes, we flew our guns all around the shop, dogfighting as we went. He would level out his 'plane' behind me and fire off a few rounds. These hit the floor or the back of my head. Running around to the other side of a bench, I caught him: my 'rat-a-tat-tat' machine-gun fire shot out several staples that pummelled into his arm and chest. They bounced off harmlessly and fell to the gun-metal floor below. Harry then 'vroomed' over to the carpet and exclaimed how he was 'hit' and 'out of control.' He made a quickly descending-to-the-earth airplane sound and then threw the stapler onto the mat. The cartridge clip hit first, and then the spring-release mechanism slid open, spewing staples in all directions—perfect hit. We 'whooped' and 'hollered' to each other, giving each other a high five and then went and picked up his staple gun. He left the loose staples on the ground for the shop boy to clean up. The shop boy came into work after his high-school classes. After Albert's late start to the morning, he had been very diligent to keep steady on the ugly K-bike. For his grumpy dishevelled self, he seemed to be doing a good job and was already done rebuilding the water pump. He was now cleaning off the mating surface of the block to apply the special BMW glue for reaffixing the newly finished pump. We usually used glue from the local auto-parts store, since it was half the price and of better quality. The primary gear for the water pump had a shaft that passed from the 'water side' to the 'oil side' via a slip-coupling seal. Not only did the slip-coupling get corroded and nasty with age, but it also literally ate away the shaft for the primary gear. Unfortunately, these primary gears were the most expensive part of the operation coming in at over two bills. This didn't even include the seals, O-rings, coolant, or time for re and re. Ahh, the joys of having a shitty, old, underpowered, heavy, clunker. Not for me, thanks. My Beemer was air- and oil-cooled, and that was enough: no need to complicate the matter further with a water pump, radiator, thermostat, hoses, extra gauges, etc.

The brilliant flashing LED that was now installed on the R-bike was angled low, so I spent a few minutes adjusting and testing the height with co-workers till content. Then she got sent up front, while I finished the paperwork. The customer drove away into the wilds of the concrete jungle. Nothing else really happened for the rest of the afternoon. A few jobs were completed, customers left satisfied, and not much bickering occurred between employees. If only some of the employees would stay away from the shop more often . . . but only in my dreams.

Bert's K-bike ran like a piece of shit. It had one hundred thousand plus kilometres of neglect. I held the tank up and out of the way for Bert's coolant system replenish. Outside, we double-teamed the bitch (excuse my language). Albert started the blue-smoking wench and got the antifreeze-glycol-mix hot with the throttle open as I kept the tank from smashing to the ground, causing unnecessary tragedy. No leaks, always a good sign. Surprisingly, the temperature gauge even worked, which meant the temperature sensor was reading correctly; hoorah, two out of the three! That is a rare happening with these beasts (probably when those customers get a hold of these writings, they will have discouraging words and letters to send to me. Oh well, the truth hurts). Eventually, after all of the bodywork was bolted back on and the coolant was checked, Albert hopped on for a test ride—his favourite part of the day. He almost fell off in the small lane beside the showroom, and it may have partially been my fault. As he slowly let out the clutch lever and started to creep forward, I grabbed hold of the tail rack. At the time, I had been behind him, cheering his departure; so at first, he didn't know he was being held up. The small resistance confused him so that he opened the throttle a bit more, and I pulled even harder. This is when, in one of the mirrors, he noticed my grinning, smiling face. He immediately told me to 'fuck off,' like the kind gentleman that he was; and at first, I did. Being unstable on the bike, Albert held his shorter-ish legs out on either side as if that would stop the 600 pounds from falling over if it really wanted to. He started forward again, and since there was no resistance, he was edging towards the gate and beyond. Just as he was sure of himself and his stability, yet still unsure about his sexuality, he pulled his feet up onto the pegs. A giant buffet of wind slammed into the gate, which in turn smashed the gate into the front wheel of the motorcycle. One split-second before it hit the bike, as I was pretty much right behind him, I grabbed once again onto the back of the bike. Albert let out a cry and started to fall off the right-hand side of the bike, sounding like an old dying dog being shot. I yelled milliseconds afterwards that I had him, but the weight of Albert and the bike was almost too much for me. My muscles strained, and an angry teeth-together cringe spread over my face. "Get on the bike, I can't hold it!" I yelled out to him, whose ass was halfway on the seat, the other half being in midair. Albert struggled and then somehow, after letting me break out in a sweat and start to ache from the heaviness of the situation, righted himself and balanced the lousy machine. While wiping droplets of uneasiness from my furrowed brow, I walked briskly over to the gate and latched it to the fence, like it should have been done in the first place. I checked the bike for damages caused by the mishap—none, good. Bert was all flustered and began to verbally abuse me for grabbing the tail rack of the bike and almost causing lawsuits and hospital time for him. Scoffing in his face, I kicked the tyre and let him ride away. He wasn't very happy, and neither was I. Bert would most likely ride around on that hunk of junk for thirty minutes, so I decided to go inside and amuse myself by looking at pictures of hot chicks on the Internet. Not porn, but pictures of beautiful girls in still frames just sometimes scantily clad or adorned with no clothes. So many out there, so many, but never porn . . .

Surprisingly, little Bert arrived shortly after he left. Most likely, he had become cold and wet because the lack of heated grips and seats on the old machine. The pegs love to vibrate, and the four cylinders heat the shit out of anybody's crotch as he told me just moments after sides-standing and hopping off . . . or after slowly dismounting, whichever you may prefer. By that time, the shop boy had arrived, and he was sternly commanded to clean the machine as the customer was waiting. News flash! The customers are always waiting because they never go anywhere or do anything! If you're riding in for an eight-hour service bud, at least bring a book or a Game Boy to entertain yourself. But that's enough ranting; everybody knows this, and nothing can be done about it. Albert finished the write-up of all the parts and labour for the job, which he scribbled over the full sheet of paper. I took it over to the computer and began entering the date. "Berty, didn't you use any coolant?" He immediately spat back, "Of course I did!" But then he brought over the coolant bottle, since he had forgotten to write down the number on the hard copy in his childlike scribble. Then he started grumbling more frequently as I found additional parts he had put down wrong numbers for, didn't write them down, and it turned into a battle between time and customer impatience. My heart was doing the whole mile-a-minute deal, and people from up front were questioning when the bike would be finished, cleaned, and the paperwork would be done. They did this about every five minutes—goddamn them! At this, I groaned outwardly a little and screamed incessantly on the inside. Just another hour, just another hour, I kept telling myself. Finally, for what seemed like an eternity, Bert and I managed to agree on the labour and all the parts used from the shop to complete the job. It was only one hundred and eighty dollars more than the original documents he had given me, no big deal! Going to the showroom, I tossed Duane the paperwork but kept my eyes low in case the customer saw me and wanted to have a 'Chatty-Cathy' time, which did not appeal to me in the least. Going back through the door to the shop, the carpet almost tripped me because of my rush, but I made it without any further complications. A couple minutes passed, and the freshly cleaned ready-to-go K-bike rolled up to the front, sparkling as though a beautiful gem in the watery air. I was delighted that this particular job was finished, for the old bikes were a lot more of a hassle than they needed to be—much more.

As the customer drove away, Bert and I were cleaning up our tools, getting ready to leave, and all was well in the world. Harry bundled his shit together and got the hell outta dodge, since he had a hot date with a missus. Albert told him to 'scram' on his way out. Harry's reply was "I'll see you in hell, biatches!" After this, I didn't see him for a whole two days until the wretched weekend was over. After putting on his fanny pack, Bert donned his revoltingly filthy 'pleasure attire' to head out. Big crusty chunks were even falling from the nice jacket he had adorned. Nice would have been a most excellent word to describe him. With my backpack full of sweaty gym clothes and my football, I finished locking up the back double doors with the chains and made my way to leave; Albert was close on my heels. We made a round and turned all the lights off in the shop, as we were the last two nitwits to be in the godforsaken facility for the night. Outside, after turning the last key in the big stainless-steel metal-gated lock, I gave Berty a hearty wave and wished him a great weekend while thinking 'good riddance' to myself. We made the walk across the parking lot in the drizzle that hadn't let up all day, and then I sat in my cold Nissan, shivering while the engine heated up. A few minutes passed, the thermostat opened, and I let the heat pour like liquid fire through the vents to turn my skin back to white from the peculiar shade of blue it had been. I worked the wipers a few times to clear off the debris and the few leaves that had accumulated during the day. It was dumb of me to drive as the walk from my house was minimal, but as a major consumer-whore, I wanted to save our environment by spewing a few more carbon monoxide and carbon dioxide particles into the atmosphere. . . oh wait, it doesn't work like that! Placing my seatbelt over my tired aching shoulders (I use a four-point harness for racing, so it does cover both shoulders), I decided to go home. Doing a safety check of the road, I watched Albert's haggard-looking truck lumbering along the asphalt at a slow pace and then pull into the parking lot that we had just left. I mulled over why he would be back: forgot his smokes, maybe a prescription, wanted to use the Internet? It could have been a whole bunch of options. "Damnit, Berty," I said out loud. This was no particular time in the day that I wanted to be dealing with problems, especially when they involved other people. From that statement, you could probably tell I didn't volunteer my time to other people much or work at the local food bank; so much for helping the community. Wipers licking their way across my windshield, I made my way over to Bert's truck. I wanted to find out his 'beef.' In the few brief minutes in my car, the clouds had blackened, and the overcast sky had started a barrage on top of me. Getting out of my car, the cold droplets hit me. Under my breath, I let out my own barrage but of foul words instead. Hustling over to Albert's door, I pulled it open and asked him bluntly, "What's goin' on?" Wearily, with his thin hair matted to his scalp from the rain and a weak voice barely audible over the noise of his truck and my car, he told me, "Got a nail in my tyre, just saw it when I got in my truck. Feel like hangin' around fer a bit?"

CHAPTER 12 — Smells Like Teen Spirit

The day was young and fresh, and Harry's cries broke the stillness of the hour. To his dismay, a thick acrid smell hung in the air of the shop. It was the chemical smell of paint, and it burned the nostrils like nobody's business. As it also stung the eyes considerably, his words were justified.

To put it lightly, the service department looked like crap. Not only that, it was crap. On the previous Saturday, the shop boy and I had relieved ourselves of motorcycle-fixing duty and went about prepping the floor for a new coat of paint. With long-handled scrapers, we peeled off a few of the old layers and eventually got down to a gross pea-green colour. This seemed to have a consistent level for most of the shop. Together we trudged down to the local paint-supply store and decided upon gun-metal gray. Just the ticket! Four cans of it ready to be liberally applied. The most chemically smelling paint I have ever bought; if only I had read the label, or rather, understood the label.

Near the end of the workday, the shop boy and I had moved all the benches and toolboxes into a far corner so that the paint could be dumped on the ground and then smoothed out with a long-handled roller. After 4:30 p.m., everyone left but me; the night shift had begun, and the painting party had arrived.

The first can opened, hit me with an instant reeling headache. It also felt like a backhand across the face. I ran like a Kenyan for the nearest face mask, which couldn't be put on fast enough. The eyes also felt as though someone had sprayed battery acid on them, and no safety goggles I owned could help. I turned the fans on in a weak attempt to bring some fresh air to me. Even with the mask, after only a few minutes, I was pretty high off the fumes, and the headache dissipated slightly. An hour or so later, after all my hard efforts and good intentions, the floor was done. She glowed like a newly polished deck on a gunship, and I just felt so proud! I left in good spirits with the fans running and was excited to see the other mechanics' expressions on Tuesday morning when they saw their brand-new-looking shop.

The opposite occurred: everyone was crying; everyone was whining; and not a single person offered congratulations on my fantastic efforts from the weekend. Of course, the complaining was translated into constant swearing. Harry was just cursing incessantly about the situation, whereas Berty was cursing at me. I'll admit that the burning sensation was slightly horrendous. Bikes did need to get worked on, but still, stop being little babies. It was only killing brain cells, and nothing they weren't used to. The service shop door had been closed over the weekend, so barely any of the burning sensation or smell reached the up-front staff. They giggled to one another that we had to suffer, which made the hatred towards them grow. Eventually, I apologized, and the other mechanics grudgingly picked up some tools to give the impression of work being done. Note to self, next time I'm painting, leave the sales-to-service door open.

CHAPTER **13** — I Love the Smell of Burnt Rubber

Harry's toolbox was halfway across the shop on its way to his truck. He was pissed; literally freakin' mad. There was no way that I was going to get in his way. Every two seconds, he would throw a few more obscene comments at the floor. They were aimed at Duane, but he had disappeared as quickly as his fat legs could take him back to the showroom sanctuary. Harry had a glass bottle of iced tea on the top of his toolbox from lunch. As he manoeuvred his box over the extension cords and black rubber mats, it fell to the floor. The bottle broke instantly, sending glass shards and cold drink in all directions. He was furious already, and this aggravated him just that wee bit more. Letting out a loud growl, he kicked the largest piece of broken glass into the closest wall. It of course exploded into more fragments, leaving carnage all over the shop. Albert huddled in the corner like a scared bunny rabbit, attempting to make himself smaller and smaller. I just sat on my red Snap-on chair, watching him in amazement. Harry had finally hit the switch, gone overboard, and lost his marbles; however you want to put it, he was leaving. Fed up with the shit and curiously after a huge verbal 'fuck you!—no fuck you!' match between Duane, Harry was cruising! Duane was an idiot and pissed us all off on a constant basis. This time, it did the job enough for Harry to see red. Damnit, I thought quietly to myself. I would much rather see Duane leave in a big kerfuffle than have Harry go. This would mean training another inexperienced turd how to work on Beemers, which was not the most exhilarating prospect to think about. When finally, after all the fighting to get the toolbox outside, Harry came back inside to grab his truck keys to load it up. After start-up, he roasted the tyres for a minute to show how childishly angry he truly was. He drove down the proper side of the road, just a little differently than most, backwards. In our parking lot, his truck flew in so fast that he almost nicked two parked bikes before coming to a screeching halt. A couple of the staff that were out of the loop had perspiration adorn their brows as they saw the taillights come to within millimetres of the expensive products on display. Leaving the vehicle, Harry slammed the door as hard as possible and stormed into the back lot to roll his box the rest of the way. Approaching me, he asked in a strained voice if I could lend a hand. Having no choice in the matter, since his mind seemed pretty made up, I accepted his gracious offer—of me helping him.

The stupid thing was friggin' heavy! Hair ball hadn't even removed any of the tools, and it must have weighed half a tonne. The top cabinet had cheap steel handles that wanted to fold into the red-painted tin it was attached to. Instead, we lifted from the underside and with its nice sharp edges left lacerating marks on both our palms. One of my afterthoughts to this was Albert: in the whole twenty minutes of Duane and Harry's fight, the toolbox rolling, and the face-off with Gerald, he hadn't moved one muscle. It was as though paralysis had taken a hold of him, and he was now stuck sitting in his chair, unable to blink or fight. The reasons for Harry's actions were not very grand, and the whole ordeal was taken way out of proportion. It went a little like this:

"Sup, man! Hows about my homeboy lend me a hand?" This was Harry's way of asking for help. "Hey, no probs, bud, lemme just finish tightening this bolt on the GT (referring to the K1200GT I was working on that had been booked in for recall work that morning). "Fine, guess I'll wait—but only for two seconds!" I was finishing up the replacement of an EWS ring, an ignition immobiliser unit that had gone faulty. The customer was a douche bag and treated our entire staff like shit because he figured he was a big shot. His wife, similar in attitude, was some blonde bitch that used a cement mixer to help get enough base and makeup onto her face each day. Ugly as fuck, but a nice body, so she thought she was just as much of a big shot as her husband. They were perfect for each other! He brought his bike in one hour late for appointment and verbally stated that he expected it to be finished and hand-polished half an hour before our originally quoted timeslot. What a piece! The showroom staff kissed his ass, like they should, before they laid the heavy news on me. I dropped what I had been doing on my bench, scrambled around to get the guy's parts, and then hurriedly began work on his bike. Man, how I would have loved to scratch it or damage some costly component on his bike. Unfortunately, it still had two years of its original warranty left, and that would mean the bike would just end up on the same bench that it was on now in two weeks' time! Those customers would love to come back to torment us; I reconsidered. In the long run, keeping a good reputation for myself and the shop was better than treating someone like crap just because they had a bad attitude.

Harry's bike was an old K100, the story of our lives. It was in the shop for a water-pump rebuild (sound familiar?). I went over and helped him take the tank and gas lines off, so he could reach the radiator cap. Seeing that he was fixing up the old clunker, I decided to save him some time. In my collection of assorted used parts and things was an older K-bike water pump that I had already rebuilt and could literally be bolted right on. Harry agreed to use my water pump on the condition of me helping to clean the gasket surfaces. "Sure," I replied. Not only did it get rid of some expensive crap out of my personal inventory but also made a few dollars for myself—a perfect scenario. Rummaging around in some bins of my junk, it was found all clean and shiny. We lined it up and found the appropriate gears for the bike (the early '80s K-bikes had a different amount of teeth than the newer '80s bikes. In 1987, they switched. If you carried both gears, you could swap to any of the bikes as the housing/bushing diameters were identical). Harry and I were both somewhat under the front wheel, making sure of the fitment when Duane came into the back of the shop. Immediately, he got on our cases. The dork (proper definition of a dork is a whale's penis, but I am using it in the slang sense of Duane just being an incompetent turd) looked at me and started to go off about the rowdy customer wanting his bike back, and I was wasting my time on the old 'flying brick' (a Beemer term for the big engine that was in the shape of a bricklike rectangle). "He's waiting up front an' tearin' strips out of each one of us while you sit here chatting with Harry! What am I supposed to tell him?" "Well, you could start by telling him to get a clue. Then you could tell him to buy a real bike. By the way, me helping Harry takes about two seconds, so don't you get your panties in a bunch." Duane did not take kindly to this 'constructive criticism' of mine. He began to tell me so, but I shut him off. "Duane, guess what: why don't you go back up there and try to sell something!" Duane also didn't like this, so he stormed away from us with his final quip being loud and agitated, "I wish I could!" right before slamming the door. Harry and I burst into hysterics. He came over to me, wrapped his dirty fingers around my neck in a mocking tone, and yelled into my face, "I wish I could sell a motorcycle!" Holy crap, did we have a good laugh. Five minutes after the fact, we were both out of breath and still making fun of the imbecile that was constantly wasting our time. Albert was strolling about by his bench, not saying anything but trouble. "Duane may be a big piece a shit," he grumbled, "but he's still the general manager. You 'ave to give 'im some try of cooperating with 'im." "Yo, Bert," Harry cut in, "The only way I'm gettin' along with hamburger joint up there is if I get a five-dollar-an-hour raise. They don't pay my ass to be on a team!" Of course, Berty did not take lightly to this either. He stammered something incoherently and also stormed up front. A few minutes later, he reappeared in the shop and held a neutral look on his face, which was a minisneer. He rarely smiled, and when he did, it was usually about something gay or if someone got hurt or if an anal joke was made, also when he stank out the shop—what a disgusting individual. We carried on working for a while. I finished up the K1200 and sent the retard on his way without even considering giving it a polish. The staff was overjoyed when they left, for they could resort back to their idle lives of drinking coffee or sitting on the new couch or bikes in the showroom. I was curious as to why Berty's mood had improved. The whole morning, he had either been scared or grumpy, and only when he had gone 'showroom side' had it elevated to a better level. Right when I was about to inquire though, the oversized demon from up front appeared! Duane was sweating profusely like usual. His first words were in a stammer towards Harry, but he then regained his composure. I missed the first words, as they were somewhat incoherent, and my ears were lacking in the hearing department. What was caught was "here at this establishment, my title is that of GM, and if you're not able to handle that, then we have a problem!" I wasn't initially sure why he was addressing Harry, as my comments earlier were the 'putdown' ones. Looking over my shoulder, it became extremely apparent: a large grin had broadened over Albert's face, and the reason he had gone up front a few moments before was to talk to Duane—most likely to refresh his memory that he had authority over Harry; some authority, mainly dealing with job descriptions and work disbursement. He obviously took this to heart the wrong way. Harry looked up finally from his seated position by his bench and coolly stated, "I do have a problem with that 'cause I've never seen you do anything or act in any way that resembles anything remotely like a general manager." Duane's eyes widened, and steam erupted from his eyes and ears. "And what's that supposed to mean?" He bellowed, "What it means, 'fat ass,' is that you don't do shit! I'm bustin' my ass back here, 'n' you're comin' back with all your hot air and negative comments all the time when you can't sell shit up front!" Harry had stood up, and they were almost head-to-head. Duane was a few inches taller and outweighed Harry by a hundred pounds. He threw a couple wrenches on the ground in his defiance towards the 'fat ass.' That comment in itself was hilarious, and I was sure at some later date, we would enjoy a decent laughing session over it. Duane in a huff straightened up his back and pushed out his massive stomach to reveal some want-to-be macho pose and trying to impose his superiority over his victim. Harry was not intimidated by this and stood his ground. He had been in many fights back in the east of Canada where he used to live, and he was getting really pissed off rather than becoming frightened, like the old man in the corner. Duane bellowed back towards the degrading comments that had been spewed at him, "Harry, that shit you just said to me is the last straw! I'm the best salesman at this shop, and you better give me a good apology right now before I fire you!" Harry had a gleam in his eyes and clenched his teeth together. He poked Duane in his gut and lowered his voice. "Listen up, you fucking piece of garbage. You're the only guy we have selling bikes, and you haven't sold any since the new owner. The only reason I'm here is to pick up a paycheck. There's no reason for me to put up with your shit—this toolbox has wheels for a reason." "You better get outta here! You're relieved from duty for the day!" Duane said this in his most manly voice as he pushed Harry's hand off of his oversized stomach. "You know what? *Fuck you*, you fat fucking slob. I don't need you or any of this shit! I won't leave for the day, I'm fucking gone! Kiss my ass!" Duane was almost blowing his gasket and yelled, "Good. Get the hell outta here. I don't ever want to see you again!" At that point, he almost ripped the doors off the hinges to get up front as fast as he could. Harry went crazy. Outside he flew with his red and black hammer, and all I could hear was the smashing of our wooden crates as he laid into them. Coming back inside, he picked up the tools he had chucked on the floor earlier and threw them into the top of his toolbox. At that point, he started to move his box outside, including the part where his iced-tea bottle became knocked onto the floor and broke.

Gerald had come downstairs from doing a bit of accounting in his office in the condominium above the shop and only caught the part about Duane being in a ragged mood. Gerald had not even noticed the truck in the parking lot with the red box being hauled into the bed. As he was filled in briefly on the gist of the story from what Trevor had heard through the door, he began to become concerned. Through the door, he went into the shop and immediately felt the tension in the air. A giant hole was in the wall where Harry's toolbox usually filled, and there was dirt and glass all over the floor. "If yer lookin' fer Hair ball, he's probably gone home fer the day." Berty piped this from the corner he had been hiding in. Gerald wheeled around and saw Bert. His voice was strained and sounding worried, "What the hell happened here? Where did everyone go?" I came back into the shop to grab Harry's air gun that had been on one of the shelves. I told Gerald that he should have a word with Duane, since he was being a jerk to everybody and not being a very good role model. He wanted to know everything right there and right then. I pointed to the twin doors leading around the lot to Harry's truck. "You better get out there an' have a word with him, or he won't be back anytime soon!" He was exasperated and moved his short body, dressed in unfashionable clothes, to find Harry.

Out by his silver truck tying up the toolbox with a few straps previously 'jacked' from the shop, he found Harry. From the truck was blaring music that drowned out the possibility of a reasonable conversation. Gerald yelled to him from three metres away, but he either didn't hear or chose to ignore him. Harry carried on tying things down when Gerald got close enough to be directly beside him. "May I have a minute of your time to talk?" Gerald's voice was strained as he was unaccustomed to yelling. Harry stopped for a second without looking at the boss. "Sorry, buds, I'm busy gettin' outta here. Can't ya see?" "Harry, I don't know what just happened in there, but we can figure it out. Just put everything down for a minute and let's have a chat." "Gerald, I've got an appointment with gettin' the hell outta here—don't have time to miss it!" At that point, Gerald started to get upset as well. Here was his employee disrespecting him, and as he was completely out of the 'loop,' he had not the faintest idea of why. He threw his hands upon Harry's shoulders, "Harry!" He bellowed, "I'm your boss and would like to consider myself a friend. Confide in me your troubles." With straight-edged lips and a gleam of uncertainty and anger in his eyes, Harry stopped. "Gerald, what's 'goin' on here' is the 'GM,'" he quotation-marked with his hands "is havin' some power trip and hit my breaker. I'm done, man, fer good." "Duane is the issue?" He seemed momentarily relieved. "Listen, Harry," he lowered his earlier aggressive-sounding tone to a peaceful consoling one. "Duane gets upset sometimes and doesn't know how to handle situations involving other people. Let's figure this out, I want to work this out. You're a great guy!" As soon as the compliments started rolling and the insults towards 'fat ass' Duane began flowing, he immediately cheered up and became sensible. "Tell me what took place between you two, and this toolbox in the truck 'gig' is unacceptable, just for the record. You come to me first before jumping up and leaving." Harry began to tell the boss of the morning's ridicule. Obviously, it was a little one sided, but when he talked with the other mechanics later on, one of us vouched for him wholeheartedly (myself); whereas Alberto grumbled and whined about character traits he did not like in the two people in question. When Harry was finished, he stood leaning against his silver truck, hesitating to say anything while the boss man took it all in. "It appears to me as though you and Duane need to sort out your differences, just not today. Right now, you can roll your toolbox back into the shop, and I'm sending both of you home for the day to cool off. And yes, you can book hours down for the whole day, I'm not worried about that. Sound good to you?" "Yah, not too bad," Harry quirked up, "But I'm pretty fuckin' pissed at that douche bag Duane. He's gonna have to dish out a good meaty apology if I'm gonna stay workin' at this joint." "Harry! Harry! This isn't' a jail cell, this is your job. Let's try to get along. Tomorrow's a new day, and let's all three of us have a bit of a sort-out. We'll clear up all the issues. Who knows, you might even come out of this financially ahead." This gave Harry the edge he wanted for a compensation conversation. "All right, mighta gotten a bit carried away back there." "Yes, from what Trevor mentioned, there was quite a lot of yelling and much vulgarity being used! That's all behind us now though!" Gerald slapped Harry playfully on his shoulder, "Now get that red box back where it belongs." Gerald walked back into the showroom to talk to 'huffy' Duane and sort him out. He was most likely still in the hating stage and also needed to be calmed down.

Harry unstrapped his toolbox and sauntered back through the alleyway to the shop. Approaching me, he grinned a big ole shit-eating grin. "Hey, buds, what do ya say 'bout helpin' me here with the ole toolbox again! Sound fun?" I threw him a perturbed look and said that Albert should lend a hand this time instead. We both knew his arms would be pulled from their sockets, and blood would pool underneath of the lifeless appendages.

Duane was all flustered, obviously. The fat retard was drinking coffee and aimlessly flipping through a motorcycle magazine faster than he could read. His mind at that moment was scattered in all different directions. Anger had welled up inside of him, and he was scared of the repercussions of his outrageous comments and actions. He was sad because he was hated so thoroughly by everyone. Gerald came through the front doors and requested his presence upstairs in his other office. Gulp, see you later, Duane.

Harry seemed ecstatic about life even after his bout with the fat one. On the YouTube, he played some fast-paced happy songs and appeared to dance his way through the actions of cleaning up broken glass, dirt, and placing all of his mechanical possessions back in order among the shelves and benches. Albert was less than pleased that Harry was back to work. It was always a two-on-one fight against Bert, and he hated it. If Harry or I was ever relieved of duty, he would be just plain jolly. Most likely, he would move out of his parents, go on a date, with a girl maybe, and stop drinking himself to sleep as often as he did. Harry went home after all his shit was back in order, and I didn't see the fat one poke his head back into the shop till the next day. Gerald came down to question us all. He wasn't 'uncheery,' but his mood seemed neutral. To me, he poked a good finger at with accusations and such coarsing through his teeth. Meh, I knew that being a partner in crime had its drawbacks, and this was one of them. Life would go on as before, and 'they' would just scrutinize our actions a wee bit more. Oooh, perhaps they would hold a general meeting again. After the first couple of meetings, they just stopped, questions remained unanswered, and problems in the shop remained problems.

After work, I felt pretty good about myself: didn't lose a good pal; Duane got some flak/bad rap; and the sun was a shinin', just a shining.

CHAPTER **14** — Run When You Hear Sirens

That sick fuck Albert sauntered over and appeared intrigued and interested in the happenings on my bench. I was intent on finishing the project at hand and gave him only a quick glance. The dirty slut had walked over just to fart on me. His face was all toothy and screwed up with maliciousness. The cackle and his run off the set was just the cherry for the shit cake he made for me. I called out to him that he was 'sick-o' and a 'pig', but it didn't help in the least the fact that a big cloud of disgust had welled up to surround me. Scrunching up my nose, I carried on my work and grumbled quietly to myself.

It was New Year's in a couple of days, and it was four-thirty on a Saturday. My bench held the remnants of a dozen screecheroos that had been disassembled. Taking out the nice combustible materials involved the use of a razor blade, a little ziplock baggy, and a screwdriver. When finished, I felt as though I was 'ballin'' with my ziplock full of nice white powder. Lines of this substance are not recommended, but coke is supposedly bad as well.

Today was bomb-making day. From the local hardware store, Harry and I purchased six rolls of black electrical tape. I had also been saving up pop bottles from lunches. Now they weren't very dangerous as we aren't full-out 'pyros.' The goal was to be able to blow up garbage bins and pumpkins; child's play without needing to outsource to expensive explosives or engaging skilful techniques.

Earlier in the day, there had been plenty to worry about: lots of bikes to work on, parts to clean, customers to take care of, etc. We had managed to work extra hard and efficiently for once to take advantage of the early evening and finish the bikes off. With an hour of shop time remaining (sounds like high school), we were creating our masterpieces.

Back in the day, Alberto had joined in wholeheartedly, buying fireworks and pounding screecheroos, and wrapping them up for terrific noises and flashes of light. Nowadays, he enjoyed watching us make pop-bottle-bombs but thought that it was rude to test them in our back lot due to the prissy neighbours surrounding the shop. Big bangs always created disturbances in the way of phone calls or upset mothers and fathers coming to the shop where the knowledge of such happenings was always denied by the involved parties.

For each bottle, a tiny hole was drilled in the cap for the wick. A plastic bag with a small amount of the magic powder was then placed through the threaded opening in the bottle with the bag entrails over the threads, and then you just put the old cap back on! Install wick through the hole in the cap, shake it up to get the powder over the wick, and voila! Apply liberal amounts of tape over the cap and the other weak parts of the bottle, and you have yourself a fun little firecracker. If using four or five screecheroos' worth of powder, you're sure to have a good time and blow up a pumpkin.

A half dozen more of them being torn apart, and my hands were getting tired. I made a few of the pop-bottle bombs for the weekend and decided to make just one more, which would be lit off right before I went home and away from this shit hole for a few days. I took five screecheroos' worth of firework powder and stuffed it into a cute little ziplock through the slender neck of a Fresca bottle that until recently I thought to possess actual sugar instead of the death-inducing aspartame. With two rolls of tape, the unit got an extreme amount of attention.

By that time on Saturday, almost all the staff had left. Duane remained up in the front to close up, and Harry and I had rolled in all the bikes and locked most of the doors. Albert had taken some aluminum for his scrap metal pile and split the scene. Putting on some safety goggles because of incidents of fireworks in my youth, I strode outside chuckling to myself, with Harry following close behind. This bottle even had two wicks for added aesthetics. We closed the door behind us and, with a cheap throwaway lighter, lit the fuse of awesomeness. My left hand held the lighter; the right held the bottle. I waited a second before throwing it a safe distance away.

It let out a great flash, and the noise was incredible. Thunderclaps seemed incomparable to this 'thing' that had been created. For some reason, it was one of the loudest explosions I had ever been a part of. It sounded as though the world had erupted and broken in two. With both our ears ringing, congratulations came from Harry, and we 'low-fived.' It literally had sounded like a jet breaking the sound barrier. Before returning indoors, I took the garden hose and splayed a bit of water over the crime scene. While this was taking place, Duane had heard the eruption and dropped what he was doing to come play harassment-daddy to us. Actually, he was extrawhiny and extrabitchy about the whole ordeal. He, being the general manager, did not condone this kind of activity going on around the shop. But because of the recent fighting that had gone down between Harry and Duane, he didn't want to raise as much of a scene. This time, after quickly telling us off, he grumbled and then returned to finishing up whatever he was doing in the showroom. I locked up the back doors, threw on my jacket, and drove off into the weekend, not once looking back.

Duane and Harry were close behind. Harry had just put on his loafers and was getting up to leave when they came in. I only heard about this later, but the memory was still fresh, and the tension was great.

Two police cars screeched into the parking lot with sirens and lights on, with all the uniformed officers being much more excited than they should be. Duane's face went completely outrageous. His jaw had dropped down, and his eyes were almost bulging out from his Neanderthal-like head. Harry was all worried at first, as he thought they were after him. The sergeant or whoever was in charge in their orderly brigade knocked on the door in a rather loud tone. Duane, still a bit dumbfounded and trying hard to take it all in, stood motionless, staring at the officers on the other side of the door. Harry noticed this and went to let them in. "What do ya got to be intimidated by, man?" Harry said with a quiver in his voice. Duane was never one to get into trouble with the law. This was probably the first time he had ever seen the red and blue lights flashing in his life. When the latch went on the door, all four of the officers, three male and one female, came barging through. Immediately, the two remaining employees got drilled by the fuzz. The police stated that they received a pile of phone calls in the past five minutes about a propane tank exploding at the nearby motorcycle shop. When I heard about the calls relaying the 'propane tank' explosion, I was overjoyed. It's not every day that you get called into the police station for a hand-made bomb. Harry also told me that I was 'wanted for questioning' by the police; put that on your resume! He told me this on Tuesday morning.

They had stated in the a.m. that they would return with some heavy fines for the individual involved in making the dangerous weapon and lighting if off in the municipality of their jurisdiction—bla bla blab la blab la. Harry couldn't remember all that had been said, but it left me nervous far into the afternoon.

Duane got on edge the second the officer described to him the reason for their visit. Interrupting the policeman (dumb move on his part), he started going off on a tangent about it being an employee that had just left. He gave them my name, hours of employment, my description, and any facts he could think of to incriminate me with the crime. When I discovered this out, holy shit, did I get pissed off! That fucking cunt had not even hesitated to turn me in—what a dirty little rat. I had strongly disliked him before, but now his guts were hated; and in my mind, he should be put up against the wall facing a firing squad.

After Duane's 'subtle hint' as to who caused the incident and the police officers finding out that it was not a propane tank exploding but a master mechanic making little bombs in the shop, they wanted to see the remnants. Harry unlocked the doors and showed them into the back lot. He at least did not contribute to the abusive and slanderous comments that had been said with my name attached. The officers saw the pieces of charred plastic that had been doused by the garden hose and were not amused. The other year's kids had blown fingers off and had excessive burns on their bodies in the same neighbourhood and at the same time of year. For some reason, they didn't want it to happen again. I was the lesson to show to others, or was going to be. The four of them took statements from Duane and Harry before heading out. That was the same time they warned of their visit for the next scheduled workday. Come say hello to me, couldn't wait! The second the fuzz disappeared from view, those two got the hell outta there.

Tuesday morning: evil looks from Duane with no comment—evil looks from the boss, but he at least opened the door; still no comment; big fucking smile from Harry and a hearty pat on the back. "So, ahh, how was your weekend, dude? Run into any coppers?" Harry was grinning hysterically and laughing at the same time as saying this. Looking at him quizzically and having no clue as to what was going on, I told him that my weekend was great: a few drinks, a few friends, nothing crazy. He then dropped the story to me about the Saturday evening right after I left. As funny as it appeared, it wasn't very funny. The cops coming to the shop to have a little 'chat' with me was not sounding very good. I changed into my work attire and awaited the expected cop cars. At ten o'clock, when they still hadn't showed, Gerald came through the shop doors and asked me to join him upstairs. I looked at him and told him I would be there in five. What a shit show this day had turned into.

CHAPTER **15** — Yahbuts and Such

One of the difficult things to comprehend when not in a service environment is the stress level. As I've been here almost ten years now, many other mechanics have passed through these doors while I have stood strong. I am now beginning to falter. Occasional breakdowns and freak-outs are occurring on a more-frequent basis. After going home, the constant nagging and psychological turmoil stays in your conscience. You know you will be back in the same little boxed-up hole in the earth the next morning.

Little twitchy eyes, muttering under their foul breath. The lovely aroma of rotting teeth combined with previous night's alcohol and unhygienic nature. Urgg, my body gets tingles throughout when I think about it, and not the good kinds of tingles.

One day, I must escape from this mess I call my job—leave and never return. Venture off to a far off island and stake a claim in the ground to call my own. Possibly build a shack, knock up a random native woman, and have naked children running aimlessly around. Nice, I like where this fantasy is going.

You could have children and Yahbuts frolicking frivolously around through the open fields. Chuckles and laughter passed on through ever-changing winds. But then again, there is always reality to consider: one intoxicated night out on the town with the boys, wind up waking early with the morning sun pouring in through the close-by single-paned window with no blinds. You gaze over with red swollen eyes and a sore neck to see the blonde white-trash bitch nestled next to you. She is wearing your 2008 *Nine Inch Nails* T-shirt from the 'Lights in the Sky' tour, sleeping soundly. Damn, all of those decisions: kill her, take your favourite shirt, and run the hell out of there with no mercy; call her back the next night and face her sober; or let her raise a bastard child all alone, since you probably didn't wear a rubber. Reality bites, and I prefer the made-up world. It could be why there are so many cracked-out retards littering this city; the weather is never *that* miserable here. They can have their own personal worlds to venture off into whenever they steal the next ten bucks from your '90s Toyota Corolla parked on the curb.

"Hey, Hobbers, come gimme a hand strappin' this cruiser down. Its lard-ass front end is too freakin' heavy!" I yelled from my red motorcycle lift in the middle of the shop. "Two seconds, man, I'm still puttin' ma clothes on," he referred to his overalls as he had got in late for work that morning. "Come on, skanky momma, I'm breakin' a sweat over here!" I strained out of my clenched teeth while keeping the bike from pummelling into the gunmetal gray-painted cement floor below; the new coat if I may add. It seemed that I always got these precarious motorcycle rolling/falling-over scenarios. Perhaps it was a sign for me to go to the gym and bulk up.

"Yah, but I can't seem to get the damned leg in straight," Harry snarled back at me." "Ahh, Hairy, Yahbuts live in the forest!" His gaze was puzzled and slightly dumbfounded as he had absolutely no idea what was going on. "What the fuck are you talking 'bout, bro?" He shook his head as he said it, shaking his straight, greasy, black hair over his ears. "What's that supposed to mean?" I replied, "Yahbuts live in the forest, so stop talkin' about them so much. Every time you say their name, another one is born." One of my past girlfriends kept on telling me this nonsense because I had been using improper grammar, and I kept starting my sentences by saying 'yah, but' whenever I was second-guessing her or using a comeback. I'm just not good at accepting constructive criticism, so I decided to bring that element of home to the joyous workplace. Harry came over to finally give me a hand, and as he helped strap down the bike, he gave me that snarky tone again. "Dude, there's no such thing as a Yahbut, 'n' you just made that shit up. It's fuckin' stupid." I grinned back into the unshaven hair on his face, "I'm totally serious. I've seen them before. You just have to go out past all of the houses until you get deep into the forest, and if you stay really quiet, you can sometimes see or hear one." He groaned and moved back over to his bench while rolling his eyes, "Uh huh, okay, whatever you say, 'Bert'!" He insulted me by calling me this since Bert always makes up the most ridiculous stories about his weekends. Harry and I hear them endlessly, and we constantly harass him to stop lying; he doesn't.

He heard Harry and me blabbering from across the shop. He hollered out in his rag-tag redneck voice, "Hey you, what do those things look like?" I kept a straight face, which is really difficult for me and one of the reasons I'm bad at playing poker, and quickly envisioned what a 'Yahbut' looked like. "Well, if you ever *do* see one, which you won't, 'cause you guys are so damned noisy, they are about, ohh, two feet tall, pretty round, kinda like a peach, but superfuzzy. They're yellow, same colour as a Post-it note, and have two tiny little legs and no arms." I decided all of this on the fly. "How you tell them apart?" Albert hollered at me again. Obviously, it was easier to coax him into believing fiction than Harry. "Let's see, it's pretty simple, Alberto. The males are brown and superfuzzy, and the females are yellow fuzz and just a bit smaller. They both have two beady eyes and mouths similar to those from the *Critters* movies in the '80s. Bert had no idea that I was basing my characters entirely on those creatures. "Never seen them shows," Bert said. "K, how about *Gremlins*?" I was becoming exasperated. I had just given him their entire description, which I had just made up a minute ago, and he couldn't even imagine what they looked like. "I, I might 'ave a long time ago. I don't 'member, too long ago." After he said this, I hopped over to my desk and grabbed the nearest stack of Post-it notes that were lying underneath today's work orders. Mutters, swears, and insults being said under my breath towards Albert, I did a quick sketch of a female Yahbut, since the Post-it note was the perfect colour. Pacing myself over to his toolbox, I slammed it down over top of some of his perverse cut-outs posted on the toolbox lid. "There, you happy now?" I asked in a raised tone. "You've got your own personal picture of a Yahbut. Now if you ever run into one on your property, you'll know what it'll look like." He turned his head from the crouched position on his red Snap-on bike lift and scrunched both his eyebrows down to get a clearer view of the cute little drawing. "Huh? I see crazy shit like that all the time when I'm wasted out in the woods at my place!" Bert stated this as though he was deep in thought, dreaming of the tiny ten-foot-by-ten-foot single-story wooden pallet shack out on his parents' property surrounded by trees and darkness, with a case of cheap beer beside him on the porch, searching his eyes out into the nothingness. "Knowin' you, I bet ya have!" belched Harry from his end of the shop in a sarcastic manner. "Bet it's not the beer you're drinkin' up at your shack either!" He added, "Not unless they sell moonshine down at the liquor store these days!" Harry howled right back at him. "Yah, but what goes on up there goes on up there, 'n' not down here. 'Sides, them stuff won't make you see shit like that. When I'm moon tanning up at my shack, I can drink whadever I want," Berty snarled out before we both jumped on his case. "Moon tanning? Fuck you Bert," Harry chortled. "Berty, what are yah doin'?" I yelled. "Wha?" His eyes went wide as if he had placed his hand on a hot exhaust pipe. "You're talkin' about Yahbuts again," Harry kept it up, "they're gonna be everywhere at this rate!" "Listen here, slut wench," Berty snapped, "get outta here an' go do some work. We've got a whole bunch o' jobs, 'n' I gotta go to the eye doc," he defensively said this because he knew that he had just been caught saying it and hated it.

Albert is old; he has done a lot of drugs and has been drinking every day since the young age of twelve. It is very simple and easy to manipulate his mind, yet when you overload his circuits (another simple task), he goes whacko. "Just stop it, okay?" he started getting crazy. "Bert, start what? What are you talking about? You're gettin' all crazy, just calm down, man, take it easy." Harry was pestering him in a serious voice, but that was also partly what made it humorous. This makes Albert even more psychotic—when you tell him to take it easy. It was one of his most despised expressions. "Stop that!" his voice rose to a whiny shriek when it was said this time. When it escalates to that certain point, you know that the hamster is spinning on its wheel as fast as possible. We both know, referring to Harry and me, at that point with Alberto, you have to back off. He starts yelling death threats or remarks about quitting the shop. Both are used regularly by all the service staff here, but it's just not as far over the edge as you like to go with Bert. It upsets me too much.

Then Dillen opened the door with another Down-syndrome expression on his face. "Ummm," he mumbled out of the large gaping orifice he called a mouth, drooling as he went. "There's a bike here to work on, and umm, he's waiting in the showroom." Dillen, the epitome of a retard, in case you had not gathered; I despise him to put it lightly. You would think a slacker that gets nothing done in a two-week pay period would not bother another individual since he is not doing anything! Why in the world is it completely opposite then? The only time his mouth ever stops flapping up and down is when he's sleeping; in this manner though, I might be mistaken, for he most likely blabs there as well. . .

Albert looked through his glowing red eyes over into Dillen's stare. "So what the fuck are you starin' at, jerk wad? Go open the gate and roll the bike around." His wheezing kept everyone from taking him seriously as he finished his sentence. His dry raspy voice was high pitched as he yelled back into Dillen's direction, "Get movin' fuck bag, you said the guy's waiting, so hurry!" As Dillen's arms dangled loosely next to his sides, he clomped his hooves through the gate and forgot to pick up the keys from the rack on his way through. Steam seeped from Alberto's thin tangle of mangy hair at the top of this head. While closing his eyes, a thin whine pushed out from between his teeth. "If he comes in here again, I'm gonna go mental!" Dillen trotted through the gate and pulled his head around the service doors, "Hey, hey you, uhh, guys seen the keys for the bike outside? I think the steering is locked." Berty's snarl echoed through the service bay. Harry was chortling to himself from where his bike was being worked on. Meanwhile, I wasn't doing anything 'cause it was too damned funny. Man, do I love it when Bert gets all upset at the adolescent. "You fucking shit face!" Bert spat from his mismatched teeth, "They're on the key rack you never bother looking at!" His voice was at an alarmingly loud screaming volume now. "Why don't you just go home, you useless turd!" He said as a finale. Dillen took a step back, and it appeared as though some tears had welled up in his eyes. It was hard to tell because of the distance. "Why don't you shut up, Albert!" he burbled back at him. "No, you shut up!" Bert shot back. "Take it easy, you're being a jerk," Dillen mumbled, not having the effort to talk loudly as he began to ball his eyes out. "Thought I already checked the key rack." Albert's eyes dug into his, "Well, I guess you didn't, you retard!" He turned and, with his back hunched over, shuffled back over to his toolbox, mumbling as he went. He stood with his forehead throbbing in and out. "Okay, I'll pop the bike behind your bench for you when you're done that one." "Fine! Just do it!" Bert yelled across the shop, "And take the fucking garbage out too, ya do-nothing!"

In the next couple hours, I finished off my service, and the shop atmosphere began to cool down. Harry kept to himself and texted some of his slutty friends to keep himself occupied, while Albert mumbled away in his half-drunken stupor, slowly chipping away at the bikes infiltrating his bench. Dillen didn't come back again, since he knew it would mean trouble. Bert would have beaten him with a torque wrench. He let the customers wait.

I polished off a couple of services after putting on my iPod. The left-hand strap of the overalls gets the Nano zip tied to it. The ear buds go under the toque (hat) to keep them in place while moving about and under bikes. Not much talking goes on between me and others because they can't be heard. Turning the music up helps, since you become 'one' with the artist playing. It helps you understand how they were feeling when they were writing down their powerful lyrics and guitar masterpieces. Doom and death metal usually fit the mood brought on at the shop.

After a couple of albums passed through my ears, I decided it would be best to chat it up with Berty and make sure he wasn't still all grumpy pants. In addition, I hadn't gotten to use the 'Yahbuts' gag to the full extent today, and we both know that there were plenty more rounds to be put in the chamber. "Yo, Berty," I monotoned from my bench, "You need a hand over there, or are you doin' fuckin' fine?" Great movie, great line. "If I w's home right now, it would be great," he snaked out from his forked tongue. "That mot'rbike shop out by the ferries offered me a new position by the ferries. The drive is long ass ta here ev'ry day 'n' too far to the ferries ta drive." How many times can you say 'ferry' in a sentence and not even think about what you're saying, or just notice anything at all for that matter! "Berty, you're not leaving. Dude, you could like never leave." Harry said between some text messaging. "I've already quit once, and you've talked about doin' it like six times as much 's I have!" He added to get the point across. "Well, I can't put up with the stresses from you freaks in this joint," Berty stated defiantly. "Ahh, Bert baby," I said as my iPod went on pause, "most of the stresses are caused by you here anyways." He looked back in desperation, "What are you talking about? Those, those stupid people up front, Dildo and Duane, are what keeps stress'n' me out. Jest fed up with them, ahhh!" "Herm, herm, you do have a point there, Albert-o," Harry called from across the benches. "If those retards were gone, I probably wouldn't 'ave quit that first time. Better work as a mason anyways, 'cept most of 'em are drug addicts or some other thing they're doin' messin' with their heads. They couldn't remember anything. I'm like, the only one that knew what he was doin'! (Harry, the year before, had quit after the summer months to make more money in masonry. In the springtime the following year, he had talked to the boss and got rehired. He had stayed ever since.) Berty muttered 'Yeah right' under his breath at Harry's idea of himself knowing what he was doing. That idea was a little far-fetched. "They're gonna have to be some changes around here if I'm gonna stay. *Got it*?" He put a bit of edge on the last word for emphasis. "I said *got it*?" he squealed, since no one responded to his long motivational speech. Harry and I both piped up in an exacerbated overenthusiastic tone, "Oh yeah, Berty, we are so down with that. Totally awesome! Good call, man, right on!" He raised his upper lip in an exasperated manner, "Listen up, slack jobs, don't be givin' me that crap! I put up with a lot of yer guys' crap as well, don't ever ferget that!" Harry chimed in, "Bert, ahh, we also gots to deal with you, man, 'n' you 'n' I both know that's no easy shit. Not so perfect angel either, dude." I decided to add a thought too, just for fun. "Hey, both you guys, I think we all have our problems, and we're all hard to deal with in our own ways, understand what I'm sayin'? We are all difficult people, and we just have to try to put up with each other the best way possible." Albert glared back towards me, "Why you gotta make it sound all gay, you fruit loop? Next thing, and you'll be tryin' to suck me off in the back room or somin' queer." "Berty, you'd like that, can't get dick off your brain for two seconds!" I shouted at him, "You know I'm not homosexual, and the only way you're getting me in the back room is with a big friggin' jug of chloroform." "I don't even know what that word is!" Bert said back to me, "Alls you gotta do to get in the back room is by smellin' a bottle cap of beer! Cackle cackle cackle!" "Hey, Harry," I turned my head around, "why's it always sound like a witch is here whenever Bert laughs? He's like a big cackling machine." Albert interjected, "You got big right, that's fer sure!" "Yah whatever," I finished. Harry continued, "At least you're better off than the boss, the little fellow." Albert began cackling aloud again, "Just imagine how 'is old lady feels! Not much goin' on down there!" He raised his voice up to a high squeaking level again. "They probably had to use a funnel to make a fucking baby!" At that point, I cut him off with my hand, "Bert, you dork," I said quietly, "Take it easy. You know there is about one foot of drywall and a few two-by-fours between us and his office, right? Since he can hear almost all of our music at low volume, he can probably hear every word you're sayin'." Berty scrunched up his forehead, which showed off a preposterous amount of wrinkles, "Can't help sayin' shit like that when it's funny." I groaned. (Once upon a time, the boss and the other two mechanics were all having a couple of brewskies in the shop after work back in the good ole days. With a few in them already, for some reason, they started yabbering about a middle-aged bald mechanic that had worked at the shop a few years back. The bald little fucker was absolutely useless in all manners of life. His claim to fame was that when he was having intercourse with a lady, he couldn't hit the bottom but could 'sure as hell bang the shit out of the sides.' Good conversation starter maybe? So anyways, the boss spewed out that his dick was three inches long. I'm not sure if he was joking or maybe he got a little more taken off during circumcision than needed as a child; but really, if I had been in the shop, I would have been in hysterics. Good thing I wasn't there . . . That was the exciting news that was told upon my arrival in the shop the following day.)

"For the record, I gotta leave at exactly five thirty," Harry piped up, "I've got a tanning appointment, 'n' I can't be late. They don't hold the spots fer you." "You little girl," I snarled at him, "Gonna get your nails painted while you're there? Make them all puurdy?" Whenever someone else is being made fun of, Berty joins in eagerly; since for once, it wasn't him being picked on. "Come on, Sally, when did you get a sex change?" Harry quickly retaliated towards us, "At least I'll be gettin' all the hot ladies on my boat and on the beaches this summer. They'll be creamin' all over me with my sexy tanned body there." Beginning to cackle again, Bert quickly reverted back to his normal mind-set, "The only thing that'll be creamin' on ya are a bunch of dudes! Ha-ha-ha-ha!" "Well, fuck you guys," Harry snarled back, "Still gonna be gone at five thirty, and *no*, I ain't pickin' up any guys, you fruit baskets. Chicks dig tanned dudes, 'n' that's the end o' that!" Albert wanted the last word by saying 'chicks with dicks' quietly in my direction. I gave him a quick smirk to let him know I had heard him; everything back to normal.

CHAPTER 16 — A Winter Marshmallow Roast

The fresh snow glistened in the moonlight. The streets were covered in a layer of white powder. All is quiet; all is calm. The evening is beautiful, unhindered by the chatter and noise of the day; a tranquil environment. The roads have yet to be touched and destroyed by the courageous drivers of the night. It is peaceful; it is perfect.

When 2:00 a.m. rolled around, the citizens of the town were asleep minus a few junkies and deadbeats. The call disturbed me from my drunken slumber, and the incessant ringing continued until the phone could be located. The bright light-emitting diode display felt as though it was burning my retinas. It was as strong as a laser. The phone slid open and immediately answered the call. At first, all that could be heard was 'garble garble.' My head swam, and I asked the caller to slow down and tell me his name. The person on the other end seemed momentarily taken aback and hesitated before beginning again. He called himself Gerald. The name seemed to ring a bell somewhere underneath that sleepy alcohol-induced state I was in. Gerald, Gerald? Ohh, and then it came back to me—crap. "Gerald! How are you? Sorry about that! I was asleep 'n' stuff" His voice was strangely upsetting. He sounded shocked and sad and had a sense of urgency pouring off his tongue. Before I could finish my unstructured sentences, he began talking again. "Calm down! This is important!" Gerald was telling me to calm down, and I was the one almost in a comatose, unlike the crazy man on the other side of the phone line who was the one that needed the 'calm down.' "There's been a fire." Well, those words most definitely got my brain functioning. Gerald had kept on talking, but those four words had caught, and it was all I heard. "Gerald, Gerald, Gerald," I yelled in quick succession, "Did you just say there's been a fire? Slow down, what are you talking about?" I sat up in bed and pushed off the covers. It was nastily cold in my room, and it felt like a dozen hands slapping my body. My boss's voice was still jabbering, "The security company called me and said the shop's fire alarm went off. They already called the fire department, and they're most likely already there." He mentioned himself attempting to get to the shop to access the situation and damages, but as soon as he stepped outside, he knew there was absolutely no possible way of getting further than fifty feet. I was the first number he had called. Gulp, responsibility. "You have to go down there, since I'm dug in." It felt like he was standing and perspiring directly above me, bellowing incessantly as though two minutes of hysterical yelling would fix anything. "What am I supposed to do? How bad did they say it was?" "I have no idea! I just know that they called and said they were sending police and fire trucks and astronauts and the army!" Gerald had gone crazy. No astronauts or scuba divers or military would help anything. Damnit! Harry's and my own motorcycle were in the showroom! Those better not be getting crumpled by falling timbers and burning pieces of dealership. "Gerald, I gotta get some pants on! I'll check it out right away. Call me in, I dunno, like ten minutes." He agreed to this. He wanted to keep on talking as though it would help the unusually circumstanced situation. My response to get him off the line was to tell him not to worry—maybe not the best choice of words for the exact time?

I put some pants on, and it was the most productive thing I had done in days—not literally, but it sounded good. The world was spinning slightly, but once I walked out into the snow, I hoped that the feeling would subside. Snow? Fuck me. It was going to be cold as shit outside! Why the hell did it have to be so damned early? It was supposed to be my weekend with a wake-up at noon or one o'clock the next day, followed by some lounging and watching of reruns on television. After the pants, I found a hat, scarf, and my big poufy down-filled jacket; I was going to need it. Stepping out the front door, there was a bit of snow. Yesterday, I had shovelled my walk, but there was a layer of ice underneath that had been forgotten about. The leg went left, the other leg went left also, but with my palms, I was caught before hitting the ground. Mmm, cold hands now, but my bottom was fine. The sky was light gray, and perhaps the white snow was reflecting off the clouds and lighting my path. Littered on either side of the road were a few streetlamps setting off an eerie glow. My Adidas running shoes crunched over the fresh downfall and slid around on wet patches lurking below. Hands got shoved as far as they would go into the down-filled jacket. My head I tried to scrunch up to my shoulders in an attempt to keep my minimal amount of body heat in; it didn't work.

No one else walked where I walked. The streets seemed empty. At that moment, it would be nice to have a smoke. I didn't smoke, but it would fit the mood well.

A lonely night, he takes a drag from the lit cigarette and holds it in, then exhales through clenched teeth. From a passerby he would appear intimidating; a lone wolf out for the kill, chilled to the bone, but with no fear and no conscience to his actions; a real man.

A block away from the shop I saw the lights, lots of lights. I wanted to run or to do something to prevent these bad things from happening. Of course, it wasn't going to turn out that way. Maybe it wasn't as bad as Gerald's excited comments sounded. At the intersection, I looked both ways and crossed, not bothering with the walk button or the red lights above.

Fire trucks had left deep tracks in the snow. The peaceful evening with its tranquil environment had been broken. An ambulance and a few squad cars had also made it out to the happy gathering. The sirens were unnecessary, and they remained off. At the early hour of the morning, not much traffic was needed out of the way. Neighbours of the shop had come out of doors to see the lights and try to take in what was going on. They wore nightgowns and pyjamas, most draping jackets over their children to protect them from acquiring colds; others did not. Dogs on leashes were eating snow, and I supposed they had been inside their whole lives and never had this experience before.

The closer I got, the more things became apparent: The showroom was not the area that was hit first. The shop still had smoke billowing out from the roof. If there had been any windows, perhaps it would have been easier to maintain. One wall of solid reinforced concrete, impenetrable! The others were made from shit-wood material that would light up instantly. Not only the cheap materials but oodles of petrol, brake cleaner, and other highly flammable substances. Attached to our welders were oxygen and acetylene tanks. I wasn't sure if the heat was high enough to make those explode, but it was definitely something to think about; I wondered if any of the firefighters had; it would be a beautiful sight!

Two giant red trucks with ladders and hoses pumped water or fire-retardant material on the burning building. It was pretty dark, and I couldn't tell what it was. Mingled with the snow, it looked like a blizzard. Coppers were all around talking on their radios and with one another. From my vantage point, it was all incessant babbling.

The firemen had broken down the back gate for access to the rear lot. As it was simple plywood and two-by-fours, it was not exactly a demolition man's dream. The fire truck's lights, red as they were, left the snow along the walkways the colour of blood. They were as blinding as my phone had been when waking up. Little bodies moved to and fro among the trucks, cars, and buildings. I had made my way to the scene finally, and of course, I went up to the first fire marshal I could find. My inquiries seemed to bother him, and he asked me to give distance to the accident scene. He made it sound as though a mass suicide had taken place or some sort of hostage situation, not a fire at a local motorcycle shop. My questions went unanswered, and I kept asking new ones in vain. Then my phone rang again.

"What have they told you, son? How bad is the damage to the shop?" Over the ten minutes in between the calls, Gerald had cooled considerably. His voice was not as shaky and was easier to comprehend. "Umm, not much to tell really: shit-load of cop and fire vehicles an' a bunch a smoke. The fire guy won't tell me the damage. Won't tell me anything actually." "Put me on to the chief. I wanna know what's happenin' to my business!" Gerald's voice went to a high-pitched mouselike squeak when he started getting upset again that morning/evening, whichever it was now. I walked back over to the head fire dude and yelled that the owner of the 'on-fire' business was on the line and wanted a word. My goodness was he ever grumpy. That guy definitely needed to get laid or fire a gun or go on a waterslide. Unhappy people agitate me immensely. I might sound unhappy in my writings, but that's just words on paper and not an actual mind-set! From my cold white hand, he snatched the mobile. As soon as this took place, he jumped into a nearby truck to exit the noisy surroundings—the fucker! I waited impatiently watching him talk through the passenger-side window of the truck. Other firemen ran back and forth, and I would occasionally get in their way, apologizing. They would ignore me and carry about the business end of their work. For nearly six whole minutes, Gerald and this other random man with the large reflector-covered coat talked. With one hand holding the phone up to his ear, the other flapped around incessantly. I guess he was a hand talker.

Being not as drunk anymore, I decided that feeling cold sucked, since my entire body began to shiver. When 'reflector-wearing macho fireman' eventually exited from his truck, he seemed to also have cooled down a bit. "So it looks like you work here then?" The guy's voice was not as deep and gruff as it should have been. He was built like a tank though and could have easily thrown me around as if I were a bowling ball. Bushy red beard mixed with a head of red hair. His question was more of a statement, as he already knew the answer. "What did you tell my boss about this place?" I asked, pointing to the shop by tilting my head in its direction. He offered me back my phone, which I shoved down into the left pocket of my pants. Gerald had hung up and obviously had nothing else to say to me even though I was the only person representing the company and monitoring the situation. "He mentioned his neighbour might be able to get 'im here. Looks like you got a few weeks off from sellin' bikes though." I soured when he said this. "I'm actually a mechanic here and work on the bikes." I swatted down his pesky comment, referring to myself working in sales. The 'dude' most likely had some knock-off Harley, a Suzuki, or Yamaha, with loud pipes and a V-style engine to blat around on. Make fun of me? Well, fuck you, asshole. Go shove that fire hose right where it's real inconvenient. "So how bad was the fire inside?" I wanted some straight answers for coming all this way from home. Obviously, he had just told my boss everything, so he should be able to tell me. "It's not as bad as it could have been. Pretty mild to the fire we took care of last week." He went off about it being an electrical fire. Then he carried on about the real issue. Over a few days of hot-and-cold weather fluctuations in the neighbourhood, snow had accumulated on the soggy old roof and then started to melt. After a few times of doing this, the weight was more than the old shoddy construction could take. During the previous eve, the heavy ice and snow that had accumulated collapsed the roof. We found out later that it had happened right over the toolbox against the concrete wall—Albert's toolbox. This caused a few good laughs. Above Bert's toolbox was a mother lode of incandescent bulbs with their appropriate ballasts. They had all been drywall-screwed into the ceiling and wired into the same circuits with cheap Marrette connectors.

If you admire the handiwork behind the breaker box, you will find a giant mass of wires and a shit show with cheap 'do-it-yourself' from one of the old owners. The breaker box contained relics of breakers. Occasionally, with all of our welders and parts-cleaner tanks and microwaves running, breakers would trip. On a really fun occasion, smoke would even rise out of the box.

This breaker box was right above my toolbox. I would be gathering tools for a job and enjoy the aroma of burning electrical. Man, does that sting the nostrils. Anyways, the roof caved in, and the snow, ceiling, roofing, and electrical stuff fell right on Bert's toolbox. Fires started out in two places at once: one with Berty's electrical 'shmauze,' and the second right near my box. As there was a rather large gaping hole in the roof, lots of oxygen was to be had to help the spread of flames, but it also let the smoke and flames escape into the neighbourhood.

It was the weekend. Next door to the shop are many houses. One of those houses was having a birthday party. It was cold outside, so this small gathering of thirty-some-odd-year-olds was being held inside. It was just a regular old drunken fuck fest with loud music and all the other condiments for a fantastic house party. At one thirty, the party was coming close to an end. Lots of people were passed out, had left, or were asleep with random people they had met during the evening. The few hard-core partiers and drunkards that remained awake took a break and went on the balcony of the two-storey house to smoke a joint. British Columbia: the home of Mary Jane. Lots of snow made them all huddle in a circle and take in deep hits from the J. A twenty-seven-year-old named Jerry Tolskine sucked in way too much and went on a coughing fit. He turned from the group and kept on for a good minute or so as his friends made fun of him for being a 'pussy.' His eyes watered and, after brushing some snow off the pine railing, leaned his arms on it. He took in a few long breaths to calm himself. Looking out into the gray night, he could see the outlines of commercial buildings and other residential houses. No other lights were on except the streetlamps, the service department roof, and all of the vehicles.

Jerry was a bit stoned after his tokes. He had slowed down, and he was mellow and happy. Watching the fire made him smile, and it seemed to warm him up. Giving off a light chuckle, he turned to his friends and got their attention. "Hey, dudes," his voice was drawn out and docile, "looks like they're havin' a blaze too." He pointed over to the roof on fire and started giggling hysterically at his own joke. Tom McGrath, his faithful friend from the second grade, actually understood what was going on. Getting all panicky, he found his cell phone and called 911. Because it was just a town, he received the answering machine with a bunch of local police-station and fire-station telephone numbers for him to call. The police later took down this information from the group of friends when they were looking into the idea of foul play being involved. Tom and Jerry, who had been teased every day of their lives for the names they held, never dialed the other numbers. In the state they were in, both of them and the other surrounding friends couldn't locate any paper to write down the fire-department's number. As the fire alarm had gone off shortly after, the police decided it wasn't worth pressing charges as it was all covered by insurance anyways . . . maybe. The group outside on the patio/balcony got bored of the fire and went inside to get back into the heat, the reek of booze, and find somewhere cozy to sit.

At 1:45 a.m., the fire crew being only three blocks away from the shop rolled up and break down the gate as the smoke is pouring from the back lot. The ole trucks with all those fancy hoses get used, people start running around in an organized fashion, damage assessments start coming in, and everybody's working; it's the real shebang. And that's also about when I get the annoying and disturbing phone call waking me from my pleasant slumber.

Harry's palace built on sand was somewhat close to the shop. When I was done talking and listening to the fireman, he was the first person I called. Being that he was most likely still up, he probably wasn't even at home. I didn't think about this during the continued ringing. My second attempt at reaching him was successful. He opened his phone, but at first, all I could hear was groaning and rustling. I yelled out his name several times before he put his head next to his phone. His quiet snoozly tone was not very audible overtop of the running and noises I was dealing with at the fire scene. Fire trucks, even when they are parked, are surprisingly noisy with all of the generators and other things running. "Goin' on, dog?" Harry's voice sounded as though a truck had run over his vocal chords. In the background was a girl's voice inquiring about the caller's identity (me), and she sounded sleepy as well. They both might have been . . . doing things until late. "We've had a little problem at the shop tonight, 'n' I thought I might give you a dingle." "Dude," he dropped the word out as if I was asking him for a kidney, "it's like probs three in the morning." I heard some random shuffling sounds on his side of the line. "What the fuck, man, it is like three in the goddamned morning!" "Harry, Harry, there was a fire at the shop. Where are you?" "Ha-ha, you fuckin' with me? You need me to pick you up from a club or somin'? "Hobbers, I'm serious. I'm down at the shop right now next to the fire chief, and Gerald's at home 'cause he can't get through the snow." Harry let out a laugh, "Yo, man, I'm like right next to the shop. I'm totally gonna check this out!" More rustling of Harry moving around. Once again, I heard the young lady in the background, "You should put some clothes on Harry, it's cold out." I couldn't even laugh at this but was able to let out a smile. "Man, the whole roof's on fire!" Harry was at the house party behind the shop on the same balcony where Tom and Jerry had been an hour or so before, and he was naked! "How did I not hear about this? Dude! The whole roof's on fire! There's sooo many fire trucks, holy shit!" "Umm, Harry, where are you? How did you see the fire so fast?" He let out a tired sounding 'guffaw' in-between his excited jabbering. "I'm just behind the shop, man! I'm watchin' the whole thing at this house party with a bunch a' people. This is crazy that our shop's on fire!" We ended our somewhat one-sided conversation that mainly involved Harry explaining to me how insane it was that out motorcycle shop was on fire as though I was unaware. Approximately twelve minutes passed, and in that time, he managed to become decent, put on some pants, say goodbye to his friend, and make his way over to join me in the excitement.

Upon seeing me, he approached and gave a giant bear hug. His breath smelt of tequila, and he was swimming in alcohol. Harry only had a light sweater on with jeans for pants and flip-flops on his feet. The pumping adrenaline kept him warm for a few minutes as he babbled on in excitement and experienced all of the lights and sounds. Together we watched the smoke and water show unfold. Only a few minutes had passed before Harry's heart rate slowed, and he began bitching about the temperature. I was pretty cold even with my down jacket and wasn't about to give him mine. We walked over to one of the smaller fire trucks and asked for one of their blankets.

Gray, thick, and warm, he got wrapped up nicely by this hot little firewoman whom he attempted to hit on—one girl to the next, that Harry. I had trouble finding just one decent girl that I enjoyed talking to that didn't turn out to be a slut. Unfortunately, for this young lady, she appeared to be a lesbian, and his charm did not work. Or maybe that was unfortunate for him? "So, Harry," I chuckled out loud while talking to him, "who was your fine-feathered friend you were sharing a bed with and didn't have any clothes on with last night?" For a moment, he blushed, and a large grin spread across his face. "Oh, ya know, just one of those friends that I've got around this town." I knew the names of a couple, but there were others who had been seen and whose names had yet to be mentioned.

A little after three, my phone started ringing again. I was all docile and ready to leave, as nothing was really going on. It was Gerald. His neighbour had managed to help him out, which was a very kind thing to do at such a late hour of the night. With the snow, it was taking them a while to get down to the shop, but they would be there shortly. Harry and I hung out until then. Since the situation was not as serious as I would have liked, boredom began to set in. The distance brought far-off lights from an approaching truck. The vehicle parked in the middle of the traffic lane ten feet behind the cop cars. I heard Gerald before he could be seen.

The lights from the top of the trucks were glaring up my vision, and he was rather short. Only a few meters from me, he came into view and was sobbing rather heavily. Gerald saw the two of us and threw his arms around both our shoulders. "My boys! My boys!" He sobbed loudly, "What have we done to deserve this?" How in the world are you supposed to console a fifty-five-year-old man? This I asked myself as my hands automatically patted his back. "Gerald, it's not as bad as it looks." Harry took off his blanket and tossed it over Gerald's shoulders. "Thanks for being here for me," he cried. Moving away from us, he walked over to the front door of the shop. There was not much risk anymore, as none of the firemen approached him. I suppose they had gotten used to the lot of us rowdy characters being about. Gerald fell to his knees and raised his hands up to the shop. After he moaned, "Why have you forsaken me?" I began to think he was being melodramatic. "Dude, I am so done with this crap tonight." "I know, man, jest wanna get into a bed and close my eyes." I liked how Hair ball said 'a bed' as opposed to his bed. My eyes were difficult to lift, and all my plans for Sunday had gone to shit. It seemed as though a few free days in the following week might make up for that. "Hey Harry, looks like we might have time for a hike next week." Harry was cold and tired, but we had been overworked that week, and a break might be nice. "Hah! Can't say I've ever been laid off 'cause the old dealership caught on fire!" "Yah, true that, something good to tell the friends at church tomorrow." "Church . . . the only church I know is the strip club! Ha-ha, back on the East Coast, that's what we used to call it." "Yah, I was actually talking about a real place of worship and not the one between a set of legs. But I do know a cool place we can go for a hike in the snow if you've got some boots." "Yah, that would be cool. I'll get back to you once I can see, hear, and think properly again."

Gerald was chatting again with the fire chief with a morbid look spread over his face. I wanted to leave so badly! Ten minutes of walking and home-free I would be. They parted ways after their 'talk,' and Gerald returned to the two sorry souls waiting around doing nothing. "Well my boys, they are going to have a team of inspectors in first thing Monday morning. But he said the work space for you is unusable until all the damages have been fixed. There's a very large hole in the ceiling near the concrete wall. Looks like I'm going to have to give you a week off of work at least. This is horrible for business! They said I can't even use the showroom to sell bikes until the smoke damage has been taken care of. It's going to ruin me!" Gerald moaned, whined, and groaned for another couple minutes about insurance most likely not covering anything due to all of the faulty wiring and light fixtures. He then went on like a babbling brook about his business crumbling. It was a good thing Harry and I didn't work there, or we might also be upset about not being able to work for a while or having all of our tools ruined or about our bikes in the showroom that we couldn't access . . .

Once Gerald was finished his annoying but understandable rant, I sneakily snuck in the lateness of the hour and how long some of us had been there for looking over the whole situation. He agreed and said we would be called after the inspectors had informed him of the situation. "Umm, what about Bert and the others? When are you going to let them know 'bout this?" Harry mentioned, "Oh, I can't even think about them right now. I'm far too emotional about the whole ordeal. Why don't you two make the calls in the morning? That would be much easier." Urgg, there would be so many questions. "All right, Harry, I'll call Bert and the shop boy if you call Dillen and Duane." Harry looked at me with disgust, "Thanks, asshole." "Okay, Gerald, we'll take care of them for you." He momentarily cheered up after hearing that his employees with the ruined shop were so devoted. "Fellows, that's great. I couldn't ask any more from you. Now go home and do your best to get some sleep. We'll get through this, we must if we are to carry on." At that, I felt like rolling my eyes. Whoa are we! But I refrained from doing so. I gave the short bald man a hug—a manly hug. Harry and I put out our fists and 'pounded' each other. With one final look at the horror scene, my walk back to home began.

A few minutes into the walk, I realized how damned exhausted I was from the whole night. Quickening my pace to get some more blood moving through my body helped the chill, and it also got me back to my place quicker. The porch light was the most beautiful thing ever to be seen. My key turned in the lock, and I swung the door wide open. It smacked into the door stop and made that weird 'boing' sound quite loudly. I kicked off the shoes, tossed the jacket on the carpeted stairs, and used the last of my energy available to crawl up them. Fifteen seconds later, under my blanket, I was zonked out and fast asleep. The devil himself could not have awoken me from my slumber.

CHAPTER 17 — Let There Be Light

One week had passed since the horrific fire. The people that were in the 'loop' stated that it was unsafe to be on the premises until work had been completed and the structural parts had been repaired. Yellow tape was covering the front door, the rear gate area, and the rear shop doors. With the boss being as vague as possible, what was known about the shop was very little. Customers had acquired Gerald's personal telephone number from somewhere and wanted to know the state of their motorcycles. They were given dismissive answers as well and resorted to finding employees' e-mail addresses and pestering them, including my own.

I telephoned Harry that Sunday morning. We had hung out earlier in the week just to drink and blab. This call was about something else. "So Harry, how ya doin' this morning? What do you have planned for the day?" "Actually not much. This is like the first weekend I'm not hungover in forever." He actually had the whole previous week free because of the fire. "You feel like going for a ride today?"

During the week off, all the crap weather we were having decided to lift. A few light rains washed away the snow, and the sun dried up the aftermath; it was gorgeous.

"Yah, I could be down fer that, 'cept our bikes are locked in at the shop." "Meet me there at noon." He agreed and then hung up.

To be honest, since talking to the 'boss man' and watching him cry and pray to the heavens, I hadn't set foot in the motorcycle dealership parking lot. Getting there a few minutes before noon gave me time to ponder. The parking lot was deserted with no form of life but my own. The yellow tape that I had heard about made the place look like a crime scene. All of the walls that usually had a bright white appearance to them seemed grey and bland. The whole picture was sad, and it started to depress me. At the point of me going all 'emo,' Harry's truck drove into the lot. He hopped out, "Check me out, man! I've got the whole place to park where I like!" "You know it's Sunday, right? You could have a circus here if ya wanted!" He ignored me and got to the point, "Brought my helmet 'n' jacket, 'n' I'm ready for business." "Oh god, you've checked this place out, right? No business is gonna happen here for a while." "Don't you go bein' a douche. We're both here for the same thing." "True enough, I don't need no arguing. I have no idea if the alarm is still working or if all that 'jazz' has been disabled." Harry thought for a quick second, "Eh, only one way to find out. Grab yer keys while I get this shit outta the way." He was referring to the 'Police Line Do Not Cross' tape. 'Jingle

jingle' of my keys. Gate open, door open, and no sign of alarm yet. It did smell like a campfire inside though, which was obviously not surprising. Three steps into the showroom, and the countdown to the alarm going off sounded. Harry ran over and hit his code into the lit screen, "Well, this baby is still dangerous." I walked over to him, "Hey, hey, that just means we're free to get our stuff. Let's get 'er done! I guess the alarm doesn't care that there is a big-ass hole in the roof of the shop? Whatever."

Our bikes had been piled inside behind a whole lot of others. Harry and I rolled about eight bikes into the parking lot before our own Beemers could be pulled out. Blue bikes, ugly green bikes, and white bikes filled the parking lot. Then of course there was my silver bike and Harry's orange bike, which were the only two good bikes out of the lot. I had brought my spare helmet from my house, but my own jacket was back in the service part of the shop. Now was the time to see what condition the area would be in. I made a few jokes with Hair ball about the state of affairs in the back and then entered into the burnt-out domain.

My cell phone had a built-in LED flashlight 'cause with the electrical problems, it was doubtful that any lights would be functioning. Trying out switches and getting zapped was not in my best interest. The LED was not very adequate in letting us see the whole ugly situation. There was so much blackness that it swallowed up most of the light. During the past week of being closed, the fire peoples had put a tarp over the gash in the roof, which covered the 'gigantoid' hole that had begun to let rain and snow inside. I found my jacket unscathed as she was at the complete other end of the shop from Albert's toolbox. Bad was her smell though, and it would take a while to get it out. Alongside were my boots, and I grabbed them both before having another look around.

On the three benches had been three bikes, nothing fancy. Only one of them currently appeared rideable. Piles of ceiling and wall material were scattered about on the floor and also mingling with other 'rolled-in' bikes. Harry was over by his toolbox, which looked fine. My own just looked a bit overheated with a thick layer of ash covering the lid and tops of all the drawers. "Dude, this place looks like shit. Let's roll out." I wanted to hang out for a while and take in this graveyard, which I called home for so long. I could still count on both hands how many years of service had been put in, but it sure as hell felt like it had taken a chunk of years out of me. Harry had been outside for a minute before I joined him. "All right, cool your jets! I turned the alarm back on, so you can't go back in." Harry looked like a small child and started dancing around as he had to urinate. "Ya could 'ave asked me first man, fuck!" I barked out a laugh as I leant over to put my stinky riding boots on. "Just go down the drain. Like you said, no one else is in the lot. Oh, and open your truck, so I can toss these shoes in." Harry went into the alleyway and pissed into one of the gutter drains singing 'Brown-eyed Girl' as he did so; weird and random. "Okay sunshine, get your damned gear on, 'n' let's go for a cruise. Hopefully, that piece-o-shit still starts. What, like three weeks a' snow? That's three weeks she's not been runnin' for!" Both the big-ole boxer R1150Rs thundered to life with those big pistons pounding away in the cylinders. "Yeehaw!" he exclaimed. "Yeehaw," I answered back. This was going to be cold, invigorating, and fun. Harry put some crap in his truck and then locked it up. The Aria helmet on my head could have used a visor clean. I had looked at my everyday work helmet, but it would either need some serious attention or be thrown in our big green bin of refuse. "So Tiger-toucher, where you thinkin' about goin' for today's ride?" Ponder, ponder, "If we go down to Hillbeam Crescents, that'll take thirty minutes each way after the lights (referring to the stoplights; and Hillbeam referring to an out-of-the-way abandoned industrial park from the '60s. I don't think the Crescents actually meant anything, and Hillbeam was just an old guy that started the place up and, when his family died and he sold out, moved away. His whereabouts were unknown to all). "We could do that," Harry stretched out his words, "or we could hit up Links pass, which ends up at Hillbeam." "Hobber, just 'cause all our snow's gone down here, don't mean that up at Links pass is the same deal." "Naww," Harry brushed that idea away with his gloved palm. "You know what? Let's do Links, but if I go down 'cause of some shit road-clearing salt of somin', you my fine sir, get to pay for that crap." "Ahh, that's what insurance is for. Come on, we both know I can't afford to fix a fancy motorcycle like yours . . ." The joke was that 90 percent of the parts were the same on both our bikes.

Harry smoked off on his machine. He always just wanted to be in front, at least at the start. I let out the clutch and chased after him. It felt great to be on my bike during winter months. Most winter riders had filthy R1200GSA bikes, which had not seen their own paint in over a year; hence why I didn't ride mine during the nasty months. Whenever riding, I received compliments on how beautiful and clean my bike was.

Moseying through town helped warm up the machines. I don't want to sound like a pussy, but I put my factory-heated grips to the higher setting. Harry probably had his on as well. It actually took a good fifteen minutes to get past and through the stoplights. Cities, pfff, what a waste of time. The cold weather continually fogged up my visor. I hadn't bought a pin lock yet or reapplied my antifog solution lately. A young dude on his BMX bicycle on the sidewalk pulled a catwalk and then looked over and gave me the thumbs-up. As he looked over, I realized at once that he was about thirty-two. This made me release a laugh. The dork was way past his youth and on the prowl to sell drugs to kids in the neighbourhood. There wasn't really anything to be done about it at that moment in time, so my right hand just rolled on the throttle, and he was erased from my mind. The heated rubber under my hands felt good. A big downfall about me was that I got cold easily especially when riding.

Side by side, we cruised into the good road areas where seeing five hundred feet in front of you was impossible. The corners started coming faster and closer together. Where the streets and roads were dry in the city, this rural area with less traffic and more foliage and trees on the 'sidelines' had damp patches here and there. It reminded us that it wasn't even springtime yet, and the weather was not always to be reckoned with. Into a long left corner we dove, with neutral camber and water covering the whole stretch. We blasted through, but I left a small amount of distance so Harry's rooster tail stayed off my foggy visor. The turn straightened out before another slowly tightening right-hander. The asphalt was dry after the straight, and it carried on that way for the next few slow-sweepers.

As we carried on our ride, the elevation rose, and it became wet on all the turns. Scraps of snow from the previous weeks began to appear around the edges of the road. The sun was shining, but going up and over Links pass was not a hot experience. We began a few of the switchbacks. Pretty slow going as I watched the lean angle of Harry's bike in the wet compared to what was possible in the dry. I dropped down into a low gear for the low speeds; high rpm for nice control. Throwing the bikes into another right-hand turn, the chance to shift up came to me again, so I took it. The roar of the torquey engines pounded deep into the depths of my skull. Harry attempted to pull away. His rear wheel slid around as he downshifted into the next turn. He gave his orange bike more gas and pulled out as he straightened. My shield was becoming splattered with particles of 'goulash' and road mud. I rode up beside him as we carried on. The snow on the side of the road was becoming extremely thick as we both became higher and higher going over the pass. I cracked open my visor again for more airflow. We crested over the highest part of the pass and from the top could see the industrial park off in the distance below. Pulling over, Harry and I chatted momentarily about the shitty roads and the huge amount of crud on them. He guessed that it would take fifteen minutes to reach the bottom, about 2:00 p.m.

This time I went in front. The winding roads took us back to the tree line and to the flatish ground at the bottom. With my left glove, I used the small finger-wiper to clean off some sludge, but it streaked it more than cleared it. Racing on ahead at an appropriate speed for the conditions, Harry and I played cat and mouse until reaching the Crescents.

Piles of warehouses and industrial buildings with huge parking lots took up the area. Tall wired gates surrounded some of them, while others had absolutely no security or cameras whatsoever, not that there was an interest in entering any of them today. There was a mile-long stretch that ran between the industrial complexes, so we drag-raced until the end. My silly R-boxer started doing a tank slapper after reaching 220 km/h. This was because, unlike the older R251 series R1100R models, mine and Harry's did not come with steering dampers. Hair ball's Rockster, the naked roadster, made a huge amount of air rush into his chest, making it harder to gain high speeds. His top-end speed was far more diminished than mine. These bikes were in no way compared to newer R1200 models or any of the newer K-bikes or S100RR bikes that we test rode every day for services, but they were still entertaining and got the job done.

As we approached the last parking lot at the end of the strip, I realized we hadn't eaten anything, or at least I hadn't, all morning or afternoon. It would be a good idea to do something about that and soon. I dropped a gear and, as I rolled into the lot, dropped my side stand to rest my bike. Harry followed closely behind. "Brr, man, I'm as fuckin' cold as a polar bear! Shoulda brought another layer." Harry jogged on the spot to warm up. He then sauntered over to a big pile of crates to look out over the street. "Fuck you, industrial park, I own you now!" Feeling around in my BMW jacket pockets, I found my emergency supply of food: two granola bars. "Hey, slut lips, you want a little snack?" Harry looked down at me and jumped down from the pallet castle he thought he was king of. "Yah, totally man; sweet." With one swoop, he grabbed the bar from my outstretched hand and, after quickly unwrapping it, devoured it in one fluid motion. He literally shoved the whole bar down his throat in one bite. "Whoa, buddy, take it easy. That's the only one I got to share. You'll probably end up choking on one of the almonds!" Harry let out a burp once his breathing tube was once again clean. "Arr, that would be amazing to have a cheeseburger right now! Let's roll out in five. We'll take the same route back and double-time this one. None o' that pussyfootin' like we did comin' down here." "Yes, Harry," I interjected, "You realize that it was snowy, rainy, gravely, and nasty the whole way out here, don't ya?" He shoved his pointed finger into my chest in a mock aggressive style, "Slut mamma, I don't want no trouble, but I think yer lookin' fer some." I grabbed his collar to emphasize the mock aggressiveness a bit more. "No, you listen, biatch rider, I don't really wanna die today. I just want one of those cheeseburgers." He got the message. "Fine! We'll have it your way, Burger King!" He threw down the Burger King's old motto, and it got me visualizing grease dripping from double beef patties. Ohh, those beef patties sounded good. We both dropped our fists/hands/whatever we were doing to each other. "You wanna go to Burger King? It's gonna take us a bit to get there. Let's medium pace it over there." Harry dropped his voice as low as it could go, "At a medium pace." One of his favourite lines from the old Adam Sandler skits we used to listen to on compact disc. "Suit up boys!" I yelled to him, "Let's go fer a ride!" This I bellowed in the most Western cowboy drawl I could. It followed with a "yeehaw!" Mounting the bikes brought no trouble, but in the distance were some dark menacing clouds. They loomed over the pass, taunting us and telling us that it was going to be shit to ride the S-turns and go up into the high elevation.

My bike roared to life with her two cylinders pounding away. The firing rocked the bike from side to side and made me steady her with my legs firmly planted on the ground. To show me his excitement and sporadic nature, Hairy busted off a quick burn-out, which filled the parking lot with rubber debris. I yelled "Come on, show-off" to him, but he just threw a goofy look out to me. He rolled onto the main drag and busted off a long wheelie. "Blah," was all I said, mainly to myself. My wheelie experiences sucked because of how bad at them I was. The act of balancing a 400-pound motorcycle without flipping upside down was never figured out by me. For the most part, less wheelies meant more practise on the twisties. Slamming the shifter down into first, I blazed out on the road after him in hot pursuit.

The clouds had blacked out the sun's rays, and all the shadows on the road had left to be replaced by a consistent grey. The few first turns brought us back to remembering turn-in speeds and lean angles. The next couple brought self-confidence and full concentration back.

The tyres that were being run on my R1150R this week were the Metzeler Sportec M5s. I had burnt off the rest of the Interact Z8s and was trying these on for size. Even though it was a 180/55-17 profile tyre, my rear wheel I had replaced with an R1100S 5.5-inch rear wheel. They were only meant to fit 170/60 tyres on, but my persuasion managed to help. At first, I did not think that the swing arm could manage the profile, but once installed, she performed beautifully. Buying a front to match made for a great sticky set of tyres. My old Michelin Pilot Race set would have been jealous.

The tyres were still hot from the ride out to the Hillbeam Crescents, and right away we could appreciate the corners. I dove into a tight left-hander and could just see Harry's taillight disappear around the bend. This gave me motivation to plunge into the next few with a higher speed. The feelers on my left foot peg dug into the asphalt and raised up my foot a wee bit as I stayed on course. As my heart rate increased, I entered into the 'speed zone.' I love that zone. You barely blink, and your concentration is at 100 percent while you ride your absolute best. A quick straightaway brought me closer to Harry as I reefed the throttle back to the stops, trying to make the old brute pull harder than she was. Diving into a long nicely cambered right-hander was sensational; the whole way I just laid into her, and I hit the apex perfectly. There was light rain starting to sprinkle which was mildly upsetting. The oil on the road would be brought up to the surface. No amount of sticky tyres would help in that situation. Being only a few hundred metres from Harry's tail made me a crazed man, and I had to catch up. For some reason my life seemed to depend on it. Ahead of me, I could see him turn his head around to see what state I was in. Since his position was ahead of mine, he didn't really have much to worry about until I had caught up to him. This I was trying very hard to do. That idiot Harry, blasting away and doing a wheelie and now ahead of me, grrr. In front, there was a slope that almost narrowed to a one-lane road. At the top, it quickly flattened out, turned ninety degrees to the right, and then after ten metres, proceeded to do another forty-five-degree turn to the left and into an off-camber S-turn that you could not see the end of as it became hidden by the trees. On this spot, I managed to gain a lot of ground on the motorcycle being pursued. He was a stone's throw away from me. I had almost gashed my knees by kneeling my body so far off the bike around those tight turns. A few gentle rolling hills brought us further into the elevation of the pass. The rain had come up above a misty sprinkle now, and I had large drops that were extremely close together but the kind that had enough space between them to let you see in between the drops. My windshield caught most of the water that would right now be hitting Harry's chest and going underneath his helmet and onto his neck. The little wiper on my glove came once again in handy. That M5 slid around a bit while downshifting but only because of the water. I pushed harder, much harder than usual in the rain.

Another five minutes, and I was upon his tail. The switchbacks to the top were almost done, and since he enjoyed smoking and drinking much more than me, which is somewhat hard to believe, his energy had to be running out; it just had to be. I may have consistently done bad things to my body, but a lot of cardio was done at the gym in between those. This kept me somewhat fit.

At the top was a long stretch of road. This was the same stretch that we had momentarily stopped at before. This time we did not, and instead we carried on at ridiculous speeds for the conditions. We had to have those burgers! It seemed the faster we rode, the hungrier we became—understandable as we burnt piles of energy to keep up the fast pace.

We reached the end of the straight, and I was still riding his ass in a nonliteral fashion. As soon as the straight ended, it threw down some fast-paced switchbacks. On the way up this side of the mountain road, there was an extreme amount of crap that had not changed coming back on the other side. The snow was still evident, and the rain was not helping. The water had moved over the visor on my helmet, then over the top, followed by dripping down the back of my neck—a grossly uncomfortable feeling.

Our lean angles were the same for four of the switchbacks. I cracked open my helmet vents again as the breathing became faster and heavier. As we straightened out and waited impatiently for the next corner, I grabbed a meaty handful of throttle. As I passed by Harry, he seemed surprised to see me. I had a lot of speed, and perhaps it was too much. Another left-hand corner came upon us. At an extreme lean angle, with my left leg pressed almost to the ground, the situation was entirely in control. As the corner started going downhill, it also tightened, and visibility became worse. Harry had given himself a generous amount of space between our bikes. In the split-second that I was entirely sure the situation was indeed mine to control, God threw an interesting variable at me: gravel. There was absolutely nothing that could be done. It was the other side of the road from our coming the other way, and we were unaware it was going to be covering the lane. A dirt road that came out of the bush had its head directly open onto this paved section. The previous day, it was entirely feasible that any number of ATV or dirt-bike riders had brought their trucks down that road. In addition, it was entirely feasible that these hooligans loved to spin their big mud-bogger tyres when entering off of the gravel and dirt road. Sucks for me.

I came into that part of the corner at break-neck speeds, and that's almost what it did. There was enough time for my eyes to go wide and for me to think 'oh no' to myself before I hit the gravel. Instantly, my Beemer low-sided and flung itself off the road. I landed on my left shoulder and kept going the same speed into God-knows-where: a tree, off the mountain, into a boulder; I have no idea. The world went absolutely black to me as I crashed my motorcycle.

CHAPTER 18 — Finding the Light

"Poor sod, bandaged up like a fuckin' mummy." "Hah! Least he don't 'ave to feel the pain his body's in right now. I'd be downin' so many drugs if I was conscious in that bed." "Yah, an' he's still lyin' there with a big old shit-eatin' grin on his face. I've never seen him so damned smiley." "He's so happy 'cause he don't 'ave to go back to work in a week when the shop reopens." "Yah, Bert, they said it'd be a week, but those idiots are slow as fuck. My buddy worked for that construction company for two years and said that the disorganization was horrendous. Probs be done in a month when we're all broke-ass an' can't afford to drive." Albert gave him a sour look, "Ain't you the fuckin' optimist. I'm 'avin the most amazin' time of my life not drivin' every day! Get up late, do whadever, have a few beers." "But you shoulda been done work 'n' retired like ten years ago. I still gots a few years a' that to go."

A cute nurse featuring the nametag 'Melanie' walked in and escorted the two belligerents out of the room. She was a pleasant height and had curly brown hair that spent its time wandering over her shoulders. Her eyes lit up when she saw Harry's handsome contrasting features. Bert shook his head as Harry began to chitchat with her while they left the room. Yes, she worked nights and was in the ward full-time. And yes, she would be there on Thursday. "Well, I guess we'll be bumping into each other again soon." They let her return to her duties as they took the elevator to the main floor and walked outside to have a smoke.

Epilogue

It was deathly hot. Sweat beaded down off my brow and under my sunglasses to mingle in my eyes. Removing the darkened lenses, I wiped the droplets from my face while the sun dove ferociously into my pupils. I blinked a few times rapidly to adjust as the glasses went back on. The cold beer in my left hand was perspiring more than I, but it was still as warm as piss. Beside me on the beach chair that I rented for the day was a fabulous book I had been taking in for the past few hours. Applying sunscreen twice, the SPF 30 seemed to be helping keep the cancer off my skin, but I sure looked like a grease ball. The cheap sunscreen at the local ping-pong whatever store was the only one without 'skin-whitening' formula—white enough, thanks, none of that for me.

It was turning out to be a beautiful day: pad Thai for breakfast, beers on the beach, a little sun, a book, and nothing to do but let my mind wander for the rest of the day. That was before she showed up . . .

Just minding my own business, or lack of business, I was rudely and loudly interrupted by these two young ladies throwing about a bright red plastic Frisbee. It was strange as one of them looked vaguely familiar. She was wearing a vivid two-piece bikini, and her flowing brown hair brought back distant memories. She apologized, and smiled a guilty smile, as though they had thrown the disc at me on purpose. No, I thought to myself, only guys pull those kinds of antics on the beach, right? It was definitely not that girl's idea, for after her sensational smile, she quickly turned and, at an almost run, joined her friend after I returned their red Frisbee. Shy she was. For a moment I kept my eyes on her as she joined back up with her blonde friend. Their words escaped me because of the distance, but I got the point. They could be seen bickering back and forth before the blonde one turned to look at me and then walk over.

It was a lovely European accent in which she used to address me; very pleasant it was. She asked if I would like to join them in their Frisbee-throwing. Obviously, I was disgusted with the thought . . . Two beautiful bikini-clad young ladies, one of them shy and very cute; the other, the straightforward-minded one, very pretty but not my style. Glug-glugging down the rest of my Chang beer, a tasty formaldehyde-filled beverage, I managed to remove my body from the relaxing lounge chair. It wasn't easy, as I hadn't left it in a number of hours. "All right, girls, I'm coming!" The three of us made bad chitchat together. All I was really interested in doing was talking with this amazing brown-haired girl, but we had to toss this silly round thing about. I was bad at throwing them and, combined with the heat and a few beers, very bad. They may have picked up on that . . .

After fifteen or so minutes, I gave up. "Could I take you girls to lunch? This whole sports and fitness aura about me is just an act to pick up unsuspecting traveling girls." A quick laugh and they agreed. Surprisingly, their bungalows were rather close to mine. Just across the street was a vivid assortment of markets, restaurants, food stalls, and vendors, offering a variety of places for us to go. Nearing the bungalows, the blonde faked being tired and ducked out from having to spend lunch with the two of us. I stated it was nice to meet her and then asked her friend if she still wanted to join me. She blushed a dynamic rouge against her elegant white skin—a delicious contrast. A small peep of a 'yes' escaped her perfect lips. Her delicate arms waved quickly to her friend as she walked away. "Shall we?" I asked while holding up my arm for her.

Together we walked away into the distance, hand in hand.

Edwards Brothers Malloy
Thorofare, NJ USA
August 21, 2012